Sarah Bennett has been r[illegible]mber. Raised in a family of bookworms, her love affai[illegible]oks of all genres has culminated in the ultimate Happy Ever After: getting to write her own stories to share with others.

Born and raised in a military family, she is happily married to her own Officer (who is sometimes even A Gentleman). Home is wherever he lays his hat, and life has taught them both that the best family is the one you create from friends as well as relatives.

When not reading or writing, Sarah is a devotee of afternoon naps and sailing the high seas, but only on vessels large enough to accommodate a casino and a choice of restaurants.

You can connect with her via twitter @Sarahlou_writes or on Facebook www.facebook.com/SarahBennettAuthor

Also by Sarah Bennett

The Butterfly Cove Series

Sunrise at Butterfly Cove
Wedding Bells at Butterfly Cove
Christmas at Butterfly Cove

The Lavender Bay Series

Spring at Lavender Bay
Summer at Lavender Bay
Snowflakes at Lavender Bay

Summer at Lavender Bay

SARAH BENNETT

ONE PLACE. MANY STORIES

This novel is entirely a work of fiction. The names, characters and incidents portrayed in it are the work of the author's imagination. Any resemblance to actual persons, living or dead, events or localities is entirely coincidental.

HQ
An imprint of HarperCollins*Publishers* Ltd
1 London Bridge Street
London SE1 9GF

This edition 2018

1
First published in Great Britain by
HQ, an imprint of HarperCollins*Publishers* Ltd 2018

A catalogue record for this book is available from the British Library.

ISBN: 978-0-00-831003-5

This book is produced from independently certified FSC™ paper to ensure responsible forest management.

For more information visit: www.harpercollins.co.uk/green

Typeset by Palimpsest Book Production Ltd, Falkirk, Stirlingshire
Printed and bound in Great Britain by
CPI Group (UK) Ltd, Melksham, SN12 6TR

It's not the first love that counts – it's the last.
This one's for M, my last and truest love

Chapter One

Welcome to Heathrow. Eliza's stomach churned at the words emblazoned on the large silver sign dominating the roundabout. They were really going through with it. After weeks of debate, of ever-more outlandish promises from Martin about how relocating to the Middle East would be a fresh start for both of them, they'd finally reached the point of no return. She placed her hand on her uneasy middle, assuring herself it was merely butterflies of excitement rather than a sense of impending dread that had made it impossible to choke down more than a couple of mouthfuls of tea.

Once they'd checked in, they'd find somewhere for breakfast. Martin wanted a blowout—a full English with all the works—to say goodbye to the UK in style. The thought of all that grease did nothing to help her queasiness, but he was excited about their new adventure and she owed it to him to be supportive. She'd manage a plate of scrambled eggs on toast and hopefully something to eat would settle her down.

'Here you go, mate.' The taxi driver's cheerful voice scattered her wayward thoughts. Blinking, she realised the car had drawn to a halt outside a huge glass and concrete building. 'That'll be twenty quid. Do you need a hand with your bags?' The taxi driver half-turned to complete the transaction with Martin who began to fumble with his wallet.

From Eliza's vantage point in the back seat, the contrast between the two men was marked. The driver was an older man, closer to her dad's age than theirs. His tanned skin crinkled around his eyes, giving her the impression he laughed a lot. He'd been chatty during the journey and seemed genuinely interested to hear about their relocation to Abu Dhabi. She'd left it to Martin to carry the majority of the conversation, although she'd managed a smile and a few words of agreement whenever either of them had aimed a question or remark in her direction.

Eliza's stomach started doing that unpleasant swirling thing again—like she was filled with water and someone had yanked out the plug, sending it spinning as the water drained away. It was the same feeling she had every time she thought, heard or saw the name of the country where they'd be living for at least the next three years.

'I'd like a receipt please,' Martin said as he handed over a crisp note fresh from the cashpoint machine. He looked pale, almost wan, next to the older man. The sallowness of his skin owed more to the hours he spent locked inside staring at his laptop rather than genetics. He'd catch the sun soon enough; he always did whenever they returned to their home town of Lavender Bay to visit their families. Not that she could persuade him to go there much these days. He was always too busy—although it was never clear to Eliza exactly what it was on his computer that took up so much of his spare time.

With the driver paid, there was no excuse for her to linger in the cab any longer, so she took a deep breath and forced her shaking hand to open the door. It *was* nerves, nothing more. Anyone taking such a big leap into the unknown was bound to be a little apprehensive, right?

The hem of the long, flowing skirt she was wearing caught on the low heel of her patent red shoes, and she had to pause to extricate it. She'd chosen muted colours, floaty layers over dark leggings and a thin, long-sleeved T-shirt, with a scarf around her neck which could be pulled up to cover her hair if needs be. Martin's employer had provided them with suggestions of acceptable attire, and although it had been stressed to her the authorities were entirely reasonable in their approach to Western visitors, it was important to her to be respectful towards the culture of the country. The fact her milk-pale, freckled complexion could burn at the first hint of strong sunlight meant she was used to covering up. Her Dorothyesque red shoes had been the only indulgence when selecting her outfit, a splash of the rich colours she favoured; a touch of courage.

Feeling a bit useless, Eliza hovered out of the way whilst Martin and the driver wrestled their luggage out of the boot. With a smile, the driver placed a large and small suitcase in front of her then tugged the handles up and locked them in place. 'Chin up, sweetheart, it might never happen.'

She laughed at the well-worn phrase and the kindly wink, ignoring the whirlpool inside her. He was sort of right. It had already happened, so she might as well stop sulking about it. 'Thank you for your help.'

'My pleasure. Have a good flight.' With a cheery wave, he was gone.

'All set?' Martin's question turned her head towards him, and she nodded. His laptop bag dangled precariously from one shoulder, his hands already filled with the handles of his two cases.

Stepping forward, she lifted the bag up so she could lengthen the strap and hook it over his body cross-wise. 'It might be easier like this.' Her own personal items were secured in a small rucksack already strapped to her back.

'Thanks.' She lifted up on tiptoes to kiss his cheek, but he was already turning away from her. Like he had been for months. *Like they both had been*—she corrected herself. It wasn't all Martin's fault if things between them were flat. They'd been drifting apart for ages, a slow slide of conflicting work schedules and a lack of shared interests. It hadn't seemed important when they were kids, flush with the excitement of young love and too naïve to understand how the little things they found easy to shrug off would slowly grow into rocks of resentment neither of them seemed willing to clamber over. Instead of addressing those problems, their answer had been to divert themselves from the rocky path of their marriage by veering off in an entirely new direction. A fresh start, a new life in a new country with new opportunities. Not ready to give up on nearly a decade of commitment, Eliza had let herself become swept away with it.

'Come on, Eliza. Stop daydreaming.' Eliza—short for Elizabeth. A name she'd chosen for herself on the same day her two best friends had chosen their own nicknames. The quirk of fate that saw certain names become popular each year, had seen the three of them all christened Elizabeth within a handful of months of each other. That might not have been a problem in a big city, but in the tiny seaside town of Lavender Bay where there were only enough children to fill one class each year, it had been a problem. Fed up of the confusion, they'd sat on Eliza's bed one evening during their first year at secondary school and decided to become Beth, Eliza and Libby. And so they'd remained for the next fifteen years.

Shaking off the old memory, Eliza noted Martin had already trundled away with his share of the luggage, forcing her to grab hers and hurry after him. The cases were mismatched in both size and weight and had seen better days. They'd invested in a new set for Martin because he'd need his suits and shirts to be halfway presentable on arrival as he would be heading to the office the next morning. Eliza only had to stay in the hotel the firm had allocated them for the first few days—the keys to their new apartment not being available until the end of the week—so it didn't matter much if her things were a bit crumpled. There would be plenty of time to sort and iron everything, it wasn't as though she'd have anything else to do once they moved into the new place.

She finally caught up to him at the barriers just before check in, and only because he'd stopped to rummage in the front pocket of his bag for their paperwork. Withdrawing the pre-printed boarding passes and their passports, he split them and handed hers over. 'There you go. Just join the back of that queue and I'll wait for you here once you're finished.'

'Wait for me? What are you talking about. We can just check in together.'

A dull blush added spots of red to Martin's pallid skin. 'I… umm…I'm going business class.'

All those times he'd brushed off her enquiries about their flight details, insisting he had everything in hand, suddenly made horrible sense. 'We're not sitting together? We're not even in the same section of the bloody plane?' she hissed, not wanting to make a scene in the crowded hall.

He adjusted the bag over his shoulder, glancing away, but not quick enough for her to miss seeing him roll his eyes. 'Why do you always have to get like this?' he sighed, as though he were the most put-upon husband in the history of the known world. He looked back, but his gaze didn't meet hers. 'Look, the company were generous enough to pay for us both, but their policy doesn't cover business travel for family members. I didn't think it was worth wasting money from our savings on an upgrade for you. It's a big day for me tomorrow. I'll be working for most of the flight so I need to be able to focus on that. Besides, economy on these big planes isn't exactly a hardship and I thought you'd understand…' His voice trailed off, the tone a perfect blend of confusion and disappointment.

He'd thought she'd understand. Which was why he'd deliberately avoided discussing it with her until now. How very like him to put off anything that might involve a difficult conversation. He'd clearly practised his list of excuses and settled on her being a distraction. Like she was some five-year-old child incapable of sitting still for a few hours. It was a bloody night flight, for God's sake, and she'd intended to spend it catching up on a few movies she hadn't seen, and sleeping.

Staring up at him, Eliza wondered, not for the first time, who the hell he was. This was supposed to be a new start for them, the next step in their life together; it wasn't unreasonable of her to expect they'd be taking it side by side. The twisting tension inside her made her snap at him. 'And what happens after check in, I suppose you're going to use the business class lounge rather than sit with me and the rest of the plebs in the departures area?'

He folded his arms, the corners of his eyes narrowing the way they did when he got angry. Martin wasn't a great one for losing his temper, but she knew the look. If avoidance and cajoling wouldn't work to talk her around, he used it as a last resort. If he thought he could intimidate her into backing down though, he was in for a shock. 'What is it about this that is so difficult for you to understand? When we get to Abu Dhabi tomorrow, I have to work. You can go to the hotel and sleep, or laze by the pool, or whatever the hell you want to do with yourself. Why are you making this difficult?' *Oh God, that tone in his voice!* It took all her self-control not to slap him for it.

Conscious they were blocking the entrance to the check in lanes, Eliza towed her cases a few feet away, then waited for Martin to join her. He rolled his eyes again, and her fists clenched over the handles as the swirl in her belly turned into a vortex that threatened to suck the life out of her. 'I thought we were in this together,' she said, pitching her voice low. 'You knew about my reservations about leaving my family and friends so far behind, about having nothing to do but stay at home and keep house for you. We *talked* about this and yet now you're treating me as some kind of hanger-on. This is supposed to be you and me, and baby makes three, remember? The Wilkinsons vs the World.'

Martin shoved a hand through his hair. 'You can do whatever you want for the next three years. I'm making enough money to set us up for life. Most women would jump at the chance to do nothing but "keep house". It's not exactly an onerous task, is it? You'll be free to spend time on your projects. Christ, we don't even have to have a kid if you don't want one, I just thought it would make you happy.'

His words struck her like a blow. All those hours spent talking about this move, when she'd thought they were finally making a proper connection again, and he'd been humouring her? 'Make me happy? Nothing about this makes me happy, Martin, but you went ahead and did it anyway! Applied for the job without telling me, then accepted it before we'd finished discussing the pros and cons.'

Another flash of understanding sent her reeling. 'Do you even *want* to have a baby?' She'd had her own doubts, not about having children—she'd always dreamed of a brood of chubby little babies growing into gorgeous, happy children surrounded by the same love she'd always known growing up—but about the timing of it all.

He shrugged. 'I'm not bothered either way. I just thought it made sense given how much time you'll have on your hands.'

Like bringing a child into the world was on a par with one of her 'little projects'. 'We're talking about creating a new life together, not knitting a bloody jumper!' She was shouting now, but it was that or start crying.

The vortex shifted into a hurricane, and it was all she could do to cling on as her reality shredded into a thousand tiny fragments and blew away. 'Who *are* you?'

Martin tutted loudly. 'Lower your voice, for God's sake and don't be such a drama queen. I'm your bloody husband, that's who I am. We can talk about this later. Let's just get checked in, okay?'

No. It wasn't okay. Nothing was okay, and it hadn't been for a long time.

Eliza took a step backwards. 'I'm not doing this.'

'Not doing what?' Even now, he didn't get it. He wasn't her husband. He was nothing like the shy, idealistic boy she'd fallen in love with. And she was nothing like the naïve girl he'd sworn to love forever. They'd been children, playing at love. Things might have been different if they'd found some common ground along the way, a fertile plot to plant the seeds of that first love so it could flourish and grow. They'd grown up, but not together, and all that bound them were words they'd said without understanding the importance behind them. 'I'm not going with you.'

Furious now, if the muscle twitching in his jaw was anything to go by, he snatched for her arm. When she twisted to evade his grip, he circled around until she was trapped between his body and their luggage. 'Don't be so bloody stupid. You're going to stop this nonsense, right now. Get your bags and come on.'

Her hands shook at the harshness in his voice, but she knotted them in the folds of her skirt, refusing to back down. 'I'll go with you, on one condition. Tell me why you love me.'

'Christ, Eliza. I don't have time for these games. I love you because you're my wife.' He glanced away, and she could see his chest rise and fall as he sucked in a deep breath. When he looked back at her, the anger appeared to have gone, but where? No one could switch moods that quickly, so why was he trying to hide it from her? She was derailing his well-laid plans and he had every right to be mad at her. And what else had he been hiding? How much more resentment had he swallowed down hoping for an easy life? Probably as much, if not more, than she had.

Feeling like she didn't know him at all, Eliza raised her hands in a placatory gesture as she edge out from where he'd crowded her against their bags. 'That's not enough, don't you see? And it shouldn't be enough for you, either.'

Martin put his hands on his hips. The muscle in his jaw had started twitching again, but his voice carried that same weary, patronising tone. 'Couples have their ups and downs. Life can't be all hearts and flowers.'

'Trotting out a couple of trite old sayings isn't going to fix this.' With every second that passed, the certainty grew within her—it was over between them.

His eyes narrowed. 'Just what do you expect me to do about it then?'

Eliza shook her head. 'Nothing. This is a good opportunity for you, you should make the most of it. It's not good for me, though, and I hope in time you'll come to see that. You'll be so busy getting to grips with everything, you won't even notice I'm not there.'

'This is ridiculous.' He reached for her again, and she tucked her arm behind her back away from him. 'The bloody house is leased out; they're moving in next week! Where the hell will you go?'

That he even needed to ask told her how little he knew and understood her. The fact she hadn't even considered returning to the little starter home they'd shared for the past five years only served to reinforce to her she was doing the right thing. Seizing the handles of her suitcases, she turned away. 'I'm going back to Lavender Bay.'

'I won't run after you.' *Good, she didn't want him to.* 'Eliza? Jesus Christ!' His frustrated shout faded beneath the rapid beat of her shoes striking on the tiled floor of the airport. Refusing to look back, Eliza kept walking until she'd cleared the automatic doors and joined the end of the queue of travellers waiting for a taxi.

Staring at her shoes, she watched as a tear splashed on the shiny red patent and rolled off. With a sniffle, she fought back the tears and clicked her heels together three times as she whispered. 'There's no place like home.'

Chapter Two

The screaming had become so much a part of Jack's life over the past month that he was out of bed and halfway across the landing before he was even properly awake. He'd just flipped on the light when the door to his mum's room opened, and she appeared next to him with one arm hooked in the sleeve of her dressing gown, the rest of it trailing behind her. A section of her short grey hair was flattened against her scalp, the other side standing up in a lopsided wave, showing how she'd tossed and turned in her sleep. The circles beneath her eyes stood out like bruises against her pale skin. She looked terrible—at least ten years older than the fifty-seven she was due to turn in a couple of weeks. She was a ghostly shadow of the vibrant, robust woman who'd filled his life with laughter since the day he was born.

When was the last time he'd heard her laugh? The stray thought was shattered by another gut-wrenching scream. Jack shuddered, then braced his shoulders. 'I'll see to him, Mum. Go back to bed.'

Tears filled her eyes. 'Poor little lamb, I wish there was something we could do.'

'Me too, we just have to give him time. We have to give all of us time.' Jack turned the handle and slipped into his nephew's room. The night-light Jack's brother Jason had purchased for his son when Noah had been tiny cast soft blue stars and moons onto the wall and ceiling. Having been declared 'too-babyish' just six months previously, it had been retrieved from the cupboard when the nightmares had started the night Jason died.

Ducking down next to the figure huddled beneath a *Star Wars* duvet, Jack touched a gentle hand to the rigid shoulder. 'Noah? Shh, now. Uncle Jack's here, everything will be okay.' The lie curdled on his tongue. Nothing could ever be right for the poor kid, not since that terrible early-April morning when all their lives had been turned upside down and shattered by the terrible car accident. One bitter twist of fate had robbed Jack of his elder brother and made him into a surrogate father overnight. The fact that Jason had entrusted his son to his keeping was a weight he didn't know if he could carry—and an honour he would spend the rest of his days trying to be worthy of.

It feels daft to be writing this, Jack, but the solicitor told me I needed to make my wishes clear should the worst happen, so here goes. In the event of my death, I want you to be the one responsible for Noah's well-being and upbringing. You're the only person I can trust to give him the life he deserves, to raise him how I would. A normal life. Give him the choices we never had, Jack...

The words of Jason's letter to him, left with the solicitor for safekeeping together with his will, were etched into Jack's memory in indelible ink. He knew they'd hurt their mum with their not-so-implied criticism of the way she and their dad had raised them. Jack had been not much older than Noah when his parents had decided to escape from the rat-race and start a new life in the country. It had been one big adventure to his ten-year-old self. At fourteen, Jason had been devastated to leave his friends and life in London behind to move to an old farm in the back of beyond, and he'd never quite recovered from that initial resentment, though it'd been almost twenty years ago. *And now he'd never be able to heal the rift with their mother.*

Growing up on the farm it had been the Gilberts against the

world, an isolated existence thanks to his parents home-schooling their sons. Jack had loved the cosy security and been perfectly content with it just being the four of them most days. Jason had chafed against it, especially when his plans to escape off to a job in the city after finishing at university had been thwarted by their father's early passing. Jason had given up a promising position with a trading house to help manage the farm. Though he'd never said so, it was clear he'd rather be anywhere else and every free moment he could manage, Jason disappeared somewhere. He'd never talked about what he got up to, and never invited Jack along either which had hurt more than he'd ever admitted.

Pain sliced through him, and Jack rubbed his chest to ease the phantom ache. It was ridiculous to be upset over something that had happened a dozen years or more ago, but he'd have followed Jason into the bowels of hell given the chance. Things changed abruptly when his brother had returned at the end of one trip with a visibly pregnant woman in tow. The pain vanished at the mere thought of Lydia. God, Jack had hated her pouting face on first sight.

Those mysterious weekends became a thing of the past, and Jason seemed to grow up overnight. He started taking things at the farm more seriously, started making all these plans for the future, but Lydia was having none of it. Country life was boring. *Everything* was boring, especially being tied down with a baby. She'd lasted all of three months after Noah was born before packing her things and leaving Jason literally holding the baby. The last they'd heard of her, she'd moved to New York with her new, obscenely wealthy, older husband.

Though he'd resigned himself to remaining at the farm Jason had been determined to give Noah a very different upbringing to theirs, making sure he was properly socialised through nursery attendance then enrolment in the local primary school.

Noah whimpered, but didn't wake. Smoothing his hand in slow circles over the boy's back, Jack kept up a litany of soft whispers. Sometimes it would work, and his nephew would settle again, sometimes not. There was nothing he could do but wait and see. The ache in his knees spoke of another long day on the farm, and Jack stifled a groan as he shifted position to sit on the floor.

It might have been the change in pressure against his back, or some dark terror conjured by his mind that disturbed Noah. Whatever it was, the boy turned over suddenly and opened his eyes. 'Uncle Jack?'

Jack brushed the sweaty strands of hair off Noah's forehead. 'I'm here, buddy.'

Noah's face crumpled. 'I couldn't find Daddy. I looked everywhere, but he wasn't there.' The last word came out in a strangled whisper.

'Ah, buddy, come here.' Jack opened his arms and his nephew slid from beneath the sheets to crawl into his lap. Thin arms wrapped around his neck, and Noah burrowed his damp face into Jack's chest. Bitter, painful experience told him the best thing to do was to let Noah cry it out of his system, so Jack set his jaw and let the boy soak the front of his T-shirt as he rocked him gently.

The back of his own eyes burned, but the tears remained unshed as they had since the moment the police had knocked on the front door and told him Jason was dead. Anger kept them at bay. At the driver of the heavy goods vehicle which had jack-knifed on a dry, clear day causing a horrendous pileup on the motorway. Jason had been in the middle lane preparing to over-take—according to the eye-witness accounts the police had related to the family—and had stood no chance.

Jack was furious with himself, too, for sending his brother on an errand he couldn't be bothered to run, and at Jason for dashing off in that ridiculous bloody sports car he'd insisted on buying as an early mid-life crisis present. From the moment Jason had pulled up in the yard in the sporty red car, Jack had hated the damn thing.

A waste of bloody money—money that could have been invested in one of the new side-ventures Jack wanted to try but Jason had refused to consider—and completely impractical for driving up and down the dirt lane that led to the farm. Thanks to ruts left by their tractor and the thick mud that formed every time it rained, the stupid vehicle spent more time parked up than being used.

Noah's sobs quietened into the odd sniffle, and Jack forced the anger back down once more. Touching a finger to Noah's cheek, he smiled when the boy raised his head. 'A bit better now?' When Noah nodded, Jack lifted him onto the edge of the bed, so he could stand up. 'Do you think you can sleep again?'

Noah's bottom lip disappeared between his teeth. Recognising the precursor to more tears, Jack bent down to scoop the boy up. 'Oof, you're getting heavy, buddy, I'll have to tell Nanna to lay off the cakes.' In truth, Noah was a wisp of a thing, all joints and gangly limbs from a recent growth spurt which had burned off the last hints of puppy fat. He'd been such a roly-poly little lad, a miniature buddha, all smiles and sweet cuddles until last summer when he'd converted all that girth into height.

There was no mistaking him for anything other than a Gilbert, now. If he kept on growing like this, he might even outstrip his dad who'd topped Jack's six-foot frame by a good inch. If it weren't for the four years between them, Jack and his brother could have been alike enough to be taken for twins at first glance, and staring into Noah's hazel eyes was like looking into a mirror of the past. Even the grief etched on his face was familiar, although Jack had been three times six-year-old Noah's age when his own father had died.

There'd been mutterings of a family curse by some old biddy at Jason's funeral which Jack had shut down with a filthy glare. People loved that kind of crap, though he hadn't realised how much until his family had been on the end of the gossip.

Settling Noah on his hip, though he was almost too big to be held that way anymore, Jack pressed a kiss to his forehead. 'How about some hot chocolate?'

Noah perked up considerably at the suggestion of his favourite treat and even managed a little smile by the time Jack negotiated his way down the steep stairs and into the square hallway on the ground floor. Wincing as his toes touched the chilly flagstone floor, Jack made his way to the large sprawling kitchen-diner that was the heart of the old farmhouse. He deposited Noah on one of the ladder-back kitchen chairs, sighing in relief to be standing on one of the cheerful rag rugs which covered the bare stone floor.

A sleepy woof greeted them from the large basket tucked close against the Aga as Sebastian raised his head to greet them. Leaving Noah's side, Jack crossed the room to flick the kettle on, pausing to bend over and scrub the chocolate Labrador in his favourite spot behind his left ear. Bastian rolled his eyes in bliss, tongue lolling. 'Silly thing,' Jack said, affectionately, and the dog wagged his tail as though in agreement.

Retrieving a box from the overhead cupboard, Jack scattered a couple of biscuits into Bastian's bowl then gathered a pair of mugs and the instant hot chocolate mix while he waited for the kettle to boil. His mum always made the whole thing with hot milk, but it was too late for Jack to be bothered faffing around with pots and pans. Besides, Noah wouldn't mind—the distraction of being out of bed and away from the nightmare would be enough to set him to rights once more.

The dog scoffed his midnight snack then ambled over to the table where he placed his head on Noah's knee. He'd become attuned to the boy's moods, offering gentle comfort whenever he sensed Noah was upset. Casting a quick glance over his shoulder, Jack couldn't help but smile at the image the small boy and the big dog created together.

Jack mixed their drinks, adding a generous splash of milk to increase the creaminess of the flavour and to make sure it wasn't too hot to drink. He wanted Noah settled back in bed as soon as possible so he'd be rested enough for school in the morning. Both Jack and his mum had agreed it was important to keep Noah to his regular schedule, and with the support of his teacher, he seemed to be coping okay during the day. It was the nights which were the real problem.

Placing the mugs down on the scarred surface of the block pine table, Jack took the chair next to Noah. Bastian immediately circled around Noah's chair to wriggle his broad body in between them. Jack shifted his seat over to make room. The dog nudged his cold nose into Jack's hand, a silent demand for more ear scratches. Obliging his beloved pet, Jack sipped his chocolate, keeping a weather eye on Noah who seemed a lot calmer now, his attention all on his own drink.

When only the dregs remained in his cup, Jack placed his hand on the back of Noah's head. 'We've both got a busy day tomorrow, are you about ready to get some more sleep?'

Noah gave a little nod as he placed his mug carefully on the table. 'Uncle Jack, would it be all right if I came in with you?'

Christ, the hope and worry in his big hazel eyes was enough to break a man's heart. 'Of course, it's all right.' He held up a finger and wagged it at his nephew in warning. 'No farting though.'

His nephew giggled. 'Bastian farts much worse than me.' They both looked at the dog wedged between them.

'You're not wrong there, buddy. Remember when Nanna gave him cod liver oil to help when he got itchy skin?' His mother had embraced her new holistic life to the full and it wasn't only the human occupants of the farm who were subjected to her home-made remedies. Jack didn't think he'd ever smelt anything so bad in his entire life. Luckily, after speaking to the vet, they'd switched it out for a spoonful of sunflower oil mixed in with Bastian's food which had eased his skin problems with less dire side-effects.

Noah wrinkled his nose. 'He was so stinky!'

Bastian turned his head from side to side, giving them both

his best innocent face. Jack tugged the dog's ear, fondly. 'Yes, mister, we're talking about you.' He stood, put their mugs in the sink to soak then turned to hold out a hand to Noah. 'Come on, then.'

The dog trailed them to the kitchen threshold, his face a picture of pure misery when Jack tried to nudge him back enough to pull the door closed. 'Forget it, mate,' he said.

Bastian whined, making Noah tug on Jack's fingers. 'Please, Uncle Jack.'

The dog thumped his tail as the weight of two pairs of hopeful eyes bored into Jack. 'Oh, bloody hell,' he muttered under his breath. 'All right, but when Nanna tells me off in the morning, I'm telling her it's totally your fault.'

His nephew skipped up the stairs, one spoiled dog in tow while Jack turned off the lights and closed the doors. By the time he'd followed up after them, they were already occupying most of his king-size bed, together with the raggedy teddy Noah had had since a baby, leaving a thin sliver down one side for Jack to crawl onto. Wrestling enough of his duvet from beneath the dog to cover his back, he then rearranged the sprawl of little boy limbs until Noah was mostly vertical on the mattress.

A foul smell hit his nose, followed by a giggle. 'Naughty Bastian,' Noah said, fooling no one.

'Yeah, right. Go to sleep, stinky boy.' Jack punched his pillow into shape, then settled his head onto it with a sigh.

Little fingers curled around his forearm. 'Night, Uncle Jack.'

'Night, buddy.'

Soft snores followed not long after, a counterpoint to the dog's snuffling breaths. Careful not to move his arm and risk waking Noah, Jack rolled onto his back and willed himself to join them in sleep. It wasn't to be. The first hint of dawn showed behind his bedroom curtains before he finally dropped off.

'Jack?' A soft hand on his shoulder shook him awake. 'It's past eight o'clock.'

Feeling as though he'd only just closed them, he forced his gritty eyes open to find himself nose-to-nose with Noah's teddy bear. He flinched back at the unexpected sight. 'Huh? What?'

His mum, Sally, crossed the room to open the curtains, causing him to fling an arm across his face to shield himself from the already bright sunlight. 'Have a heart, Mum!' Two seconds later he was sitting bolt upright in bed. 'Where's Noah?'

His mum finished opening the top window, then turned to regard him. 'He's downstairs finishing his breakfast. I popped in earlier, but you were dead to the world, so I thought I'd let you sleep a bit longer.' Her nose wrinkled. 'It smells dreadful in here.'

Adjusting his pillows so he could lean against the headboard, Jack reached for the steaming mug of black coffee on his bedside cabinet with an appreciative sigh. 'We're men, we smell. It's the law.'

She laughed. 'Apparently so.' Her expression sobered. 'Noah's a bit quiet this morning, did he say anything to you?'

Jack swallowed a mouthful of the hot, bitter brew, grateful for the energising power of caffeine. 'Only that he had that dream where he couldn't find his dad again. He went straight off to sleep after a hot drink.' The next slurp of coffee finally kicked his brain into full gear, and a feeling of dread stole over him. 'What time did you say it was?'

'Just after eight.'

He threw back the covers with his free hand, almost spilling his coffee in his haste to get out of bed. 'Bloody hell, I need to get a move on. I'm supposed to be planting the top of the south field.'

The weather had taken a dip after the Easter holidays and had only settled down over the past couple of weeks. A decent stretch of sunny days had dried and warmed the soil sufficiently for him to be able to transfer last year's cuttings from the greenhouse to the fields. Clearing the old plants in preparation had been miserable, muddy work so it would be nice to be out there and feel the sun on his back.

'I'm sorry, Jack, I just thought an extra hour would do you good, especially after you'd been up with Noah.'

Though he appreciated his mum's intentions, he wished she hadn't let him sleep in. With Jason gone, there never seemed to be enough hours in the day to get everything done. He'd have to bite the bullet and hire some extra help soon, but he couldn't quite make himself do it yet. They had seasonal helpers at harvest time, and he hoped that between him and his mum they could make it through until then.

Taking the step to replace Jason would be a final acceptance of everything they'd lost, and he just wasn't ready to try and work alongside someone else. They might not have seen eye to eye on everything, but he and Jason had lived and breathed lavender since they were children and knew the inner workings of the farm by heart.

Catching sight of the worry lines on his mum's brow, Jack finished off the last of his coffee then bent to brush a quick kiss on her cheek. 'It's fine, Mum. You did the right thing. Thanks for the coffee, and for seeing to Noah.'

Sally took the mug from his hand. 'Give me that. Go and have your shower. I'll rustle you up a bacon sandwich and a thermos to take out with you, and then I'll get Noah off to school…' She paused by the door. '…Or he can stay home for a few days? I can make sure he keeps up with everything.' The hope in her voice was enough to break his heart. She'd given up her career as a university lecturer to pursue a dream of raising her sons away from the rampant consumerism of modern life. Having missed so much of their growing up thanks to long hours spent climbing the corporate ladder, their father had been in wholehearted agreement at his wife's decision to home-school both Jack and Jason. Their lessons had been scheduled to fit around working life on the farm and had involved as much about life as they did the curriculum.

The isolation had never bothered Jack. After being a latchkey kid, he'd been thrilled to have so much of his parents' attention, but it had been another thorn in Jason's side and something he'd been determined not to repeat with his own son. Feeling torn between honouring his brother's wishes and the naked need in his mother's eyes, Jack clenched his fist against his thigh. 'I think it's important to keep Noah to his regular routine, don't you?'

She flinched as though he'd struck her, before fixing on a bright smile that failed to get anywhere near her eyes. 'You're right, of course. I'm just being overly sentimental. The last thing he needs is me fussing all over him.'

This was his life now, it seemed—hurting one person in order to honour his promise to another. Ignoring the stab of guilt in his heart, Jack faked his own smile. 'You can fuss over me anytime, Mum.'

'Get on with yourself.' She shooed him towards the bathroom, her smile genuine this time, much to Jack's relief.

True to her word, there was a foil-wrapped package and a thermos waiting on the kitchen table for him, together with a large water bottle, an apple and a banana. Jack finished rolling back the cuffs on the old checked shirt he'd slung over jeans and a T-shirt, then scooped up the food and drink to stow it in the rucksack he used to cart his bits and pieces around. Exiting the kitchen via the boot room, he stomped his feet into his work boots, tied the laces and headed out the back door.

Jack stowed his bag in the front of the sky-blue compact tractor parked in the yard, then pulled out the safety checklist book from beneath the seat. Their dad had been fanatical about safety, and his sons had carried on in the same tradition.

Nothing moved until it had been checked, even on days like this when Jack was running behind schedule. Satisfied the flat-bed trailer behind the tractor was hitched correctly, he circled both trailer and tractor, checking the tyres as well as the general condition of the bodywork. The engine came next—oil and fluid levels, connections, belts and hoses were all surveyed for wear. Last came the cab where everything was in order, well, once he'd cleaned the mirrors and wiped a layer of dust from the inside of the front window.

The greenhouse lay beyond the main farmhouse on the other side of the distillery, next to an old farmworker's cottage. Jack trundled out of the yard, pausing to check the driveway in front of the house was clear before he ventured further. Their old battered Land Rover was nowhere to be seen, so the school run was already underway. Confident he could move around without risk to anyone else, Jack followed the driveway to his destination. Pulling up outside the cottage, Jack made a mental note to track down the keys for the place and have a nose around.

He and Jason had used it as a hideaway when they'd been kids, but it had been empty for a long time. His mum had talked about moving in there—said she wanted her own space away from all the testosterone in the farmhouse. Only they'd lost Jason, and she'd put her plans on hold to help Jack. Perhaps it was time for him to pick up the slack. Noah wasn't the only one who would benefit from sticking to a routine. It was time to stop fire-fighting and accept the new status quo. The farm was his responsibility now and so was Noah. If he could get the cottage into a habitable state it would give his mum the space she craved whilst giving Jack room to breathe. He knew she only wanted what was best for them all, but if she kept making decisions about Noah without consulting him they could end up on a collision course.

A waft of warm air greeted him as he tugged open the greenhouse door. After propping it open, he dropped the tailgate of the trailer and began to transfer the first row of black plastic pots from the greenhouse. He'd taken the cuttings from the previous year's new plants, a process they followed annually to ensure they preserved the quality and consistency of their crop. Although small now, the plants would spread and thrive within just a few short weeks, filling the air with their distinctive heady perfume.

Half an hour later the trailer was full, and so was his stomach thanks to the sandwich and a mug of hot tea. The steady work had warmed his muscles, so he paused to strip off the checked shirt before heading up to the south field. It would be a back-breaking day, and as he jolted along the trackway, he was already promising himself a long soak in the bath at the end of it.

He got the last of the plants in just as the sun was going down, his back screaming in protest as he bent over one last time to tamp down the sandy soil around the bush. With a groan, he gathered the empty plant pot and stowed it with the others in the trailer. Heaving himself into the cab of the tractor, Jack switched on the lights and chugged his way back down to the sprawl of buildings that were the heart of the farm.

Parking the tractor in the rear yard, he grabbed his bag and headed for the back door. The pots and trailer would both need washing out, but that would be a job for the morning. Bending to unlace his boots elicited another groan, and he all but hobbled into the kitchen to find his mum and Noah sitting at the kitchen table, a book held between them. The scent of something delicious rose from a large pot on the top of the Aga.

'All finished?' his mum asked as he paused at the sink to wash his hands.

He nodded. 'Just about. I'll need to take the water truck up there tomorrow, and give them a soak, but then it's done. Have you guys eaten?'

She shook her head. 'Noah wanted to wait for you, didn't you, poppet?' She stroked her grandson's cheek as he tilted his head to glance up at Jack.

There goes my dream of a soak in the bath. 'I'd better jump in the shower, then. Five minutes, all right?'

Sally pushed to her feet. 'No rush, love. I need to put the bread in to warm, yet. We're having Irish stew.'

His eyes practically rolled back in his head. Part of his parents' back-to-nature kick had been cooking everything from scratch. No more Pot Noodles or takeaway pizzas for the Gilbert family—something else Jason had resented when they'd first moved down to the bay. Jack had pretended to be miffed in an act of brotherly solidarity, but he'd loved every meal his mum or dad had placed in front of him, even the burnt ones. 'Sounds heavenly. I'll be right back to set the table.'

True to his word, he was showered, changed into tracksuit bottoms and a T-shirt and back in the kitchen in a flash. The heat from the power shower had done wonders for his stiff back, and he moved around freely, laying out mats, cutlery and glasses as he chatted to Noah about his day at school.

'I got a smiley in my book today,' his nephew said with a shy smile. He'd never had to know much about Noah's schooling whilst Jason was around, other than pitching in with the school run, so he was still getting to grips with how it all worked.

When he cast an enquiring glance towards his mum, she said, 'Noah stayed behind at break time to help his teacher clear up.'

'We did painting. I put all the brushes in the big sink and put the paints in the cupboard after Miss Daniels put the lids on them.'

'That's great, buddy. I bet she was glad to have you help her.' Jack held up his palm. 'Give me five.' Noah patted his little hand against Jack's, practically glowing with the praise.

'And he helped me to make dinner, didn't you?' his mum added.

'Wow. I reckon all that helping out deserves a reward, don't you?' Jack crossed the kitchen to tug open the freezer. 'Ah, ha! I knew we had some left.' He turned around to show the tub of brightly striped ice cream. Neapolitan had always been his and Jason's favourite, and they'd passed their love down to Noah. 'What do you say, Nanna? Has Noah earned an after-dinner treat?'

Smiling fondly, Sally nodded her head. 'I should say so! Can you give a hand with this, Jack?'

He put the ice cream back, then took the oven gloves his mum held out to him and transferred the bubbling pot of stew from the cooker top to the thick cork mat on the table. Removing the lid sent a waft of delicious steam teasing his nose. 'This smells amazing.' His mum took her seat with a smile and the three of them settled down to enjoy a delicious family supper. Jack glanced from his mum to his nephew, filled with love and pride for both of them. In spite of the horror of their loss, their little family was pulling together.

It would be getting busy around the place soon and he'd have even less time to spend with Noah, best to make the most of it while he could. 'How about we walk to school tomorrow, Noah?' Even with Noah's shorter legs it wouldn't be more than half an hour from the farm into Lavender Bay, and it was all downhill. The exercise would do them both good and would also give him the chance to give Noah his undivided attention. 'If we get up a little bit earlier, we can take Bastian down to the beach to play. Would you like that?'

When Noah beamed at him, Jack knew he'd made the right call. The feeling of contentment stayed with him through Noah's bedtime routine, Jack's late evening walk with Bastian and on until he'd managed to read about five pages of the paperback thriller on his nightstand before his eyelids were drooping. *We made it through another day*, was his final sleepy thought as he turned out the light.

The screams from Noah's room jerked him awake at 2 a.m.

Chapter Three

Libby Stone came bursting into Eliza's old bedroom, a bottle of wine in one hand and a white carrier bag in the other. 'I bought emergency supplies,' she said, brandishing both. She stopped in her tracks, dropping to sit on the edge of the bed and when she spoke again, her voice was much gentler. 'Oh, Eliza! Oh, don't cry, darling, we'll help you sort everything out.' Dumping the wine and the bag on the floor at her feet, she gathered Eliza into a hug.

'I'm okay,' Eliza managed to say around the tears which had come on unexpectedly earlier that evening. Five weeks to the day since she'd left Martin in the airport and it felt like she'd lurched out of one rut and fallen straight into another. Her parents had welcomed her with open arms, though with more than a little concern about her snap decision. They'd danced around the subject, her mum's comments rather more barbed than those from her dad, but accepted her request for space to sort things out. Only she hadn't sorted anything out, just slipped into helping out in the pub, and now they were acting like she had a job for life behind the bar.

She knew how upset they'd both been at her brother Sam's decision to pursue his dream of opening his own restaurant rather than taking over running the pub as previous generations of Barneses had, and now it seemed to be falling to Eliza by default of her return. And she didn't want it any more than Sam had. In a fit of confusion, she'd texted Libby for help.

Another set of arms enfolded her from behind, and the soothing tones of her other best friend, Beth Reynolds, murmured against her ear. 'Of course you are. We've got you now.' Knowing it to be true, some of the desperate panic seizing Eliza's heart eased.

She sat up a little, and her friends eased back from the embrace to look at her. Beth offered her a tissue, and the three of them laughed when Eliza blew her nose, making enough noise to put a baby elephant to shame. Libby stood up. 'I'm going to raid the kitchen for some plates and glasses, be right back.'

Eliza heard her talking to someone on the landing, her brother, Sam, from the deepness of the tone, and sure enough he followed Libby into the room. 'I'm not stopping,' he said. 'Just making a contribution to the cause.' He held up his hands to show a chocolate fudge cake, then placed it on a free space on her dressing table. Bending at the waist, he brushed a quick kiss on Beth's cheek and whispered something in her ear.

It had been weird for Eliza at first when Sam and Beth had started dating that spring. But seeing the way they gravitated towards each other every time they were in the same space, it was clear they were head over heels. Although Sam kept his bedroom at the pub, he spent almost all of his free time at Beth's and Eliza doubted it would be too long before they were living together officially. Her heart twisted. As much as she adored them both and wanted nothing but their happiness, the easy way they had with each other served only to drive home how much Eliza had lost.

Returning with plates and glasses, Libby sent a mock-pout towards Sam as he straightened up from Beth's side. 'What about me?' She puckered her lips at Sam, making kissing noises.

He blew her a kiss then ruffled her wild, spiky hair. 'What are we calling this, seasick green?'

'Mermaid, actually.' She poked her tongue out at him. 'Why are you still here?'

With a grin, he held his hands up in surrender as he backed towards the door. 'I'm leaving, I'm leaving.'

The light-hearted interlude provided enough of a distraction for Eliza to calm her tears. She mopped her face dry whilst Libby removed three parcels wrapped in white paper from the carrier bag and placed each on a plate. She handed one to Eliza. 'Small haddock and chips, and—' she pulled a Styrofoam cup from the bag '—Mushy peas.'

She wasn't the least bit hungry, but not wishing to offend her friend, Eliza tugged the paper open. Her mouth watered as the smell of hot chips and vinegar hit her nostrils, making her realise she hadn't eaten anything beyond half a slice of toast that morning. Tipping the contents of the paper onto her plate, she dumped the pot of peas next to it and her stomach gave a rumble of approval. Libby offered her some cutlery, which she accepted with a grateful smile. 'Thanks for this.'

Libby shrugged. 'With the kind of staff discount I get, it's no big deal.' Given that Libby's dad owned the local fish and chip shop just a few doors along the promenade from the pub, that was something of an understatement. Libby handed Eliza a glass of wine. 'And I scored this from your mum on my way through the bar, so freebies all round.' She clinked her glass against Eliza's. 'Cheers.'

Eliza returned the gesture, took a large mouthful then placed her glass on the bedside table. Silence settled over the three of them as they each began to eat. She knew they must be full of questions, but the fact they didn't push her to talk proved once again how important the bond between them was. She should never have let Martin talk her into moving so far away.

The food in her mouth formed into a hard lump and she

reached for her wine to wash it down. 'What am I going to do?'

Beth set her knife and fork together. 'About what?'

A bitter laugh escaped Eliza. 'Everything. You know, I lie on this bed every night running over the last ten years of my life and I can't tell you what Martin's honest opinion is about anything. I used to credit the fact we never argued as a sign of a healthy relationship, but now I realise he just said whatever he thought I wanted to hear.' She rubbed her aching eyes. 'If he wanted to do something, he just went ahead with it and then would make out he'd done it for our benefit. If it was something I wanted, and it didn't interfere with his plans then he just let me get on with it.'

Their house was a prime example. Martin had found it, even gone so far as to research the mortgage payments, access to local facilities, how much money they could save compared to renting because of the cheaper cost of living—everything to make the fact he'd already accepted a job hundreds of miles from their home town seem perfectly logical. When it came to the interior, he'd given her free rein, saying she was the one with the creative streak and could use it as a template to show off her skills. She'd been so excited at the prospect, she'd planned every room down to the smallest nick-nacks, all the while believing it was Martin's gift to her, his way of making her as happy and as settled as possible in their new environment. In reality, he'd already got what he wanted when she'd agreed to the relocation so he didn't care whether she painted the kitchen blue, cream or flamingo pink. He'd said as much when she'd asked for his opinion, taking the sheen off her happiness in the process.

And he'd done the same thing when it came to Abu Dhabi, making her believe he was only exploring the possibilities when in reality he'd made it as far as the final interview stage before mentioning it. When he did raise it, he'd bamboozled her with stacks of information, from how much money he would make over three years, to brochures about winter cruises around the

Arabian Gulf, to estimates on the monthly rent they'd get by letting their home out.

Some might call the effort he'd gone to thoughtful, but Eliza had felt powerless under the onslaught. There were so very many good reasons for them to do it, the fact she simply hadn't wanted to go felt selfish. *Though not as selfish as walking out at the last moment.* Her guilty conscience had a point. Martin had only gone ahead and done those things because she hadn't stood up to him. Not quite sure what she wanted to do with her life beyond some thing creative, she'd chosen a university course which covered a broad spectrum of art and design hoping to settle upon a specialty eventually. She'd dabbled in everything from pottery to dress-making and loved it all.

Then Martin had been headhunted in their final year while she'd still been uncertain which direction to go in. After much soul-searching they'd agreed she would put her further studies on hold for a couple of years until Martin was settled in at work and she'd found herself a job working for the local council as an administrator.

She'd channelled her creative interests into their house and making her own clothes. After taking a few commissions from people she worked with who admired her style, she'd branched out into selling online via *Etsy*. Her little shop had ticked over thanks to word of mouth recommendations, but she'd never quite got to grips with marketing it properly. Somehow, two years had stretched into four, and still the timing hadn't been quite right for her to go back to school.

And now here she was with a wasted degree, a raft of general office skills and no idea what to with herself. She threw herself back on the bed and stared up at the ceiling. 'What am I doing with my life? What was the point in leaving Martin to end up back here pulling pints night after night?'

Beth took her hand and shook it gently to draw Eliza's attention to her. 'You don't have to justify your decision to anyone in this room other than yourself. And, whatever you decide we will support you.'

'But—'

'Whatever.' Beth cut off the protest from Libby with a glare past Eliza's shoulder.

'All right,' Libby grumbled. 'But I still think Martin is a wanker.'

A snort of laughter bubbled from Eliza as Beth simply shook her head. Libby had always been the most plain spoken of the three of them, and Eliza hoped that would never change. She didn't want them to pretend around her, she needed their honesty, even if it hurt sometimes. She owed it to them to be honest too. 'My marriage is over. It's not about the move to Abu Dhabi, that was just the final straw. I haven't been happy for a long time, and I'm as much to blame for that as Martin. I'm twenty-six years old and I've got absolutely nothing to show for my life. I can't go backwards, but I have no idea how to move on, or what I want to move on to.'

Silence settled over the room for a few minutes as they all absorbed the import of her statement. Eliza waited for her heart to reject her admission that things were over for good with Martin, for her soul to cry out in protest and insist what they'd had was worth fighting for. There were no tears, no flutters of panic, just a deep sense of calm settling over her. It hurt. God, did it hurt, to know she was closing the door on what had been her day-to-day reality for the past ten years. But it didn't feel like she was making a mistake. She knew what she *didn't* want, now if only she could work out what she did.

Two weeks after her outburst, Eliza found herself round at Beth's place hiding out from her dad who wanted to talk her through the orders for that week. He and her mum were still gung-ho about teaching Eliza the ins and outs of the pub, and she hadn't plucked up the courage to tell them not to pin their hopes on her. It didn't seem right turning them down until she could offer a better reason than that she didn't want to do it. She needed a life plan, and she needed one fast.

'And you still haven't heard a word from Martin?' Beth paused in the act of cleaning the glass display cabinet behind the counter of her shop to stare incredulously at her. She'd inherited the old emporium on the seafront at Lavender Bay when her friend and childhood guardian, Eleanor, had passed away earlier in the year. Beth had updated the place to reflect her own tastes, but it still carried the eclectic, fun-loving spirit of the original owner, whose name now graced the business.

Eliza shook her head, glad for the way the tumble of curls shielded her face from Beth's intent look. Martin was refusing to acknowledge any of the emails and messages she'd sent him. Until they could open a dialogue, she was stuck in limbo. Frustration gnawed at her gut. 'Nothing.'

She'd sent him a message to let him know where she was, and then followed it up with several requests to talk. The last one she'd sent had been a couple of days ago after she'd transferred the funds from her ISA into her bank account—the interest rate was so low it wasn't worth hanging onto it—and updated her passwords. She'd felt guilty about it as she and Martin had always had access to each other's account details but had heeded Libby's advice to make sure she had sole control over what was rightfully hers. Living at the pub covered her bed and board for the time being, so she just need a bit of spending money to cover incidentals. They'd have to sort out all their financial stuff in due course, but the rent from their house covered the mortgage and she was happy to let the current lease run its course. Hopefully, Martin would come around in time. It would be a lot easier on the both of them if he did.

Eliza flicked a feather duster over the spinning rack of postcards. 'Can we talk about something else?'

A soft hand touched her shoulder, and Eliza turned to find Beth had abandoned her cleaning. 'Of course we can, I didn't mean to pry. I'll stick the kettle on and we can have a brew…' The bell above the door jangled, indicating the arrival of a new customer. 'I'll be right back.'

'I'll make the tea,' Eliza offered.

Beth nodded then turned to the couple who'd entered. 'Welcome to Eleanor's Emporium!'

Leaving the couple to browse, Beth accepted a mug from Eliza and rested her hip against the counter. 'Have you thought any more about what you're going to do if running the pub is out of the question?'

Eliza took a sip of tea, winced as the too-hot liquid burnt her tongue and shook her head. 'Not really.' Setting down the mug, she adjusted the shoulder of her peach cotton blouse where it had slipped down to reveal the edge of her bra-strap. With loose sleeves which stopped just above her elbows, and a row of gentle pleats down the back, it was one of her favourite styles and perfect for the sweltering weather that had settled over the bay. She'd adapted the design from an old pattern she'd found and had built a summer wardrobe around a half-dozen versions of it in various pastel shades.

'Oh, I love your top, it looks so cool and comfortable!' Startled, Eliza looked up to find the couple had made their way to the counter with an eclectic selection of items, including a couple of the floaty scarves. It was the woman who'd spoken, and she gestured to the scraps of material. 'I'm hoping these will keep the sun off without making me any hotter.'

As someone who caught the sun easily, Eliza had every sympathy for her. 'It's certainly a scorcher out there. I have to cover up too, or I'll be red as a lobster.'

The woman smiled, then cast a pretend glare at the man with her. 'Some people tan to perfection, it makes me sick.' There was no malice in her tone, and the man flashed a bright grin showing he wasn't in the least bit offended. Turning back to Eliza, the woman eyed her blouse. 'You must tell me where you got that lovely top, is it somewhere local?' She sounded hopeful.

'I made it myself, I make most of my clothes.' Eliza stepped back to show the long, tiered skirt she'd paired with the blouse.

'They're beautiful, you should sell them,' the woman said. 'I'd snap them up in a second.'

The man nudged her shoulder. 'Come on, you. Let's find an ice cream and a spot in the shade before you convince this poor girl to give you the clothes off her back.'

Brain whirring, Eliza took another step back while Beth finished serving the pair who left with cheery waves. Her eyes roamed over the cluttered shelves of the emporium. Beth already stocked jewellery and other small artworks from local craftspeople, perhaps she might find room for a few bits and pieces…

'Are you thinking what I'm thinking?' Eliza glanced up to find Beth giving her a Cheshire cat grin.

'Maybe…' Eliza bit her lip. 'But I wouldn't want to impose.'

'Oh, rubbish.' Beth waved away her comment. 'I'm a hard-headed businesswoman these days and you know it. I'm only interested in stock that will sell, and from the covetous looks that woman was giving your outfit, I reckon I'd be on to a winner.'

'It would be worth a try,' Eliza mused. 'And in addition to selling them here I can set up online. It's pretty straightforward, and I've still got my *Etsy* store.' She'd put her account on hiatus, but a couple of clicks and she'd be back up and running.

And it didn't have to be just clothes. She could run up some pretty cushions and other soft furnishings. Or make some soaps and scented candles. People loved to buy homemade things, and she could even rent a pitch at car boot sales or craft fairs. It would be a lot of work, but it would be *her* work. And if she could add a local twist to some of her products, something to tie them in to Lavender Bay…of course! When the idea came to her, it was so obvious she could've smacked herself for not thinking of it sooner. 'I need to pay the Gilberts a visit. What do you think about a range of beauty products and scented candles using lavender from their farm?'

Beth sipped her tea, eyes sparkling with excitement over the rim of her mug. 'I think you've got yourself the makings of a fantastic business. You'll need a hook, though. A brand that reflects who you are and the fact everything is homemade, not mass-produced.'

'I'm not very good at marketing,' Eliza confessed. It had been what had held her back before. She'd never been great at pushing herself forward into the limelight.

'I didn't have a clue when I took over this place, but it's a lot easier than I expected it to be.' Beth reached for her phone. 'That Instagram account Libby persuaded me to open with Banana Monkey was a stroke of genius. He's got so many followers, it's ridiculous!'

Eliza's eyes strayed to the giant wooden banana standing pride of place just inside the door. The monkey perched on the top was modelling a pair of fluorescent pink sunglasses and a floppy sunhat. Eleanor, the original owner of the emporium, had purchased the monstrosity and he'd been a firm fixture ever since. 'I love the photos you post on that account.'

Beth grinned. 'Exactly! I linked it to Facebook and Twitter so everything I post gets shared there automatically. I've even had a few customers pose with him and got them to hashtag the emporium.'

'I'd need something of my own, though…' Eliza rested her elbows on the counter as she thought about it. 'If I can get the Gilberts on board then I can make lavender the central theme.'

'Yes!' Beth scrolled through her phone. 'Look, there's lots of popular lavender hashtags already. What about *Made in Lavender Bay*?'

'Hmm.' It had possibilities, but Eliza wanted something more personal, something to reflect the care and attention she took over the things she made. 'How about *With Love from*

Lavender Bay?' She wrinkled her nose. 'Or is that too cheesy?'

'Oh, I love that! And I don't think it's cheesy, I think it's adorable. You could make a little logo, like a heart made from stalks of lavender twisted together.'

Eliza couldn't help but giggle, the excitement building inside her was too much to contain. If she made the logo simple enough, she could stitch it onto the clothes as well. 'I've got to go and write all this down!' She'd made it halfway around the counter before she spun back to peck a kiss to Beth's cheek. 'You're amazing. Thank you.'

Feeling positive for the first time in months Eliza practically skipped through the front door of The Siren. A familiar sandy-curled head appeared from behind the bar, followed by a set of broad shoulders as her brother rose to his full height. 'Hey, where've you been hiding?'

The smile on her face threatened to split her cheeks. 'Not hiding, plotting my new venture with your gorgeous girlfriend.'

A dreamy look crossed Sam's face. 'She is gorgeous, isn't she?'

Eliza rolled her eyes at the goofy expression, though secretly she was delighted to see her big brother so clearly smitten. He'd always been a bit of a rolling stone when it came to previous girlfriends, but Sam had fallen hook, line and sinker this time. 'I'm guessing she's about the same as when you left her this morning.' She'd only meant to tease him, but wondered if she'd missed the mark when a frown crossed his brow.

'Is everything all right with us? You don't mind about me and Beth being together, do you?'

Hurrying around to the other side of the bar, Eliza threw her arms around his waist to give him a hug. 'Of course, I don't mind. It was a bit weird to begin with, but you guys are so good for each other—anyone can see that.'

Sam squeezed her back. 'I'm really happy, Eliza.'

She loosened her arms to look up at him. 'Good.' A lump

formed in her throat out of nowhere. She seemed to teeter on the edge of tears at the slightest thing, and it was getting on her nerves. Leaving Martin had been the right thing to do, and she still had no regrets over it, but that didn't stop her mourning for what might have been or feeling guilty over her own part in the failure of their marriage. If it had been unremittingly awful—if he'd cheated on her or treated her badly—then things might have been easier. Instead it had been a slow, steady decline, as the bonds of love frayed away until nothing remained but a few strings of familiarity and a legal tie rather than any meaningful remnant of those vows they'd said to each other.

'Ah, Eliza, don't look so sad, I can't stand it.' Sam tugged a lock of her hair. 'Besides, crying makes you look ugly.' He danced back out of reach with an evil grin on his face.

Outrage at his teasing chased away her sadness, exactly as he'd intended, no doubt. 'At least I'm only ugly when I cry, mister, which is more than can be said for you.'

'Ouch.' Sam staggered back clutching at his chest, then grinned at her. 'So come on then, tell me all about this new venture of yours.'

As she helped him set up the bar for the day, Eliza explained about the customer admiring her clothes and how that had snowballed into plans for her own creative empire. 'I'll have to supplement it with working here at first because I'll need every penny I can lay my hands on to invest in materials and equipment.' Some of her excitement ebbed away. 'Mum and Dad won't be thrilled about it, I think they have their heart set on me taking over this place now you've got your restaurant and everything.'

Sam paused in the act of wiping down the bar and fixed green eyes the exact same shade as her own on her. 'And they'll get over it the same way they did when I told them about Subterranean. All they really want is for us to be happy and successful. Speaking of which…' He pulled a thick white envelope out of his back pocket and placed it on the bar between them.

'What's this?' Flipping it over, she spotted the name of the local council on the post mark, and excitement bubbled inside. 'Is this what I think it is?' A trained chef, her brother wanted to convert the pub's old skittle alley down in the cellar into a high-class restaurant. The plans had been drawn up and submitted for planning permission, and Sam had been on tenterhooks ever since.

Sam scrubbed the back of his neck. 'Yep.' The look on his face was an agonised combination of hope and worry. 'What if they said no?'

Coming home to help run the pub after their father fell ill had meant a lot of sacrifices for Sam. The Grand Diplôme from the Cordon Bleu he'd worked so hard towards should have been his ticket to a dazzling future, but life got in the way. His plans for Subterranean offered the perfect solution to achieving his dreams.

She lifted the envelope, feeling the thick wad of paper inside as though she could somehow fathom its secrets. *It wasn't just a single sheet, so that had to be a good thing, right?* 'If you don't open it, you'll never know.'

Sam laughed as he approached to pluck the envelope from her hand. 'Thanks for the deep and meaningful advice, Yoda.'

'You could always take it next door and open it with Beth.'

To her surprise, her brother shook his head. 'No. If it's bad news, I'm going to need some time to think about it before I talk to her.' He tossed the envelope back on the bar. 'Christ, just when it seems like everything is falling into place.' Tucking his hands on his hips, he blew out a breath.

Her heart ached for the dilemma he might be facing. Give up his dream career, or give up his new-found love. Beth might have been ambivalent about taking over the emporium at first, but it had become obvious to Eliza in the past weeks since her own return to the bay that her friend was here to stay. And if Sam didn't get the approval for his restaurant, she couldn't see him sticking around for the long term.

God, she was as bad as Sam, borrowing troubles when there might be no reason for it! The idea for the restaurant was a sound one, and surely the council would be keen on something that provided a new attraction for visitors to the bay. Picking up the envelope, she thrust it at her brother. 'Open it, so we can start celebrating.'

'When did you get so pushy?' He was smiling though as he eased open the self-adhesive flap.

Eliza flipped back the curls hanging over one shoulder and stuck her nose in the air with a sniff. 'It's the all-new assertive me, do you like it?'

He chuckled. 'I kinda do, but don't go changing too much, I'm very fond of my sweet little sister.' He sucked in a breath. 'Okay, here goes.'

Impatience gnawed at Eliza as she watched his eyes flicker back and forth as he scanned the top page of the stack of documents. A frown creased his brow, and she had to force herself not to wince. Damn, she'd been so sure it would be good news. Reaching for him, she forced a smile. 'It's only the first attempt, we can try again. If they don't want you to use the pub, we can look for an alternative venue.'

Blinking, Sam looked up from the papers. 'What? Oh no, it's good news. They have a couple of alterations they'd like me to make, but I have approval subject to those conditions.'

'You do? Oh my God, that's amazing!' Eliza clapped her hands together, relief flooding through her. It was about damn time their family had some good news.

'It is, isn't it?' Sam grinned brighter than the sunshine flooding through the front window. 'I've only bloody done it!'

Laughing, Eliza flung herself into his arms. 'You bloody did it!' They danced around in a circle, almost falling over each other's feet in the small space behind the bar.

'What's all the noise?'

Eliza turned at their mother's question, and it was on the tip of her tongue to blurt out the good news. She stopped herself just in time and nudged Sam in the ribs. 'Tell her.'

'Subterranean got the go ahead from the council.' He held out the letter to Annie.

'You did? Oh, Sam, that's wonderful! Your dad will be so thrilled.' There was no mistaking the relief in their mum's voice as she joined them in a group hug. Her cheeks were streaked with tears when she pulled back to regard them both. 'Looks like you're here to stay then, Sam.' When he nodded, Annie turned her full attention to Eliza. 'And what about you?'

Knowing it was time to bite the bullet, Eliza took a deep breath. 'I'm not going anywhere for the foreseeable future.'

Chapter Four

Jack chugged along the ruts on either side of yet another row of lavender, muttering curses over the sweltering weather. Even with the side windows fully open, the glass windscreen of the tractor magnified the heat of the mid-afternoon sun leaving him drenched in sweat. Since the first night after he'd transferred the new plants to the field, there'd been not a drop of rain and the forecast for the week showed little sign of any materialising. After chatting it through with his mum, they'd decided to water manually—well, mechanically. Reaching the end of the field, he turned the tractor and the water bowser attached to the towing hitch, lined up over the next row, then parked up and turned off the engine. The sudden silence came as a relief. Noah had suffered another terrible nightmare and another sleepless night combined with worry over his nephew had left Jack with a banging headache.

After clambering from the cab, he rummaged inside the rucksack beneath his seat and pulled out a bottle of water. He placed the bottle against his aching forehead. Sighing in relief as the chilly surface eased a little of the tension, Jack opened the bottle and drank. The cold liquid soothed his parched throat and he drained half the bottle before capping it again. The cloth he'd tied around his neck to protect it from the glare of the sun was soaked. He tugged it off to wring it out, using a bit of water from the bottle to rinse the worst of the sweat from it, then draped it over the bonnet of the tractor. The combined heat from the engine and the sun would dry it out in no time.

His shirt was in a similar state, and he tugged it away from the base of his back in the hopes of allowing the faint breeze to cool his skin. It did little to ease his discomfort, so he quickly unbuttoned the soft denim and shrugged out of it, shuddering a little as the clammy material stuck to his skin. He tied the sleeves in a loop around the side mirror on the tractor to hang in the sunshine, then took another long draft from the water bottle.

Squatting on his heels, he sighed as the body of the tractor offered a respite from the heat and studied the nearest lavender plant. Strong pale green stalks radiated out from the base, forming a dome with the first hints of the spears which would soon be laden with tiny purple flowers showing. A few more days, a week—maybe two—and the whole farm would be transformed into delicate blankets of every shade from palest lilac to deep imperial purple. There was plenty of work to be done between now and then.

With a soft groan, he stood and stretched his arms over his head to loosen the kinks in his spine. Another couple of hours bouncing around in the tractor's seat would leave his body vibrating from scalp to toes, but it had to be done. Gritting his teeth at the state his head would be in by the end of the day, he reached for his shirt, intent on untying the sleeves when a soft, feminine voice hailed him. 'Hello! Mr Gilbert?'

Jack spun on his heel, catching his elbow on the jutting out mirror in the process. 'Shit!' He rubbed the sharp pain and studied the small figure waving at him from the other side of the field. Shrouded beneath a huge floppy straw hat and swathed in layers of white linen, it was hard to distinguish much about her, other than her diminutive size.

Shading his eyes with one hand, Jack cast a glance down the

sloping path she must have followed. Plenty of locals—and tourists—liked to stroll along the public footpath which led them out of the bay, along the edges of the farm and back towards the cliffs that tumbled into the surf marking the far end of town. His unexpected visitor had strayed far from that route though, ignoring plenty of 'Private Property – Keep Out' signs in the process.

Striding along the top of the field, he closed the gap between them. 'Are you lost? The public footpath is back that way.' He gestured impatiently hoping she'd take the hint.

The wide brim of the hat tilted up, revealing a pair of pale green eyes and a small, slightly upturned nose spattered with freckles. She was a lot younger than he'd expected from the way she'd buried herself under layers of white cotton and linen. There was something familiar about her, but he couldn't quite place her. For a brief moment he wondered if they'd dated in the past before dismissing it. She looked too sweet for his tastes. A shy smile lifted the corners of her delicate mouth, confirming his instincts. *Definitely too sweet*. For some reason that only served to irritate him further.

'Not lost.' Her smile faltered for a second before she tried again. 'I knocked at the farmhouse, but there was no answer. I looked for a shop, but you don't seem to have one.'

Well, she'd certainly had a good nose around the place. Jack folded his arms across his chest, remembering belatedly that his shirt still fluttered from the tractor's wing mirror. 'This is a working farm, as you can see. We're too busy to play bloody shopkeepers.'

Her eyes seemed to follow the motion of his arms, then skittered away as a ruddy blush brought roses to the pale cream of her cheeks. 'Oh…um…I assumed you'd have one to sell your lavender. That's why I'm here…to buy some, I mean.' Her hand waved vaguely towards the field at his back.

Hot and tired, and with still several hours of work left to do,

Jack felt the reins on his patience slip. 'We already have a wholesaler we deal with, and I'm not in the market to change. Especially not to some random cold-caller who can't be bothered to make an appointment first.'

Her face flushed, her embarrassment at his sharp words etched plain in her shocked gaze. Jack shrugged away his momentary discomfort. *It was her own bloody fault for trespassing.*

Her next words wound his frustration levels back up again. 'Oh, I think there's been some kind of misunderstanding. I'm not from a company, I was just looking to buy a few things for myself. I want to use it for making soap, scented candles, that kind of thing…' Not even a company rep, then. Just some woman with a new hobby looking to buy a tenner's worth of product—twenty quid, tops. He scowled. This conversation with her had cost him more than that in wasted time.

A sudden gust of wind tugged at the brim of her hat and she clapped a hand on top of it to hold it in place. 'Well, I can see you're busy. I'm sorry to have bothered you…' The woman took a sidestep which placed her directly in the line of the sun, turning the diaphanous drapes of her skirt almost see-through. His attention strayed to the shapely curves of hip and thigh, then to the way the angle of her upraised arm strained the cotton of her blouse over her breasts. Who'd have thought so many secret delights lay beneath all those layers?

God, she's lovely.

The thought completely blindsided him, and he faked a cough as an excuse to turn away from her. When he looked back, her eyes were fixed on him, her bottom lip trapped between her teeth. That hesitant expression making it clear she hoped for some reassurance otherwise, but she *had* bothered him, and in ways he wasn't ready to analyse. There was too much going on in his life, the last thing he needed was a distraction—not even one as pretty as this delicate beauty. It wasn't like he was in a position to ask her out, or any other woman for that matter. The sorry state of his romantic life added another layer of frustration to his already frayed temper.

Jack rubbed his aching temples, wishing like hell he'd never got out of bed that morning. 'If you've finished wasting my time, I assume you can find your own way back out?'

He was already striding away as more stuttered words of apology spilled from her lips, and he hunched his shoulders as though to ward off the guilty waves lashing him over such rude behaviour. It didn't matter how attractive she was, after that display she'd likely run a mile if she ever laid eyes on him again.

Frustrated, hot, and overwhelmed by a sudden sense of longing for simpler days when his only responsibility was to stick in a hard day's graft, Jack snatched his shirt from the mirror and thrust his arms into it, then grabbed his now-dry neckerchief and knotted it around his throat. He swung into the cab of the tractor and turned the key, wincing as the engine coughed, shuddered and rattled into an ominous silence. *No, no, no, don't do this.* He tried again and the starter mechanism whirred, but didn't catch.

Flinging himself back down to the ground, Jack stomped around to the side of the engine block and unlatched the cover. A hint of white caught his eye and he turned to watch the woman disappear around the corner of the hedge edging the field. He didn't believe in karma, or any of those flights of superstitious fancy…but if he did, then the universe had just given him a serious kick in the arse for his behaviour towards her.

Covered in grease, dust and sweat, Jack finally parked the tractor in the rear yard. He was in such a foul mood he couldn't even be bothered to uncouple the bowser and return it to its storage spot. He just stomped into the mud room and kicked off his boots. Turning the tap over the metal sink on with his elbow, he reached for a thick bar of soap and began to lather his filthy hands and lower arms under the stream of water. The tangy scent of the mass-produced soap stung his nostrils, and his mind strayed unwillingly to thoughts of the woman from earlier. He could picture her delicate little nose wrinkling at the overpowering smell, and—he gave himself a rueful sniff—not just from the bar in his hands.

She'd been too far away for him to catch a hint of her perfume, but he would bet his last pound on it being something as pretty and fresh as she'd looked. Something sweet and tempting—cherry blossom, or roses. One of the ideas he'd had for expanding the farm had been to turn the old, neglected vegetable patch they'd abandoned since his father's death into a huge bed of roses. Good quality rose oil was in as high a demand as lavender, and the scruffy, weed-strewn patch was over half an acre. More than enough room for a trial area. If Jason had agreed to the plan they would've had their first batch of oil—something else the pretty soap-maker might have been interested in. Jack rolled his eyes; he was not in the market for tuppenny ha'penny deals, no matter how sweet her smile.

The inner door to the kitchen swung open, and Jack glanced over his shoulder at his mum. 'Hello love.' She greeted him with a smile. 'You're late tonight. I've stuck you a plate in the oven and Noah's just finishing off his reading and that's the last of his homework.'

Thank God she was there to pick up the slack. His weren't the only plans that'd been thrown into chaos by Jason's death. Their mum had wanted to take a back seat on the farm, had even talked about finding a little place to live down in the bay before setting her heart on the old farmworker's cottage. All that had gone on hold for the foreseeable future, though. 'Cheers, Mum. I've had a shit afternoon, not helped by some random woman swanning about the place thinking she can buy a couple of sprigs of lavender for some stupid bloody craft hobby, and then the tractor breaking down. I managed to get it going, but it doesn't sound happy. If I can't work out what the problem is tomorrow, we'll have to get someone in.' And that would cost a small fortune, no doubt. They had an annual budget set aside for repairs and maintenance, but still, it was another complication they could do without.

His mum gave him a sympathetic wince. 'You look fed up. Get yourself showered and then eat your dinner, hopefully that'll make you feel better.'

He nodded. 'And I might treat myself to a cold beer, too.'

Her next words depressed him even more. 'I don't think there's any in the fridge, but I'll check.'

She turned aside, making room for Bastian to come wagging out of the kitchen to greet him with a cold nose shoved against the bare skin where Jack's shirt still hung unbuttoned. Jack yelped and flicked his wet fingers at the dog. 'Get off, you daft thing.'

His mum reappeared. 'No beer, love, sorry. Why don't you take this one for a walk down into town and treat yourself to a pint and a bit of company? You've hardly stopped for days and I can see to Noah for the rest of the evening.' She closed the gap between them to cup his stubble-roughened cheek. 'I'm worried about you, Jack. You need to take a break.'

His bad mood evaporated under the deep concern in her. 'I'm all right, I promise.' Stretching his legs after a long day cooped up in the tractor sounded like a bloody good idea, though. And just maybe he could find a pretty girl down the pub for a chat, maybe a stroll along the promenade and a kiss or two if he was lucky. The image of a pair of moss-green eyes and a freckled snub nose rose in his mind before he dismissed them. If he bumped into the woman he'd been so rude to that afternoon he'd be lucky if she didn't kick him in the balls. 'A walk will do me good, and poor Bastian too, I bet. Thanks, Mum, you're the best.'

She winked at him as she dropped her hand. 'And don't you forget it. Go on, hop to, and I'll butter you a slice of bread to go with your dinner.'

As his mum had predicted, a shower, change of clothes and a hot meal had done the power of good to lift his spirits and chase the worst of his fatigue away. She and Noah had ensconced themselves on the sofa in front of *The Lego Movie* and had both seemed perfectly content to carry on without him. With a whistle to Bastian, Jack gathered the dog's lead, a disreputable looking tennis ball and a pocket torch for the way back and set off across the circular driveway towards the footpath leading down into Lavender Bay.

It was a pleasant evening, and as they drew closer to town a refreshing breeze came in from the sea, lifting his mood even further. The walk down from the farm had taken just under fifteen minutes so although his mouth was watering at the prospect of a cold pint, Jack took the time to head down onto the beach to let Bastian have a really good run. There were plenty of people strolling along the promenade, as well as a few hardy souls who were paddling their toes in the sea as the evening dusk drew trails of pink, orange and indigo across the sky. The sun had been hot, but it was still early enough in the season for the water to remain frigid.

He shared a smile with a shrieking woman and the laughing man beside her who'd got caught out by a wave splashing halfway up their calves. It was his own turn to curse as Bastian came pounding through the surf, tongue lolling around his tennis ball, sending a spray of icy water soaking the front of Jack's T-shirt. 'Cheers, mate!' Jack shook his head at the dog, who dropped the ball at his feet, tail wagging a mile a minute.

Stooping, he picked up the ball and tossed it again, making sure to aim up the beach this time. Bastian charged off with Jack in slower pursuit and the pair met near the steps leading back up to the prom. 'Enough for now? Let's see if we can get us both a nice cold drink.' He clipped the short leather lead onto the dog's matching collar and led him up the steps.

Laughter, music and the smell of hops and rich gravy greeted him in a delicious wave of sensation as Jack pushed open the door to The Siren. Pausing just inside, he caught the eye of a familiar face behind the bar and nodded down to the dog. 'He all right?'

'Jack the Lad! You're a sight for sore eyes!' Sam pushed his fringe out of his eyes as he pointed to the other end of the bar. 'Come around to the side and I'll get you a dish of water for him.'

He'd first got to know Sam the previous year after the man had returned home to help his parents run the pub. Jason and Jack had been regulars since they'd been old enough to buy a pint, but they'd never really mixed with others their own age. In the way of kids, the two of them being home-schooled had created enough of a barrier to potential friendships.

A few years of maturity on all sides had closed any gaps and once Sam had returned to Lavender Bay, he and Jack had hit it off. 'Cheers, I appreciate it.' Jack said when a large metal bowl was placed on the bare patch of tiles next to the raised section of the bar.

Sam straightened up. 'No trouble, now what about you?'

'A pint of lager, please.' Jack looked around the bar whilst he waited. It had been too long since he'd been down into town, but the place looked the same. Accepting the beer placed before him with a nod of thanks, he dug in his pocket for some change and handed it over to Sam. 'Sorry I haven't been around for a while, but—'

'Don't even mention it, mate. I'm just glad to see you.' Sam cut him off before Jack could get bogged down in a painful explanation. It was so damn hard to say the actual words and he appreciated the other man's sensitivity.

Raising his glass, he took a long mouthful of the cold lager and swallowed his grief down along with the bitter brew. 'Damn, I needed that. So, how's things been with you?'

The blond man laughed as he slung the handful of coins into the till without bothering to check them. 'Oh, you know same old, same old. Fell in love, opening a new restaurant. Nothing special.'

'Nothing special?' Jack shook his head. 'Bloody hell, I've only been out of the picture for a couple of months and you're living the dream. Tell me more…'

'Hello, gorgeous boy! Look at you! Yes, yes, you're very handsome, aren't you?' A familiar soft voice distracted Jack from whatever Sam had been about to say next and he glanced down to see a woman crouched over an ecstatic-looking Bastian. He couldn't make out her face thanks to the sandy curls tumbling around her shoulders, and she sounded a lot more enthusiastic than earlier, but he had more than a sneaking suspicion of who she might be. *Well, damn.*

The woman straightened up, one hand still scratching the dog behind his ears, and familiar moss-green eyes met his stare, proving his suspicion correct. 'Oh. It's you,' she said in the way one might observe finding a slug in their salad. 'What are you doing here?' *Make that half a slug.*

Jack gestured to his drink, trying to ignore the heat rising on the back of his neck. Embarrassment over his earlier rudeness doused his good mood. 'It's a pub, isn't it? I'm doing what most people do in one.' *Nice one, you wanker.* What was it about her that made him so defensive?

She wrinkled her snub of a nose at him, drawing his attention once again to the smattering of freckles across it. 'Not for much longer if you can't keep a civil tongue in your head.' She glanced away from him to Bastian, crouching once more to lavish the Labrador with attention. 'Not even if you've brought the most gorgeous-looking dog with you.' The tone she used to address Bastian was infinitely warmer than the one she'd used on Jack.

Sam cleared his throat. 'You remember my sister, Eliza? She's not normally this rude.'

Eliza. Memories of giggling girls he'd eyed from across the pub in his teenage years tumbled through his head. So that's where he'd recognised her from. Although if memory served him right, she'd always been with the same boy.

His trip down memory lane ended abruptly when Eliza straightened up and graced him with a look likely to give him frostbite, even in the middle of the current heatwave. 'Mr Gilbert took offence when I disturbed him at the farm earlier.'

There was enough of a trace of hurt in her voice to smack some sense into Jack, and he offered her his hand. 'It's Jack.'

'The lad, I heard.' The look she gave him said she knew exactly why her brother called him that. Jack rolled his shoulders; so he'd played the field a bit, what of it? He'd never been out with a woman who didn't share the same expectations—and boundaries. Refusing to feel embarrassed when he'd done nothing wrong, Jack decided to skip over it. 'Look, I'm sorry about earlier. I was in a foul mood, but that's no excuse for being an arse. Can we start again?'

She eyed his hand warily for a moment before placing her palm against his. Her slender fingers seemed to disappear beneath his as they closed around them, adding to his early impression of her delicacy. 'All right, then.'

Another customer hailed her, and Eliza made to step behind the bar, then froze to look back at him, then down. When Jack followed her gaze, he realised with a start that he was still holding onto her hand and dropped it with a mumbled apology. Jesus, he needed to get a grip. *Or not as the case may be.*

Finding his eyes straying towards where she was laughing over the bar at some comment from the man she was serving, Jack shook himself and turned his attention back to Sam. Now he knew the connection between them, it was obvious he and Eliza were related. Same sandy hair, same green eyes. He listened avidly as Sam described his plans to convert the old skittle alley beneath the pub into a high-end restaurant until eventually another customer drew him away.

Settling down on an empty stool, Jack snagged a copy of the local paper which sat folded on the bar next to him. A few minutes of browsing through the latest news, adverts and personal announcements got him halfway down his pint and feeling more relaxed. Bastian had drunk his fill from his bowl and flopped in an untidy heap with his head resting on one of Jack's feet. His mind strayed back to the problem with the tractor—he'd checked and cleaned the connections and topped up the water in the radiator, but it shouldn't have overheated the way it had. He would have to go over everything with a fine-toothed comb in the morning and see if he could pinpoint the fault.

A delicious waft of a rich, heady perfume caught his attention and he glanced up to find Eliza's face an inch or two from his own, that sweet smile curling her mouth at the corners. 'You don't strike me as someone who'd be fascinated by the local bowls league.'

Jack frowned, and she tapped the newspaper in front of him. Lost in his thoughts over work, he'd been staring unseeing at a breathless article about the Lavender Bay bowls team's nail-biting victory over their fiercest rivals from the next town over. His eyes lifted back up to find Eliza still leaning over the bar.

This close, her freckles stood out clearly against her milk-pale skin. The pretty mint-green dress she wore drew attention to the deeper green of her eyes. He tried not to think about touching the pad of his thumb to the dimple next to her rose-red lips. *Rose-red lips?* He'd clearly spent too long in the sun earlier and it'd cooked his brain. Shoving away the fanciful notions of her beauty, he cleared his throat. 'Bowls isn't really my thing. I was miles away.'

Eliza tilted her head, causing the wild curls of her hair to tumble over one shoulder, leaving the other one bare. Her motion drew his eyes lower to a scatter of darker freckles just below her collarbone. Their arrangement held him captive, reminding him of a constellation. He couldn't tear his eyes away, as though if he stared long enough the pattern would reveal a secret about his future the way the stars spoke to astrologers. Bloody hell, the sun hadn't just cooked his brain, it'd melted it into mush.

Knowing it had been too long since he'd spoken, Jack wet his lips. 'I…I was thinking about my tractor.' *Smooth, mate.*

She quirked an eyebrow at him, those pretty red lips pursing in amusement.

'It broke down earlier, after we…ah, met.' He scrubbed at the stubble on his chin wondering what the hell was wrong with him. He'd never been so tongue-tied in his life. 'I decided it was probably karma catching up with me.'

Her laugh rippled through him like an electric current. Jack grabbed for his pint and drained most of what remained in the glass. Perhaps he should've just upended it over his head because he was acting like some stupid boy with a crush. Yes, he'd come to the pub with half a mind to meet a willing woman for a little fun, but Sam's sister didn't strike him as the kind of girl you fooled around with.

No time. No room for this, think about Noah. The reminder doused the embers of attraction before they had chance to do much more than smoulder. The poor kid didn't know if he was coming or going as it was and needed all the stability Jack and his mum could give him. Introducing a woman into the mix would only cause further confusion to the already vulnerable boy—especially considering the way Noah's own mother had behaved towards him. Apart from cards at Christmas and his birthday and the odd guilty present in the post, Lydia had remained resolutely absent from Noah's life since he'd been a baby. Jack would cut his own arm off before he'd bring another woman into his life only to have her walk away when things didn't work out.

Needing to draw a physical as well as mental line, Jack took a step backwards, disturbing Bastian in the process. The Labrador rose to his feet with a grumbling whine, but soon perked up when he noticed his new favourite person. Installing himself behind the bar, the dog nudged at Eliza's hand until she began to stroke his ears. 'Sebastian!' Jack might as well be talking to himself for all the notice the bloody mutt took of him.

'He's all right,' Eliza crooned. 'Aren't you, gorgeous?'

Feeling like whining himself, Jack drained the rest of his beer. 'Well, I suppose we should be heading back.'

She glanced up at him, then over her shoulder at the clock on the wall. 'It's only just after eight, are you sure you don't want another drink?' Was she keen to get him to stay, or merely being a practical landlady with one eye on her profits? Either way, it was enough to make him hesitate. 'Unless you need to go? I suppose you farmers have an early start.'

It would take him quarter of an hour to walk home—less if he was brisk. Even if he stayed for another drink he could still be back by nine. He was doing the school run tomorrow because his mum was heading into Truro to meet an old friend for coffee, so he'd planned to stay close to home doing chores—and trying to sort out the tractor now, of course. There would be hours for any alcohol to clear his system, but after Jason's accident, Jack was paranoid about anything to do with driving. 'I don't have to rush off, but I'll have a soft drink this time, please.'

'Coke? Lemonade?'

Craning his neck to study the contents of the low fridge behind her, Jack shook his head. 'Nothing too sweet…'

Eliza nudged a panting Bastian back to the public side of the bar with her knee, then washed her hands at the sink below the bar. 'Hmm…we've got a nice tonic water with a hint of lime. It's lovely and refreshing.'

'Sounds great, thank you.' Jack tried, and failed, not to notice the way the short skirt of her dress pulled tight around her curvy rear as Eliza bent to retrieve a glass bottle from the fridge. She added ice to a tall, slender glass, poured over half the water and placed it and the bottle on the mat in front of him. He fished a note out of his wallet and accepted the change with a smile. 'Cheers.' He took a mouthful and closed his eyes in appreciation at the bitter, fruity tang of his drink.

When he opened them, she was grinning at him. 'Good, huh?'

She pointed to a cluster of men sitting at a table in the corner. 'My dad's a whizz when it comes to anything mechanical. I'm sure he'd be happy to take a look at your tractor if you want a second opinion.'

Caught off guard by the comment, Jack's immediate reaction was to refuse. As though sensing it, Eliza hurried on quickly. 'He's not been well lately, if it wouldn't be too much inconvenience to you I think it would do him a power of good to feel useful again.' A hint of worry clouded her pretty eyes.

He still owed her for his earlier rudeness, and to be honest it would be good to get another opinion. He and Jason had always bounced things off each other, and although his mum knew everything when it came to cultivating their crop, she'd always left the machinery maintenance to her husband and then her sons. He knew Paul Barnes well enough to say hello to, having been served plenty of times by him over the years, and he'd always seemed a decent enough guy. *What harm could it do*? 'Sure,' he found himself saying. 'Why not?'

Chapter Five

Eliza wasn't sure why she'd offered up her dad to try and help Jack out. When she'd left the farm that morning, embarrassed and more than a little upset by his rudeness, she would've been happy never to set eyes on him again. He was lucky he had such a gorgeous dog otherwise she wouldn't have given him the time of day. There was something about him that spoke to her—a hint of vulnerability lurking behind the sharp words. She didn't remember much about him from the past. He and his brother hadn't gone to the local school for some reason she couldn't quite recall. They'd come around the pub once they were old enough, but they'd not mixed much that she remembered, and she'd not had eyes for anyone other than Martin. Trying to recall them now, it was Jason she had the most distinct memory of, with his big booming laugh and ready smile. Jack had been his shadow.

Once they'd started chatting this evening, he'd opened up a little bit. And when he'd gifted her with a sunny smile which lifted the shadows around his eyes, she'd found there was a very different person lurking behind those walls of arrogance. Teasing him had come as easily to her as breathing, and who would've thought it would be so easy to make a burly farmer blush? Add in the terrible accident in which he'd lost his brother and she had no chance. Always a sucker for a lost cause, Eliza found herself wanting to reach out and help him.

Wondering if she was setting herself up for another fall, especially given his ability to blow hot and cold, trepidation set in as she wound her way through the scattered tables towards where her dad sat with Pops and a few of his cronies. With a quick glance over her shoulder to check Jack had followed her, she placed a hand on her dad's shoulder and leaned down to brush a kiss on his cheek. 'You busy?' she asked when he turned to look up at her with a smile.

'No, lovely girl, what can I do for you?' He must've noticed Jack standing just behind her from the way his eyebrows raised.

She turned to include Jack in their circle. 'Jack's from up at Gilbert's farm. He's having a bit of engine trouble with a tractor and I thought you might have time tomorrow to take a look.'

Paul Barnes stood to offer Jack his hand. 'I've seen you in here a time or two, Jack.'

He nodded. 'Haven't been down for a while, Mr Barnes, but Jason and I used to enjoy a drink here.' Always hopeless in the face of raw emotion, Eliza blinked hard at the sudden sting of tears which rose unbidden at the stark expression on Jack's face.

Her dad placed a hand on Jack's arm. 'Terrible business, that, lad.' He gave himself a little shake, then continued. 'But I'm sure you're sick of people saying so. Pull up a seat and let's have a chat about this tractor problem.' Scooting his chair back, he cleared a space at the table. 'Shove over a bit, Pops.'

Eliza's grandad—universally known as Pops to everyone in the family—obliged and Jack borrowed a spare stool from a nearby table to settle between them. Obviously not wanting to be left out, his chocolate Labrador wiggled in next to Pops and nosed the empty wrapper from a bag of peanuts. With a laugh, Eliza leaned forward to snatch up the packet. 'None of that now.'

Both dog and owner turned to regard her, making Eliza aware of how close she was standing to Jack. Hiding her blush with another laugh, Eliza busied herself clearing the rest of the table, taking orders for a fresh round of drinks for Pops and his friends. When she returned to the bar it was to find her brother regarding her with a speculative gleam in his eye. Choosing to ignore it, she dumped the dirty glasses and rubbish, then opened the fridge to retrieve a bottle of alcoholic ginger beer. Sam was still staring at her when she turned around, and it made her distinctly uncomfortable. 'What?'

His eyebrows raised at her sharp tone. 'You and Jack seem a bit cosy. I could've sworn he was the one you were ranting about this afternoon.'

Cheeks flaming, Eliza ducked her head over the steel ice tray and busied herself scooping some into a pint glass. Perhaps she ought to stick her face in the tray and cool down. 'I'm just being friendly; he's had a tough time of it lately.' She popped the cap on the bottle, then gestured with it at the taps on the bar. 'If you've enough time to be misreading a situation you can make yourself busy and pull a couple of pints of Best.'

Giving her his patent annoying-big-brother knowing grin, Sam saluted with a couple of fingers at his brow. 'Yes, ma'am.' He poured the drinks then placed them on a round tray next to her on the bar. 'So, what are Jack and Dad so intent upon?'

Sam's comment drew her attention back to the corner table to see her dad sketching something with his hands in the air whilst Jack nodded. 'He's got some mechanical problem with a tractor and I thought Dad might be able to offer him some advice.'

She added the ginger beer, a pint of cola and a measure of scotch with a small jug of water to the tray and would've picked it up had Sam not curled an arm around her shoulders. 'Look at Dad,' he murmured close to her ear. 'I haven't seen him looking so animated in ages. You did good, Sis.' His lips brushed her temple then he disengaged his arm. 'Shall I take these over for you?'

'Thanks, that'd be good.' Ignoring the little pang of disappointment at not having an excuse to get close to Jack again, Eliza made herself busy wiping down the bar. Really, what on earth was the matter with her? A nice smile was all well and good, but it didn't mean she had to act like a goose over the man. *And a very nice chest, too*. Giving her subconscious a mental swat, she grabbed a collection tray and started clearing empty glasses, cans and bottles from various tables.

Masculine laughter rose from the corner, but she refused to turn around no matter how much the deep, rolling baritone seemed to ripple through her. Her marriage to Martin might have been on the rocks well before she admitted it to herself but thinking about another man only a couple of months after she'd finally ended things was unseemly to say the least. She was just lonely, nothing more, and had sensed a similar emotion in Jack.

Since she'd been a little girl, Eliza collected waifs and strays, coming home with an array of lost kittens, upset classmates and random lone tourists she'd struck up conversations with on the busy promenade. Her mum had accepted them all with her usual brisk kindness. The kittens had been returned to their owners or handed over to the local rescue centre; her classmates fed and cossetted; the tourists treated to a friendly welcome and an evening of laughter and conversation in the bar.

This thing with Jack, not that it was a *thing*, of course, was just a variation on the same theme. She'd sensed a need in him and extended the hand of friendship. Chairs scraped on the wooden floor behind her as she lugged the full tray back behind the bar, and Eliza glanced around to catch Jack heading out the front door, a reluctant Bastian in tow. His gaze rose to meet hers and she couldn't look away. Pops called out something to Jack, rescuing Eliza from making a fool of herself by staring too long. Jack broke their connection to laugh at whatever had been said, then slipped out the door with a wave.

Eliza kept busy behind the bar, emptying and restacking the dishwasher as Sam returned. Thankfully, a flurry of customers squeezing in one last drink on a work night meant the next half an hour passed quickly. Her mum come down to fetch her dad, grumbling good-naturedly about him abandoning her on their night off. Slinging an arm around her waist, Paul gave his wife a squeeze and whispered something in her ear which made her giggle and place a hand on his chest.

Heart lifting with pleasure at witnessing the sweet moment between her parents, Eliza caught Sam's eye and they shared a grin. They'd grown up in a demonstrative household and it was good to see the pair of them looking so relaxed after months of tension caused by her dad's illness. The chronic lung disease would always see him weaker than the robust man of her memories, but the warm, dry weather seemed to be agreeing with him. Arm in arm, they left the pub to escort Pops on his walk back up to Baycrest—the retirement home situated at the top end of the promenade.

A quick check of her watch told her it was a few minutes before nine. She placed a hand on Sam's back as he leant down restocking one of the fridges. 'Leave that, I can handle things from here.'

He did his own automatic time check, then straightened up. 'If you're sure? Beth's got me hooked on this new detective drama, so I can probably make it round there before it starts.'

His eyes drifted over her shoulder, checking on the number of customers left in the pub, and she nudged him. 'Go on, I'll be fine. Give her my love and tell her I'll pop in tomorrow for a cuppa before I start my shift, I want to borrow Eleanor's old sewing machine.' Hers had gone into one of the shipping crates bound for Abu Dhabi so there was no chance of seeing it anytime soon.

Sam waggled his eyebrows. 'You going to tell her all about your new friend?'

'Oh, shut up, before I change my mind and make you stay for last orders.' That got him moving.

*

Last orders came and went with little ceremony, and the place was empty a good ten minutes before their official closing time of 10 p.m. Eliza was just reaching for the top bolt on the front door when it swung open and her parents strolled in. They looked starry-eyed and Eliza tried not to notice how the back of her dad's hair stood on end, or the red fullness of her mum's lips. 'Enjoy your walk?'

They exchanged a knowing look, causing Eliza to roll her eyes. She bet Sam and Beth were cosied up on the sofa in her flat above the emporium and smooching more than they were watching the television. Even at the height of their marriage, Martin had never been one for outward displays of affection, and it had taken her a long time to stop expecting him to reach for her hand when they walked anywhere together. For a good six months before she'd finally left, he'd not even come to bed at the same time as her—always too busy with the latest online game he'd been addicted to. Well, whatever, that was all in the past now.

Her dad reached up to slide the door bolts into place, then turned to Eliza. 'I told Jack I'd call up at the farm just after nine tomorrow. Pops decided to invite himself along, so I'll take the car. We should be back by lunchtime.'

'Oh, I was going to take a trip to the Cash and Carry first thing. We're running low on a few snacks and I need to pick up some salad and veg. I also need to get some material. As soon as I get my hands on Eleanor's sewing machine I want to get cracking.' She tried not to notice the pointed look her parents shared. They'd greeted her new business venture with lukewarm enthusiasm, although she'd promised to fit the work in around shifts at the pub to make sure she was pulling her weight.

Jack turning her down flat had put a damper on the beauty products side of things, but she was determined to get a few skirts and dresses on display in the emporium as soon as possible. If she could prove to them she could sell her stuff it would give her a bit of breathing room whilst she rethought the supply issue for her soap-making.

Her dad shrugged. 'Fair enough. Can you drop us off on your way instead, and I'll ring when we're done?' When she nodded, he continued. 'And I suppose we ought to have a discussion at our next family sit down about getting a second car.' In order to keep things running smoothly, they were getting together every Sunday afternoon to talk over how things had been and plan out the week to come.

Beth had been added after the first week, to make sure she had the support she needed to keep on top of everything with the emporium, and to keep her in the loop with Sam's new restaurant project. Juggling four businesses—even if one of them was still more dream than reality—was going to take a lot of patience and planning, and it wasn't only Eliza who was aware of the need to protect Sam and Beth's fledgling relationship.

They'd work it out though, she thought as she puttered around the bar finishing the evening cleardown. Much as her parents went on about retiring, her mum still held sway over the kitchen and her dad looked after the books. Sam seemed content to fill in wherever he was needed, his focus more and more turned to Subterranean now the revised plans had been finalised. Eliza could be as flexible as needed to fit around the others' schedules, but she was determined to make a go of things. She'd put her dreams on hold for far too long and this was finally her time to do something that was one hundred per cent by and for herself.

Gathering the cloths they'd used throughout the shift for wiping up, as well as the towelling mats that protected the top of the bar from the worst spills, Eliza gave the room a final onceover then switched off the lights and headed upstairs. What had started out as a horrible day had turned out pretty damn good in the end. With her dad clearly feeling better about himself, she could only hope things would continue to improve. She crossed her fingers and uttered a silent wish that Jack's good mood from that evening would carry over into the morning.

It was another fine, bright day, the air already heavy with the promise of the heat to come as Eliza held the passenger door open so Pops could ease himself into the car. Her dad already perched in the back, a grin of anticipation on his face. He'd loaded his enormous toolbox into the boot with as much relish as a kid going off on a picnic or some other treat. She watched Pops wrestle with the mechanism for his seatbelt, his once agile fingers twisted with age and arthritis, and winced. 'Do you need a hand with that?' she asked, crouching beside him.

'I'm not completely bloody useless, girl,' Pops grumbled as he finally managed to click the tab into the lock.

'Not completely, Pops, just mostly.' Her dad's dry rejoinder was greeted with a snort somewhere between indignation and humour, and Eliza had to bite her lip to hide a smile as she closed the door before moving around to her side of the car.

Having dropped her handbag in the seat well next to Pops' feet, she reached down for the adjuster handle and dragged her seat forwards until she could reach the pedals. It was already warm, so she started the engine and cranked the air blowers to their highest setting. A quick fiddle with the mirror brought it into eyeline, and she caught a wink from her dad which she returned with a smile. Finally ready to go, she settled her own belt across her body, adjusting the stiff black material so it didn't wedge itself between her breasts.

What passed for weekday rush hour in Lavender Bay was still in full force, meaning they had to wait behind three cars at the main roundabout. It was always busy at weekends during high season as holidaymakers came and went, but on a sunny day like this, the majority of visitors stuck close to the beach. Which would mean another busy lunchtime shift for the pub, no doubt.

'Turn left here.' Eliza bit her lip at the unnecessary instruction from Pops but didn't say anything as she took the road which led up the hill through town towards the farm. The radio was tuned to a news station, and she rolled her eyes at the irate caller ranting about national sovereignty as she flipped the control on the steering wheel to switch to a music station.

'Hey, I was listening to that,' Pops protested.

'No politics when I'm driving, Pops, that's the rule.' Eliza paused at a cross roads before turning right and then almost immediately left onto the dirt road which led to the farm.

'But I like a nice phone-in,' he muttered.

Her dad barked a laugh. 'There's nothing nice about phone-ins, just a load of ignorant people shouting at each other. Give me a bit of *Radio Two* any day.'

Eliza had to agree with him, which made her feel about a hundred years old, or at least as though she was heading for early middle-age. The radio in the kitchen at the pub was perpetually tuned to that station, and she much preferred the mix of new music with old classics she'd grown up listening to. She crested the rise, the sight of the farm buildings arrayed before them distracting her from the good-natured debate still ongoing between her dad and Pops. An old Land Rover was parked in front of the farmhouse, and she parked behind it.

She didn't have time to get her belt unfastened before the front door opened, and Jack's broad shoulders filled the frame. He had a T-shirt on this time, which should've been better, but the way the material clung to his upper body only served to bring a flood of images of him naked to the waist into her mind. Hiding her blush behind a thick curtain of hair, she took her time sorting her handbag out, which gave the men time to get out of the car and greet Jack.

He didn't seem to mind that Pops had tagged along from the warm greeting they exchanged. She watched Jack usher them over the threshold with directions towards the kitchen, noting the easy way he relieved her dad of his heavy toolbox. When she didn't follow them through, Jack raised a quizzical eyebrow. 'You not staying?'

Wondering why she'd got out of the car, she fiddled with the strap of her bag. 'No, I've got errands to run and then I need to help Mum with lunch prep before we open up. Dad's going to give me a call later for a pick-up.' She tossed her stupid bag onto the passenger seat, feeling more awkward than she had since her early teens. 'I hope they won't outstay their welcome.'

Jack smiled. 'I'll be on my best behaviour, I promise. No grumping and complaining.'

Oh, goodness, that wasn't what she'd meant at all. 'I didn't…' Flustered, she cut herself off when his smile stretched into a grin. He'd only been teasing, and she was making an absolute fool of herself. 'Well, I'd better leave you to it…'

'You're sure you can't stay? I was going to offer you a tour around the place, a bit of a peace offering. We've got some samples in the distillery, I was going to give you some to help with your soap-making and whatever.' Jack tucked his hands into the front pockets of his jeans, his eyes flicking from her face to the stones his foot was scuffing through on the driveway.

Touched by the thoughtful offer, Eliza relaxed. 'That's really kind of you, but you don't have to. It was my own presumption that got us in this mess in the first place.'

He scoffed a little. 'Nothing presumptuous about expecting a lavender farm to sell bloody lavender.'

She laughed. 'No, I suppose you're right.' She couldn't help but glance around. It would've been fascinating to stay and find out how everything worked. And the chance to spend a bit more time in his company wasn't the worst idea, either. 'I'm sorry to miss the tour, but I really should go…'

'Another time, perhaps? Things will be pretty quiet around here for the next couple of weeks until harvest. If you let me know a date that works for you, I can adjust my schedule accordingly.' He seemed sincere, and if his first offer had been a gesture made for politeness' sake, there would be no reason for him to repeat it.

'Wednesday is my day off,' she found herself saying. She'd been planning to spend the day at the sewing machine, but a couple of hours wouldn't do any harm. She might even be able to take a few photos while she was there to post on her new Instagram account.

'Great. Shall we make it the same time then?' He glanced over his shoulder then back to her. 'If your dad comes through and helps me fix the tractor, I'll take you out for a ride in it if you fancy, give you the authentic farm experience.'

She tried to recall what she'd seen of the vehicle. It hadn't seemed that big, so they'd probably be squeezed in tight together in the cab. Just the thought of it sent her pulse racing. *Stop it, Eliza*! 'Wow, you sure know how to show a girl a good time, by the sounds of it.'

Her attempted joke didn't just fall flat, it poisoned the atmosphere between them, as unwelcome and embarrassing as a fart in a lift. Jack's open expression grew shuttered, and he hunched his shoulders. 'It was just an idea, and you'd get a better view from being higher up, but we can take the Land Rover.'

'Oh no, the tractor sounds great fun, I was kidding.' She followed his gaze down to where she'd inadvertently clutched his forearm. The crisp, dark hair on his skin tickled her palm as the muscle flexed beneath her fingers. Mortified, she released him quicker than a hot coal, took a couple of stumbling steps backwards and all but jumped back into the car. 'Right then, places to go, people to see and all that.' *Just stop talking, woman*!

Grinding the gears so badly it was a miracle she didn't leave half the transmission on the driveway, Eliza drove off before she made things any worse. Not that she was sure it was possible. A quick glance in the rear-view mirror showed Jack still outlined in the doorway, and she cringed. He must think her mad. Catching sight of her own flushed reflection, Eliza sighed. He wouldn't be far wrong.

Chapter Six

'I'll take you for a ride on my tractor, what kind of a line is that?' Jack muttered to himself in disgust as he stomped across the hallway towards the kitchen. No wonder Eliza had practically burnt rubber in her efforts to get away from him. A delicate woman like her wouldn't want to be bouncing around in a dirty farm vehicle. Even dressed casually like she was that morning, she was still a vision of soft draping material and pastel shades. It didn't quite tie up with the funny, feisty woman who ran the bar in The Siren so efficiently. He recalled watching her lug a plastic crate full of glasses across the bar, the alluring sight of her bottom perfectly outlined by the fitted dress she'd worn that night. Whilst he'd appreciated the sexy, confident woman she'd been in the pub, the sweeter, slightly shier version who'd just driven away appealed to something inside him and he wondered which version of Eliza was the true one.

Well, there was nothing to be done for now other than to concentrate on his guests and see which Eliza showed up on Wednesday. Assuming she actually intended to come back and hadn't just been too polite to refuse his offer to his face. Pushing the intriguing thoughts about Eliza away, Jack entered the kitchen to find Paul Barnes and his dad seated at the table each with a steaming mug before them. 'We helped ourselves to a cuppa, lad, and made one for you whilst we were at it,' the elder Mr Barnes said. 'Didn't think you'd mind.'

'Not at all, I should've been here to make it for you. There's some biscuits in the tin if you want one.' Bastian's ears pricked at the sound of the metal lid being pried open, and Jack pointed at him. 'None for you, get back in your basket and leave poor Mr Barnes in peace for five minutes.' The dog gave him a look which plainly said Jack was wasting his breath. Bastian knew a soft touch when he saw one, and he'd had Jack wrapped around his paw since day one.

Paul glanced up, his hand still playing gently with the dog's ears. 'He's no bother; don't trouble yourself on my account. And Mr Barnes makes me feel old as the hills, so please call me Paul.'

Jack nodded as he pulled out a chair to sit next to him. 'Thanks. And thanks again for agreeing to come over here today. Mum's off seeing a friend this morning, so we'll have to fend for ourselves.'

Pops helped himself to a second chocolate digestive before putting the lid back on the tin. 'Why is it the things that are so bad for you taste so bloody good?' He dunked the biscuit in his tea, then bit half of it.

'Don't mind Pops. You'd think he's barely housetrained until you see him out on the terrace surrounded by his lady friends up at Baycrest.' Paul winked at Jack.

'There's nothing wrong with enjoying the company of a fine woman, son.' Pops turned his attention to Jack, a wicked gleam in his blue eyes. 'What about you, lad? Are you keeping company with a fine woman?'

Jack all but choked on his tea. Pops might be a bit long in the tooth, but it had occurred to Jack last night while chatting to him that only a fool would underestimate the sharpness of the mind lurking behind his wrinkles and greying hair. 'No time for women, I'm afraid, fine or otherwise.'

Pops shook his head. 'That's no way to live, lad. A life unshared is one only half-lived. You're not a bad looking boy, and a hard-worker if this place is anything to go by. Any woman would be glad to be on your arm. Take our Eliza, for instance…'

Oh, Jesus Christ! What was he supposed to say to that?

Luckily Paul saved him the trouble from responding. 'Pops!' He fixed his father with a stern frown. 'Don't start bloody stirring things up. The poor girl needs a break after everything she's been through.' His eyes flicked to Jack. 'No offence, Jack.'

'None taken.' He'd not been lying when he'd told Pops he didn't have time for a woman in his life. Hadn't he had that exact thought only the night before? Between the farm and taking care of Noah, there weren't enough hours in the day. What kind of woman in her right mind would be happy to see him maybe one evening a week? And as soon as the harvest kicked in, it'd be less than that. That's why he kept things short and sweet—that and a bone-deep fear of ending up with completely the wrong woman the same way Jason had done.

Just thinking about his brother was enough to lay him low. The pressure of his grief lurked in his mind like a constant headache. Embarking on anything that might stir up one type of emotion would inevitably lead to the intrusion of others. And he simply didn't have the time to fall apart, not with everyone counting on him.

Besides, even if he had been interested in Eliza, it sounded like she'd been having a hard time of it herself. He wanted to dig for information, not liking the idea someone might have hurt her, but forced himself to drain his tea and rise from the table. It wasn't his business; *she* wasn't his business and he needed to remember that.

So, why had he invited her for a tour of the farm? His initial reaction to her was much more in keeping with his general feelings about his home. He didn't want strangers poking about, had never liked people around who weren't part of the family. And yet here he was sipping tea with her father and grandfather. If he didn't watch out, she'd crack his defences wide open.

Wallowing wouldn't help anything, and it certainly wouldn't get the tractor repaired. 'If you want to follow me out to the yard, we can get started?' They dumped their mugs in the sink and trooped out the back. One look at the state of the tractor and bowser both covered in dust and mud had Jack hanging his head in shame, and he hurried forward to uncouple the bowser and tow it out of the way.

Neither Paul nor Pops seemed to note anything amiss as they slowly circled the tractor. Eyes bright with excitement, Paul placed a hand on the engine cover and grinned at his dad. 'She's a beauty, eh, Pops?'

'She sure is. Let's have a look at what's inside, shall we?'

Jack showed them where the release mechanism was, then opened the hatch to a pair of admiring whistles and stepped back to give them room to look. Heads almost touching, they muttered and murmured to themselves, and Jack decided to leave them to it for a few minutes. Crossing the yard, he grabbed the hosepipe and proceeded to rinse the dirt off the bowser then opened the drainage tap at the rear to allow the dregs of remaining water inside to drain out.

Glancing over, he saw they were still bent over the tractor's engine and was about to carry on with his clean up when he noticed Pops sway slightly. Hurrying back, he placed a light hand on the older man's shoulder. 'Everything all right?'

Pops glared at him, then his expression softened with a sigh. 'My old knees aren't what they used to be, lad, but no need to fret.'

Jack watched Pops shift uncomfortably for a second, then had an idea. 'Be right back.' He strode around the side of the house and across the driveway towards the distillery. Unlocking the door with one of the ever-present keys clipped to his belt, Jack paused on the threshold as a wave of lavender-scented air rolled over him. His shoulders loosened, releasing tension he hadn't been aware of until it began to fade, and he couldn't help but smile. It didn't matter what time of year it was, the aromatic smell of the plants they processed in there had seeped into the very fabric of the building. Collecting what he'd come for, Jack secured the door and returned to the yard.

'Here, how about this?' He plonked one of the tall stools they used when sorting out the cut lavender stalks ready for drying behind Pops and stepped back with a grin. He nodded at the stool when Pops glanced around. 'I think it's just about the right height for you to be able to see, why don't you try it out?'

They moved the stool until it rested right against the edge of the tractor. Jack held his walking stick whilst Pops eased himself up onto the wooden seat, then tucked it between the legs out of the way. 'Ah,' Pops closed his eyes on a sigh. 'That's better, thanks, lad. I tell you, the worst thing about growing old is my mind and body being out of sync with each other.' He settled himself a bit more centrally on the seat. 'Right then, why don't you run through exactly what happened with the tractor yesterday?'

Paul raised his eyes briefly from his study of the engine. 'Before you start, have you got a manual for this handy?'

Jack nodded. 'I've downloaded one on my tablet, hold on…' He jogged inside and grabbed the large flat-screened device from the counter top. Returning, he located the file and opened it before handing the tablet to Pops.

'No good to me with these useless claws.' Pops waved a gnarled hand at him.

'Here, like this.' Jack showed him how to zoom in and out with a basic pincer movement on the screen. 'You can drag the image around too, just pull down on the screen with your finger, and swipe across to get the next page.'

Tentatively at first—and then with more confidence—Pops began to navigate his way around the manual. When he looked up, his blue eyes were shining. 'This is bloody fantastic.'

Jack nodded. 'It's a life-saver. Mum and I use it for everything when we're on the go. The only thing we use the PC for these days is doing the accounts.'

Paul straightened up, arms folded across his chest. 'Remember when Annie wanted to buy you one of these for Christmas and you dismissed it as new-fangled nonsense, Pops?'

Pops hefted the device between his hands. 'I thought it'd be a lot heavier than this. And you can read books on it, too?'

'For sure. There's loads of apps you can download for that. You can change the font and the text size to suit whatever you like. This one has a stand, too, if you get tired of holding it.' Jack took it back briefly to show Pops how the front of the cover could be bent to support the tablet.

The old man grinned over at his son. 'It's my birthday soon…'

Paul shook his head, but he was grinning too. 'Message received and understood.'

They spent the next hour running through the daily and monthly maintenance schedules Jack followed, checking everything was in order and helping Paul to familiarise himself with the detailed workings of the engine. Working methodically, they proceeded to strip individual parts, giving everything a thorough clean as they went. The dry weather conditions had generated a lot of dust, and whether they found a fault or not it would do no harm to make sure everything was pristine.

'Right, we're happy with all the points and connections, so I say we check the hoses next.' Jack nodded in agreement and went to fetch a large bucket of water whilst Paul carefully removed them. They crouched over the bucket and tested the thick rubber tubes by immersing each section. The first proved fine, but a stream of telltale bubbles appeared halfway along the second.

'Bloody hell,' Jack dried off the hose on his shirt then studied the damaged section. There was nothing visible to the naked eye, but a second dip in the bucket produced the same result.

'That's the culprit, no doubt about it,' Pops said from his perch on the high stool.

'More than likely, Pops,' Paul agreed. 'But, if Jack's happy to carry on, I say we should check everything else to be on the safe side.'

Jack nodded. 'If you're sure you've got the time, then that'd be fantastic. I'll give the garage a call and see if I can get a replacement hose. I'd rather do that than try and patch it. Especially if this heat's going to continue.'

Paul clapped him on the shoulder. 'I've got all the time in the world, son.' He pushed himself to his feet, and his breath seemed to catch on an ugly wheeze. Bracing one hand on the tractor, Paul began to cough—a painful, wrenching sound that made Jack's throat ache to hear it.

Helpless, Jack looked over at Pops who shook his head as though to indicate Jack shouldn't try to help. The old man slipped down off the stool, and Jack stepped back out of the way as he moved towards his son. 'Why don't you get us a cold drink, lad?'

Grateful for something to do, Jack rushed into the kitchen to grab a couple of bottles of water and cans of soft drink. When he returned, Paul was half-sitting on the stool, puffing on a blue inhaler. Pops leaned against his walking stick, his head close to his son's, murmuring something too soft for Jack to catch. Both men smiled at him as he offered them a choice of drinks. Paul took a bottle of water and drained a third of it before letting out a few slow, steady breaths. 'Sorry about the fuss.'

Jack waved him off, a can of soda clutched in his hand. 'No fuss, as long as you're all right.'

Paul snorted. 'I'm as all right as I'm going to be. Now my lungs are half-knackered, I spend half my days sat on my arse and it drives me up the bloody wall. I can't tell you how good it's been to get my hands dirty. I forgot myself for a minute and moved too fast, that's all.'

He tried to stand up, but Pops pressed a hand to his chest to keep him in place. 'What did I just say to you? There's nothing to prove so rest up for a few minutes. I need to get these old legs of mine working a bit anyway.' Straightening up, he pointed the end of his walking stick at Jack. 'Why don't you call the garage, lad, while I do a couple of laps of the yard to loosen up these stiff old joints of mine? By the time we're both finished I reckon we'll all be ready to start again.'

Grateful to escape, Jack re-entered the kitchen, pulled out a chair and slumped into it, his knees suddenly shaky. He closed his eyes, pressing the heels of his palms into them. Watching Paul go from hale and hearty, to grey-faced and struggling for breath had shaken him to the core.

It only took a split second for things to change forever. Hadn't his dad seemed fine at breakfast the day he'd dropped like a stone in one of the fields from a massive heart attack? And Jason... *God, Jason.* The image of his brother's laughing face burned behind Jack's closed lids, and a shudder rippled through him.

'Hold it together, come on...come on...' Jack whispered over and over until the worst of the shakes subsided. Paul was okay. He'd been speaking, hadn't he? And Pops hadn't seemed overly concerned about it. By the time Jack went back outside, no doubt he'd be right as rain. All he needed to do was get up and walk through the door to see for himself.

It was another five minutes before Jack could persuade himself to leave the chair, and he took his time over the call to the garage. The rational part of his brain told him he was being foolish, and yet he kept his back turned firmly to the open door, not quite ready to look outside. Thankfully, the garage had a spare hose in stock, so he requested it be put aside for him to collect that afternoon and the cost added to his account. Feeling more grounded, Jack straightened his shoulders and forced himself to venture back outside.

Relief flooded him to see Paul had regained the colour in his cheeks, and his breathing had settled down to a normal rate. Pops was still wandering the yard, pausing to look at whatever caught his eye, seemingly in no hurry to re-join them. Leaning back against the tractor, Jack tucked his still shaking hands behind him and tried to look casual.

'I didn't mean to put the wind up you, Jack. You look like

you've seen a ghost..' Paul leant forward to place a hand on Jack's arm.

A ragged laugh escaped him. 'I did, sort of. Well, two actually…' Damn, why had he said that? He shrugged one shoulder, hoping to dismiss the comment. 'Don't mind me, let's get this finished, shall we?'

Paul didn't remove his hand, leaving Jack the choice of pulling away, or submitting to the tenderness he could feel through the older man's grip. His eyes flicked to Paul's, skittering away at the sympathy and understanding written deep in them. 'I'm all right,' he muttered, fooling neither of them.

Paul cleared his throat, then spoke softly. 'I know I'm not much more than a stranger to you, but if you need someone to talk to…I keep thinking how it'd be if my Sam was in your shoes—and Christ, he nearly was a couple of months ago. I'd want someone to notice. Someone to reach out and let him know he wasn't alone.'

Jack shook his head, denying the words he was hearing. Denying the comfort and care his soul cried out for contained in the big-hearted man beside him. 'I don't have time.' The words choked in his throat.

'Time for what?' Paul left his seat to stand directly in front of Jack, placing his hands on Jack's shoulders. 'Time to talk? Time to grieve? Ah, son, you'll make yourself ill if you try and keep it all inside.'

His hands pressed so hard against the metal of the tractor, his fingers ached. Jack pushed harder still, fighting to keep from reaching out. 'They need me to hold it together.' He managed to grind the words out through his stiff jaw. 'There's too much to do…after the harvest…'

'All right, son. I've said my piece and I'll leave it at that, but don't ever be afraid to ask for help if you need it. No man is an island as someone much wiser than me once said.' Paul stepped back. 'Right then, who's up for another cup of tea?'

Pops rubbed his hands together. 'I'll never say no to a brew. Reckon you can scare us up a biscuit to go with it, lad?'

Jack relaxed his death-grip on the tractor and let the tension melt from his body. 'I can do one better than that, Pops. Mum baked a Madeira cake yesterday.'

'Now you're talking, lad, now you're talking.'

When Paul laid a hand on Jack's shoulder as they walked back towards the kitchen, Jack resisted the urge to shrug it off. *No man is an island.*

Chapter Seven

Eliza tamed her unruly curls into a long pair of plaits that trailed to the middle of her shoulders, then fumbled around in the small make-up bag on her dressing table. Locating her tried-and-tested mineral foundation powder, she swept a thin layer over her pale skin with a large, soft brush. She regarded the freckles scattered across her nose with a sigh, then added another layer of the powder. The heatwave might be great for business around the bay, but if the sun continued to beat down like this, her entire face would turn into a freckle. At least the foundation contained a built in SPF sunscreen and she'd make sure to have a hat with her. A quick flash of pale, rose-pink blusher and a sweep of mascara to darken her sandy lashes, and she was done.

She snatched up the green cotton shirt from where it draped over the end of her bed and slipped it on over the white vest top she'd teamed with a pair of her oldest, most comfortable jeans. Leaving the top few buttons undone, she slipped her feet into a pair of brightly-patterned Skechers slip-on loafers and looped a delicate infinity scarf covered in pastel butterflies she'd found in the emporium the previous week around her neck. With a large straw sunhat in hand, she left her room and headed down the back stairs.

Popping her head into the bar area, she paused to watch her parents for a moment. His morning spent helping Jack had put a spring in her dad's step, just as she'd hoped and eased something inside him. It had only been a couple of days, but she'd already sensed he was more relaxed, less ready to jump to offence if anyone tried to help him. Perched on a stool at the bar, he had the order file in front of him as her mum checked the stocks.

The familiar scene brought an unexpected lump to her throat, and she had to clear it before she could call out to them. 'Right, I'm off.' It was on the tip of her tongue to add a caveat that she would stay if they needed her, but that seemed an act of hubris considering how many years of experience they had running the place. Besides, she really wanted a day off. Spending time back behind the bar of The Siren was wonderful, but she yearned for some fresh air and a bit of peace and quiet.

Her mum looked up with a smile. 'Have a nice time, lovey, I can't wait to hear all about it. I've always been curious about how things work up there.'

'They've got a great set-up from the bit I saw of it,' her dad added. 'Jack should think about having an open day.'

'I'll tell him you said so,' Eliza said with a teasing laugh in her voice. Give her dad an inch, and he'd take a mile. If Jack wasn't careful, Paul Barnes would be offering him all sorts of unasked for advice. She checked her watch. 'I'll see you later.' With a wave she left them to it and headed through the yard to wait in the alley behind the pub. When she'd collected her dad and Pops, she realised they must've had a conversation about the family only having the one car as Jack had mentioned he had an errand to run in town and would be happy to pick her up.

She checked her watch again, then pulled her phone out of her back pocket to double-check the time. It was silly to be nervous, it wasn't like they were having a date or anything. Wood creaked behind her, and Eliza glanced over her shoulder to see Beth pull open the rear gate securing the yard behind the emporium.

Clutching a large, ceramic mug she grinned at Eliza over the rim of it. 'Morning!' She took a sip, her eyes never leaving Eliza's face.

Trying to ignore the sudden flush in her cheeks, Eliza fiddled with the brim of her hat. 'Oh, hi! What are you doing?'

Beth shrugged one shoulder in a nonchalant gesture. 'Just taking in the sights.' She took another sip of her tea, then came to stand beside Eliza and nudged her with an elbow. 'So, did you forget to tell me something?'

Oh, bloody Sam and his bloody big mouth! It wasn't that she'd forgotten to tell Beth or Libby about her impending visit to the farm, she'd just chosen not to share the information. Libby loved to jump to conclusions and would tease her mercilessly the way she had with Sam and Beth before they'd got together. Not that Eliza and Jack would be doing that, of course, but that wouldn't stop her.

The rumble of an engine distracted them both, and Eliza turned to watch the black Land Rover roll slowly down the alley towards where she waited. Just as it pulled up to a stop, Beth nudged her again. 'Six-thirty tomorrow at my place, Lambrini time. Libs and I will want a full report.'

Jack lowered the car window and rested his elbow on the open frame. Dark glasses shielded his eyes, but there was no missing the glance he shot between her and Beth. 'You ready?'

Eliza nodded. 'Yes. Absolutely.' She practically ran around to the passenger side and yanked the door open. 'I'll see you later, Beth,' she called then hopped up into the four-wheel drive without waiting for an answer. 'That's Beth, she's my best friend, and Sam's girlfriend. She runs the emporium now, you know, the shop next door to the pub…' Her blathering trailed off in the face of the blank stare of the dark lenses of his sunglasses.

Jack nodded his head downwards. 'Put your belt on, please.'

'Oh, yes, of course.' Her face flamed. She tugged it on, feeling stupidly flustered. Given what had happened to his brother, no wonder Jack was hot on car safety. She should have been thinking about that, not worrying about her friends and their nonsense. It was time to put all that to the back of her mind, or it would ruin her day out. Eliza unzipped the small bag she'd hooked over her shoulder and fished out her own sunglasses. Sliding them on, she settled back in her seat. 'I'm really looking forward to today. Thanks again for sparing the time.'

Jack put the car in gear and steered along the alley. 'It's the least I can do after you introduced me to your dad. He was great the other day.' The wistful note in his voice had Eliza turning her head to face him, but he kept his eyes fixed resolutely ahead as he waited for a car to pass before he turned out onto the main road.

'You got the tractor fixed, I hear?' Her dad had been surprisingly closed-lipped on their drive back from the farm, answering her questions in monosyllables. Pops had been his usual chatty self, so she hadn't thought much more about it, especially after her dad's mood had been so good since.

Jack nodded, eyes still on the road. 'Yes, and we did a full maintenance check on it, so I shouldn't have to worry about anything when things get crazy during the harvest.' He didn't seem inclined to say any more, so Eliza let the conversation go so he could concentrate on his driving.

They were pulling up outside the farmhouse in next to no time. When Eliza would've undone her belt, Jack laid a quick hand on her arm. 'Stay here. I'm just going to get Bastian and then I thought we'd head out to the fields. I thought we'd do the outside part of the tour before it gets too hot, if that's all right with you? I'll be two minutes.'

'Sure, whatever you want.'

True to his word, Jack returned a few moments later. He opened the rear of the car to load the very excited Labrador, who poked his nose through the wide grill separating the boot space from the back seat and gave Eliza a woof of greeting. 'Hello, gorgeous boy,' she said. 'I'll give you a cuddle as soon as we get out, okay?'

As though he understood, the big dog turned a circle in the confined space then settled down out of sight.

The driver's door opened, drawing her attention and Eliza ducked her head down to look past Jack towards the front door. A short, smiling woman around the same age as her mum stood on the threshold, a warm smile on her face. She raised her hand and took a step forward. 'Hello, my dear. I was just saying to Jack it'll be nice to have a bit of company around the place as I missed your dad's visit. Do say you'll stay and have a bit of lunch with us later.'

Eliza cast a quick glance up at Jack who'd paused half-in, half-out the car. It was impossible to judge what he was thinking behind that sphinx-mask of a face, so she erred on the side of caution. 'If we have time…'

Jack's grunt was equally non-committal as he slid into his seat. 'We'll see you later, Mum.' With a quick wave they headed away from the farmhouse towards the track Eliza had walked along just a few days previously.

After parking at the top of the field, Jack opened the back of the car to let Bastian out, and the dog loped around to Eliza's side to greet her. She tried to climb out—not the easiest of tasks with several stone of Labrador leaning against her legs.

'Give the lady room to breathe, Bas.' Jack tugged gently on the dog's collar, until he yielded just enough space to allow Eliza to stand up. She bent over to scratch Bastian behind his ears, laughing at the sheer ecstasy on his face. His tail beat against her calf, so hard was he wagging it, and she was glad to be wearing jeans.

'Hold on a sec.' Jack disappeared around the back of the car, returning a moment later with a grubby tennis ball which he tossed towards the edge of the field. Bastian raced off after it.

'Thank you.' Eliza smiled, and Jack shrugged.

'You might not be thanking me later when your arm is ready to fall off. The only way we'll get a moment's peace is to keep throwing it.' Sure enough, the dog dropped the now-soggy ball at Eliza's feet and barked expectantly.

Using her thumb and forefinger to avoid the worst of the slobber, she picked it up and threw it. Jack turned in the opposite direction and began to stroll along the edge of the neat rows of plants. 'So, what do you want to know about what we do here?'

She flashed him a quick grin. 'Everything?'

Jack snorted. 'You sure about that? I can bore on about this place all day.'

'How about I promise to tell you when I've had enough?'

'Deal.' He halted. 'We grow a couple of different types here, but this is the bulk of our crop.' He waved a hand over the plants. 'It's got a fancy Latin name, but it's most commonly known as Old English lavender. This is what we distil the essential oil from.'

Even with her sunglasses on, the light of the sun was dazzling. Eliza donned her straw hat, relieved when the wide brim helped to shield her from the worst of the glare. She gazed out over the field. 'It's very neat, I'm amazed at how each row is so straight.'

Jack grinned. 'It's a bit of a nightmare to first lay it out, but we use a special kind of matting which helps keep the weeds down. We stake out the rows at an even distance, then once the matting's laid you can't veer too far off a straight line.' Hunkering down, Jack held the lower stems of one of the plants up so she could see the dark material beneath it. 'We drill holes straight through the matting to accommodate each plant. It's pretty durable and lasts the lifetime of the plants.'

Eliza crouched down to run her hand over the pale silver-green shoots covering the bush. 'And how long is that?'

He shrugged. 'It depends, really, but they average between seven and ten years. After that the yield falls away dramatically.' Straightening up, he brushed his hands on the front of his jeans before holding them out to help Eliza to her feet. 'We take cuttings from the mature plants and propagate them in the greenhouse.

It saves a fortune in buying replacement stock and also ensures the quality of our essential oil.'

His hands settled warm and firm on her shoulders as Jack turned her towards the far corner of the field. 'You can see the much smaller rows over there?' She nodded, conscious of the heat of him close to the rear of her body as he pointed over her shoulder. 'That's all new plants I put in this year. It'll take them three years to mature.'

The crisp, clean scent of whatever body spray he'd used that morning filled her nose, making it hard to concentrate on his words. The tanned skin of his forearm lay over thick muscle, scattered with dark hair, turning golden at the ends from constant exposure to the sun. There was something so vital about him, maybe because he spent all day surrounded by nature and out in the fresh air. He wasn't like anything she'd encountered before, and if she wasn't careful she'd end up making a fool of herself around him.

The dog bounded up, nosing his way between them, and Eliza was glad of the distraction. Ducking down, she grabbed the dog's ball and sent it flying off once more. The Labrador gave chase. 'You weren't kidding about him, were you?'

Jack stared after his dog, a lopsided grin on his face. 'Nope. He's been the same since I got him four years ago.'

She studied the dog as he ran towards them, trying to gauge his age. 'Have you had him since he was a puppy?'

He nodded. 'Nine weeks old.' The grin on his face turned decidedly soppy, softening the hard plains. 'He was such a tiny little thing. And now look at him.' Bending down, Jack greeted his dog with an enthusiastic rub over his shoulders. 'Nobody seeing those early pictures of you would believe the beast you've grown into, would they?'

Bastian barked once, then tried to stick his nose in the top pocket of Jack's denim shirt. Jack fended him off. 'Nothing in there, mate, I told you, you're on a diet.'

The disappointment on Bastian's face made Eliza smother a giggle. 'He looks so hard done by.'

'Spoiled rotten, don't let him fool you for a second.' Jack stood. 'Right, I'll show you the other species we grow—the one we cut and dry rather than use for oil, and then we can head back down to the distillery, okay?'

'Do you mind if I take some photos? I'm trying to boost the social media profile for *With Love from Lavender Bay* and looking for images I can post to my Instagram account.'

'Is that the name of your new business?'

'Yes, what do you think?'

Jack laughed. 'I'm the last one to ask about stuff like that, but it sounds pretty enough. If you think folks will like pictures of my fields, help yourself.' He whistled to the dog and drew him away to give Eliza space to work.

She took her time, interspersing long views over the rolling hills with close up shots of the still-furled buds. Jack was still busy romping with the Labrador, so she even sneaked in a few shots of the two of them playing when he wasn't looking. There was so much energy about Jack she soon forgot all about taking pictures and just settled in to watch him.

When he finally wrestled the tennis ball from Bastian and glanced up at her through his fringe, her heart did a funny kind of dance in her chest. 'Get everything you need?'

'Just about.' Eliza fanned her face with her hand in the hope he'd assume her red cheeks were from the heat rather than a blush. 'It's very warm.'

'It sure is. At least there's air con in the car. Come on.'

Cold air blasted from the vents the moment Jack turned on the engine, and Eliza tugged her hat off with a happy sigh. The sun was already warm, and she could feel where the vest beneath her shirt had begun to cling to the base of her spine.

As they made their way towards the fields at the lower end of the farm, a thought occurred to her, and she half-turned in her seat to face Jack. 'Do you grow the type of lavender that can be used in cooking?'

He glanced across at her. 'I can't say I've ever fancied it myself, but the Old English can be used for culinary purposes. I thought it was soap you were interested in, not baking?'

'Not me, Sam. Has he told you about the restaurant?' When Jack nodded, she continued, 'I know he wants to use local ingredients and I read some types of lavender can be used in recipes.' She paused, recalling his lack of enthusiasm about supplying her for her crafting ventures. 'But, I don't suppose that's your sort of thing if you're used to dealing with the wholesale market.'

Jack was silent for a few moments, then said, 'There'd be no harm in discussing it with him. Whenever he's ready, get him to give me a call.' He paused. 'Or I could pop down to the pub another evening when I'm free?' There was the hint of a question in his tone.

'I'd like that.' Eliza gave herself a mental slap upside the head. She hadn't even begun to come to terms with the end of her marriage; if she kept making stupid remarks like that, she'd give Jack the wrong impression. As attractive as he was, she was in no fit state to contemplate starting *anything* with another man. Even one who made her heart flutter. 'I mean…I think that'd be nice…I'm sure Sam would appreciate it.'

It took the half-hour tour of the lower fields before she finally stopped chastising herself over her inadvertent flirting. Honestly, the poor bloke was just being friendly, and she was slavering worse than Bastian with his tennis ball. Thankfully, Jack didn't seem to think anything was amiss. It was clear the farm was so much more than a job to him, and she found herself fascinated by every facet of the growing process he described. 'Dad was right,' she said as Jack pulled up outside a large building set at right-angles to the farmhouse.

'About what?' Jack brushed at the lock of dark hair that kept falling across his forehead.

'He said you should hold an open day for the farm, and I think he's right. Your passion for this place shines so brightly, and you're really good at explaining how everything works.'

'I don't know about that...' He tugged his sunglasses off, rubbed the lenses on his shirt then put them back on, all without looking at her. 'When would I have the time?'

She laughed. 'You found time for me without any problem.'

'Yeah, well...that's different.' He popped the fastening on his belt and clambered out the car.

Intrigued, she followed suit, but he didn't seem inclined to elaborate on the point as he concentrated on letting the dog out of the boot. 'Right, so this is the distillery.' He unlocked the door, then pointed to a shady spot. 'Bastian, sit there and I'll get you some water.'

To Eliza's surprise, the Labrador settled down with his face on his paws.

Jack must have seen the expression on her face. 'He knows he's not allowed in here.' Crouching down he scratched the dog behind his ears. 'And unlike the sofa, or my bedroom, or all the other places he's not supposed to go, he knows this is a strict rule.' After straightening up he opened the small door cut into what Eliza could see was a much larger opening set into a channel running through the concrete floor. 'Mind your step.' He held out his hand to help her climb into the pitch-black space. 'Don't move.'

The instruction was unnecessary. Assailed by a fragrant wave of cool, lavender-scented air, Eliza couldn't do more than stand there and draw in a deep breath. The clean, aromatic smell seemed to enfold her, bringing with it a sense of well-being and calm. She heard his boots scuff on the concrete floor, and then a soft hum filled the air as bright over-head lighting blinked on. She scanned the room, taking in the lengths of chain stretching from floor to ceiling over to the left, the silver vat and copper pipework of the still, the rows of wooden waist-high benches on the right with a large metal sink next to them.

Having filled a bowl at the sink, Jack placed it outside then pushed the door to behind him. 'Let's start over here.' He led her over to the left-hand side. 'This is where we hang the bunches to dry.' A large tub of S-shaped hooks was fastened to the wall near the rows of chains. 'We trim and tie each bunch and attach them to the chains with these.'

She nodded, picturing how the simple, yet effective, system would work. 'And that's the Grosso variety? The one growing in the bottom fields?'

His beaming smile made her feel like she'd won first prize. 'That's right. It takes about a fortnight to completely dry out, and then we ship it out to the wholesaler.'

'The scent in here must be out of this world when the chains are full.'

'It can get a bit overwhelming, but after a while I don't even notice it. We stagger the harvest as we want the flowers to be mostly open before drying it, so this part comes after we've distilled the oil from the Old English. Come July, we practically live in here.'

'I'd love to see it.' She could picture a curtain of deep purple blooms stretching from floor to ceiling as the bewitching scent of the freshly cut plants filled her nose. It would make a stunning image for an Instagram post, too. Perhaps she could persuade Jack to pose in front of it. She'd only just put up one of the photos of him playing with Bastian on her Instagram, and it had already received more 'likes' than any of the others she'd posted. She supposed she ought to tell him about that…or maybe not, considering some of the salacious comments posted underneath it.

'You can lend us a hand if you like. We have a small team of regulars who come in to help with the harvest, but I'll never turn away a bit of free labour.' His tone was teasing, but she sensed his seriousness about allowing her to come back and see it.

Excited, she couldn't keep the grin off her face. 'You're on!

Maybe you could pay me in lavender for use in my soap-making.'

'Oh, that reminds me...' Jack reached for her hand and led Eliza across the room to the wooden benches. 'I've got something for you.'

Eliza stared at the array of items on the bench before her—several bunches of dried lavender rested in gauzy net bags next to a dark brown glass bottle, and a taller clear one. Fingers shaking, she lifted the bottle to read the label 'Gilbert's Pure Lavender Oil'.

Her eyes met Jack's. 'Is this for me?'

Chapter Eight

From the look in her moss green eyes, you'd think he'd offered her the Crown jewels, rather than a few samples. 'This is too much,' she said.

Jack shook his head, feeling embarrassed. 'It's nothing, really, just my way of saying thank you for suggesting I get your dad to help out with the tractor. You didn't owe me anything after how rude I was to you.'

The morning had flown by, and Jack couldn't remember the last time he'd been so at ease in another person's company. When he thought how close he'd come to missing out on getting to know her, he wanted to cringe. If his mum hadn't suggested he go to the pub, he might never have crossed paths with her again.

She waved off his comment. 'Hey, we dealt with all that. I was trespassing, you had every right to be grumpy.' Eyes twinkling with laughter, she looked up at him and added, 'And you were *very* grumpy.'

He felt a smile tug at his lips. 'Anyway. I thought it would help with your soap-making and whatnot. The clear bottle is lavender water, it's what's left over from the oil distillation process.'

'I'd like to see that too.'

Her enthusiasm was infectious, and he found himself nodding.

'I can't give you an exact date, so it might be short notice, but I can definitely give you a call when we start harvesting the plants.'

Eliza beamed. 'That would be great. If I can swing it I'd be fascinated to see how it all works.' She traced the smooth wooden surface of the nearest bench and sighed. 'This is such a great workspace, I'm very envious. We're a bit on top of each other at the pub—especially with the guest rooms being busy this time of year. I'm not sure where I'm going to find space for my new projects. I might have to commandeer a bit of the cellar.' Her smile turned wicked. 'Or maybe I'll convert Sam's bedroom now he's spending all his time next door with Beth.'

'I bet he'd love that.' As a younger sibling, he knew the joys of tormenting an older brother. It hadn't changed over the years, and if he wanted to wind Jason up the easiest way to do it was to invade his personal space. A wave of bleakness shuddered through Jack. For just a second, he'd forgotten the reality of his life. He hadn't been in his brother's room since he'd retrieved a suit for the funeral director's.

Soft fingers brushed his forearm. 'Hey, what it is?'

Blinking the sting from his eyes, Jack met Eliza's worried frown. 'Nothing…it's nothing.' Christ, he needed to stop saying that, to stop bottling every thought and feeling up inside him. He took a breath for courage, then spoke. 'I was thinking about Jason. About how I'll never get to play the annoying kid brother again.'

'Oh, Jack.' Her fingers slid down his arm to curl around his own. She didn't say anything else—didn't need to. The small comfort was enough in its own right. Keeping hold of her hand, he turned her to the bench where the samples he'd left out for her sat. 'I think it's your turn to educate me for a bit. Tell me about your project.'

With her free hand, Eliza toyed with one of the bags of dried lavender. 'I'm not sure how it'll work, to be honest. The dress-making will be straightforward enough as I've always kept up with it, but the soap and candles is something new.'

'Dressmaking? I think I missed a bit of the conversation somewhere.'

She laughed. 'Oh, I probably didn't mention that bit. I had a chat with Beth and we came up with a whole range of creative things. The clothes will hopefully be more of a side line once I get the other stuff up and running, but it's the easiest way to get some extra income coming in.' She raised the lavender bag to her face, and her lashes fluttered closed as she drew in the scent. 'So beautiful.'

Yes. Jack gave himself a mental kick. 'So the soaps and stuff is new?'

Her eyes blinked open, the dreamy expression fading from her face. 'Sorry, I was miles away. I did all sorts of different art and design stuff when I was at university and found I preferred the practical projects, the ones that produced something tangible. You know?'

Not sure that he did, Jack nodded anyway. It was enough to see how excited she was.

'Anyway, I've done loads of research.' She glanced up at him with humour dancing in her eyes. 'And by research, I mean I've watched dozens of videos on YouTube. It's unbelievable the stuff you can find on there, I'm really excited to give it a try.'

Jack scratched his head. 'I can't even begin to imagine how you make soap. Does it look difficult?'

'Not really, it's all about chemistry. Every video I watched stressed about being accurate with measuring the ingredients, and most of the processes use an alkali to blend with the oil base so there's some safety precautions I'll need to take…' She tapped her lip, a small frown line marring the smooth skin between her brows. 'On second thoughts, the cellar beneath the pub probably isn't a good idea as I'll need somewhere with plenty of ventilation. Maybe I can just set a table up out in the rear yard.'

'If you get stuck then you'd be welcome to try it out in here, assuming it's before or after we get the harvest in.' Jack quite fancied the idea of watching her work. They'd always been strictly wholesale providers, but it never did any harm to do a bit of research. When Eliza had first shown up she'd expected them to have a shop, and he knew a lot of the other lavender farms around the country made and sold their own products. Perhaps it was time to reconsider the way they were doing things—especially as he was thinking about testing some alternative crops to complement the lavender. Jack filed the idea away to discuss with his mum at a later date.

'Oh, I couldn't possibly impose on you like that!' Her fingers squeezed his, reminding him she hadn't made any attempt to let go. He tried not to think about how nice her palm felt cradled within his. 'Don't give me an inch, Jack, or I'll be taking over the place.' He knew she was teasing, but he had to admit to himself the idea of seeing her sweet smile, of hearing her bubbly laughter around the farm on a regular basis was more than a little appealing.

When they'd chatted in the pub, he'd wondered if her friendly, open manner was a bit of a front—something to put the punters at ease, but she'd been exactly the same all morning and he was coming to the conclusion it was just who she was. Using his thumb, he stroked the side of her hand. 'You're really nice.' The words were out before he could stop them.

With a blush she glanced away before looking back at him with a shy smile. 'Thank you, so are you.'

He took a step nearer, his free hand raising of its own accord to trace the flush on her cheek. 'No, I'm a grumpy bastard with terrible loner tendencies.' He wanted to draw in some of her sweetness, take it in and keep it safe within him. 'You're like a breath of fresh air. I've spent my whole life pushing other people away, I'm not sure why. I'm not even sure I even realised it until you came along and made me want to stop doing it. I don't quite know where to start though.'

Forgetting all about not getting involved with her, Jack bent his head and touched his lips to hers. The rich amber of her perfume combined with the familiar scents of lavender to weave an intoxicating blend that his system craved more than oxygen. For the briefest of moments her soft mouth yielded beneath his and then she turned her head away. He pulled back instantly. 'I'm sorry.'

Eyes huge, Eliza held his gaze. Her tongue darted out to lick her lips. 'I'm married.'

If she'd thrown a bucket of ice water on him, Eliza couldn't have cooled his ardour more effectively than with those two words. He dropped his hand from her face like he'd been touching a hot coal. *Fuck!*

This was why he didn't let people get too close, there was always a sting in the tail. They let you down or misled you—*or did the unforgiveable and died on you.* He'd been halfway to hanging his hopes and dreams around Eliza's neck and then she dropped this bombshell on him. At least she'd done it early before he'd done something stupid like fallen for the sweet promise in her delectable eyes.

He tried to step back, but her hand locked tight around his. 'No, wait! Oh, God! What possessed me to say that?' she wailed.

Utterly confused, Jack blinked down into the shocked expression he felt sure must be mirrored on his own face. 'You're not married?' The hope surging inside him should've set off every early-warning alarm he had, but he was already too heavily invested in this. If there was the slightest chance, the faintest glimmer he'd misunderstood her meaning, he would snatch it in both hands and never let it go. But if she really was married then he'd have to walk away and forget about her because there was no way he was getting in the middle of that.

Her fingers tightened as though trying to pull him closer, but he held his ground, not trusting himself to behave in a rational manner if they reconnected. 'Stop.' He ground the word out between clenched teeth. 'Tell me what the hell is going on—are you married, or not?'

She released his hand with a sigh. 'No! Well, yes, *technically* I am but it's over. It's been over for ages, long before the physical separation happened, if I'm honest. I just…' She covered her face with her hands. 'I'm making such a mess of this. I hardly even know you, but I feel like there's some kind of connection between us, or maybe I'm so starved for attention that one decent kiss has scrambled my brains.'

He knew the bloody feeling. Still not sure what to think, Jack reached out to tug lightly on one of her plaits, making her lift her head to meet his gaze. 'I'm a simple man, Eliza, and not cut out for games and half-truths. Why don't you explain it to me?'

He played with the length of her bound hair as he listened to her halting explanation of a childhood romance turned marriage. Tracing his fingers over the woven pattern soothed him, and it was a safe way to keep touching her. As her tale unfolded, his heart ached at the sadness and disappointment in her voice. This Martin guy must've been the one he'd always seen her with in the pub. There didn't seem to be any particular deal-breaking moment in what she was describing, more the slow disintegration of her hopes and dreams.

Her words drifted over him. He'd never had a serious relationship in his life. Between the responsibilities of the farm, and Jason's disastrous attempt at living with someone, Jack could freely admit he'd been gun-shy about the whole business. And now there was Noah to take into consideration. If Jack was to consider getting involved with anyone…his eyes roved over Eliza's face. Who was he trying to kid? There wasn't an *anyone*—there was only *the one* and she was sitting right in front of him.

'The final straw came that morning in the airport when he said we should have a baby.' Eliza dropped her hands from his shoulders to fold her arms around herself, the gesture shrinking her smaller, curling her upper body in upon itself.

Stunned out of his musings, Jack's gut began to churn. 'You don't want kids?' It was a hell of a personal question, but he needed to know. Every time he thought they were getting somewhere, she pulled the rug out from beneath his feet. He might not have asked for it, but he was a father now, and nothing could come before giving Noah everything he deserved from the man in that role for as long as he needed it.

Getting involved with a woman who wasn't interested in children of her own would be a disaster in the making. Not everyone wanted children, and he wouldn't judge Eliza if that was the case, but things between them could never be more than casual. His nephew might be too young to remember the indifference and resentment of the woman who'd given birth to him, but Jack would never forget it. *Could* never forget it

When she looked up at him, there was a haunting pain in her green eyes. 'Not like that. Not as some kind of sticking plaster fix-it-all solution. Having a child should be something you both want more than anything in the world.'

He had to look away from the pain in her gaze. The pain in his own heart—well there wasn't much he could do about that. 'But what if circumstances thrust you into that position?'

'I don't think I have an answer to that, because that's not how it was with me and Martin. He only said it to keep me quiet, to get me to go along with what he wanted.' A bitter laugh escaped her. 'He was so casual about it, like I'd be taking up a new hobby, not bringing a living, breathing human into the world.' Eliza shuddered then turned away, the length of her plait slipping from his fingers as she increased the distance between them.

Trying not to notice the loss of her warmth, Jack watched her as she began to pace. With her expressive eyes fixed on the floor, it was impossible to tell what she was thinking. Being patient didn't sit well with him, but he forced himself to fold his arms and lean back against the bench, giving her the space she needed to process whatever was going on inside her head.

The silence stretched between them, wearing his nerve down to the thinnest of threads when she finally stopped in front of him and raised her eyes to meet his. Unshed tears glistened on the edges of her lids. 'Do you ever feel like you're not really living, that you're just existing from moment to moment? That's what it was like for the past couple of years, trying to pretend everything was fine, not daring to look too closely at things because I knew I wouldn't like what I saw.'

Jack knew only too well. He watched as she pressed her thumbs to the corners of her eyes, as though she was trying to hold back tears. 'It's scary as hell. You feel like you have no control, so you bury the fear as deep as you can and try not to think about it.'

'You too?' Her voice was the barest whisper.

'Me too.'

Eliza sighed. 'I have all these "friends" on Facebook and I don't have a clue who half of them are. That's one of the best things about being back in the bay, I'm surrounded by people who really know me. Having Beth and Libby close by has been the only thing keeping me sane these past few weeks. They already know the worst and love me regardless, so I don't ever have to pretend.'

Something twisted deep inside him. With Jason gone, was there a single person in the world who had any idea who Jack really was? His mum didn't count, she knew him inside out and back to front, but she had enough on her plate without carrying his burdens. When it came to his peers, was there anyone he had a deep connection to? He had business contacts, acquaintances at the surrounding farms who he could call on for help, as they could do with him, but friends? He'd always prided himself that he could stand on his own two feet, but damn, he was so weary. 'Jason was that person for me, we told each other everything.'

When she rested her head against his shoulder he sensed it was a friendly gesture intended to offer comfort. 'So who do you talk to now? About him, about what happened?' The truth choked somewhere in his throat leaving him unable to do anything but shake his head. Her arms slid around him, 'Oh, Jack, you can talk to me about him if you want to.'

He buried his face in the top of her head, breathing in her sweet scent, and that indefinable goodness that was the very essence of her. 'Thank you. I'm not ready to talk to anyone about him, I don't think.'

Eliza drew back to stare up at him. 'Well, when you are ready then?' When he nodded, she continued. 'And if there's anything else you want to talk about, not necessarily anything deep and meaningful…'

'I'd like that.' Probably more than he should. He reached for her hand, not quite sure what he wanted from her, but knowing he wanted to keep her close. The glint of his watch face caught his eye. Tilting his wrist, he blinked at the number on the digital readout. It was half past one meaning they'd been inside for more than an hour. Part of him wanted to forget about the time, to forget about all the painful things they'd both unearthed and get back to where they'd been before she'd told him about being married.

He sighed. There was no way back to that point, and he wasn't really sure what he wanted if he was honest with himself. Losing himself in the heat and sweetness of another kiss would serve a purpose, would chase the loneliness away for a while, but if they crossed the line to true intimacy too quickly there would be no coming back from it.

As much as he longed to explore whatever connection they had going on, how much better would it be once they really knew each other? Ignoring the baser parts of his brain, he stuffed his hands in his pockets before he did something daft like put his arms around her. 'Can I take you out somewhere for lunch? We could talk about lots of shallow, unimportant things.'

A brief smile lit her face before she grabbed his arm and tilted his wrist towards her so she could see his watch. 'Is that the time already? Damn, I was planning on getting some work done today…' She met his gaze. 'Oh, I didn't mean to sound ungrateful, I've had a wonderful morning…'

'You didn't, you don't, sound ungrateful I mean. I had a really nice time too. Maybe some other time?'

'Yes. I'd like that.' An awkward silence stretched between them until she turned to gather the lavender samples from the bench. 'Well, I'd better make a move, are you all right to drop me home?'

'Sure. I've got loads to do around here, so I probably shouldn't be thinking about playing hooky.' He did his best not to sound disappointed about it. It was just as well she had to go. Things had got a bit intense between them and if they weren't careful they'd end up making a stupid mistake. Digging in his pocket for his keys, he led the way back towards the door where Bastian greeted them with a lazy woof.

Eliza bent down to give the dog a pat and a little rub behind his ear which sent Bastian into paroxysms of ecstasy. 'Daft thing,' Jack said as he nudged the dog with his knee to give Eliza room to stand up.

The trip back to town didn't take long which was something of a relief as the awkward silence had settled over them the moment they were cocooned in the stifling heat of the car. Waiting at a junction, Jack jammed the air conditioning up to maximum and fiddled with the radio until he found the local station. Letting the DJ's inane chatter fill the air, he steered the big car through the winding streets of the town and into the alley that ran along the rear of the shops fronting the promenade.

He pulled up outside the back gate of the pub. 'Here we are.' Nice. Like she wouldn't recognise her home without him pointing it out.

'Thank you. I had a really wonderful morning.' Eliza bit her lip. 'I told you that already, didn't I?'

They shared a rueful grin which broke the tension between them. 'Good luck with the sewing.'

'I'm going to need it! I've promised Beth I'd have some samples for her to display this weekend.' She shook her head. 'I won't be getting much sleep tonight.' Hand on the door, she paused then glanced back at him. 'Do you think we might see you sometime soon for that drink?'

Warmth suffused him. 'I might be able to get away Saturday night for an hour or so.'

'Lovely.'

When she still didn't move, Jack twisted around in his seat so he could face her properly. 'Eliza?'

Her cheeks flushed. 'I just…I wanted to say sorry about earlier. I didn't mean to lead you on, or give you the wrong impression. I like you, Jack, but it's…' Whatever word she was looking for she didn't find it and ended up giving him a shrug.

Another time, under different circumstances he might've reached for her. Might've soothed the blush from her face with the back of his knuckles and relished the softness of her skin. Might've leaned over to brush a kiss on her lips. But they were where they were, and their lives were not their own to risk an entanglement they might later come to regret. 'Complicated?'

She glanced down at her lap then back up with a nod. 'Very. But I'd like to be friends. I meant what I said about having a great time today.'

Friends sounded good. Sounded like exactly what they both needed right now. 'Me too. I'll see you Saturday.'

Watching as she slipped from the car and disappeared through the back gate of the pub Jack clenched his hands on the steering wheel for a brief moment. There was no time for regrets.

Chapter Nine

Having worked into the early hours of the morning, Eliza dragged her aching body into bed expecting to drop off in a matter of moments. Instead she tossed and turned as her brain decided to show her a highlights reel of her relationship with Martin. From her giggling excitement the first time he'd held her hand in the school playground when the idea of being boyfriend and girlfriend meant little more than sitting next to each other during lessons, to the tremulous hope which had filled her heart as she took her place at the top of the aisle, fingers resting on her father's arm ready to take her first steps towards becoming his wife. So many good memories she'd forgotten in her disappointment over the past couple of years. They'd had something special, so why had it gone so wrong?

The early morning shadows crept across her wall, turning the room from black, to dim grey, to hints of the sunshine to come. Gritty-eyed, she turned her pillow over to try and find a comfortable spot for her aching head. Eliza squeezed her eyes shut and begged her brain to stop with its internal movie show. The little girl from the playground was all grown up now; the idealistic bride had seen too many of her dreams pushed to one side. Martin wasn't a monster, but he wasn't the happy-ever-after she hoped for either.

A pair of warm hazel eyes filled her mind's eye, the hint of a dimple skirting the edge of a pair of smooth lips quirked into a half smile. Flopping onto her back, she flicked her eyes open and stared up at the ceiling as though there were answers to be found in the stippled white surface. 'Oh, Eliza, what are you doing?' she groaned aloud.

'Talking to yourself?'

Her brother's gently mocking tone from the doorway sent her sitting bolt upright. 'What are you doing creeping about like that?'

He held up his hands. 'Not creeping, it's my turn to cover the breakfast shift and I just wanted to look in on you as you were still sewing away when I left last night. Beth sends her love and asked me to remind you that you're expected at six-thirty, just in case it had slipped your mind. She said to take your toothbrush and your PJs so I'm guessing I'll be making use of my room here tonight.' Propping one shoulder against the doorframe, he frowned at her. 'Everything all right?'

It was on the tip of her tongue to dismiss him but she found herself saying, 'Not really.'

Sympathy filled his green eyes. 'Want to talk about it?' When she nodded, he straightened up. 'I'll stick the kettle on and get some bacon in the pan. Wash your face and come and find me in the kitchen.'

Having splashed cold water on her face and cleaned her teeth, Eliza entered the kitchen feeling halfway human. A steaming mug of tea sat in front of a placemat on the table and she slid into the chair and wrapped her hands around the hot ceramic.

'D'you want a roll or a sandwich?' Sam asked from his position by the breadboard.

'Roll, please. Wholemeal.' She watched in silence as he sliced and buttered a couple of bread rolls then crossed the kitchen to place the butter back in the fridge.

Tucking his hands into the front pockets of his jeans, Sam

leaned back against the fridge and stared at her, concern etched into his face. 'Spill it.'

'Leaving Martin was the right thing to do.' She hadn't meant to phrase it as a question, but if she could hear the uncertainty in her voice, Sam surely could too.

'Are you asking or telling, because I think you know my opinion on that.' He'd never made a secret of his apathy when it came to Martin, that was for sure.

'Telling. Only…' She shrugged. 'I don't want everyone to think he's the villain of the piece. It takes two to make a marriage, and two to break it. If he'd cheated on me or been horrible then maybe it would be easier to just shrug it off and move on.'

'Move on to what?' His brow furrowed. 'Did something happen yesterday between you and Jack?'

Eliza ducked her head over her tea. 'Not really. We got a bit confused for a moment, but we've both agreed it's a bad idea.'

'But you like him?'

There was no censure in his tone, but that didn't stop her face burning. 'That's not the point. It's too soon. I need to get things sorted out with Martin before I even think about getting involved with anyone else.' She forced herself to sit up straight. 'Besides, I've got too much to do setting up the new business.'

'I think the lady doth protest too much.' Sam muttered the old phrase just low enough for her to pretend she hadn't heard it.

Taking a mouthful of tea, she tucked her leg underneath herself and shrugged. 'I didn't sleep well so you can ignore my nonsense. This pity party is officially cancelled. Now, where's that bacon roll you promised me?'

Thankfully, he let it go though she was sure she hadn't heard the last of it. Once Sam got the scent of something he was like a bloodhound. His question about Jack had caught her off guard, she would have to be better prepared before she sat down with Beth and Libby later for their girls' night in. Especially once the wine started flowing.

The scent of hot bacon filled the air and within a couple of minutes her brother was setting a plate down in front of her. 'Why don't you take that and the rest of your tea back to bed? I can cover things this morning and you can try and get some sleep if you've had a rough night.'

Smiling gratefully at his understanding, Eliza gathered her plate and mug. 'You're not all bad you know, Sam Barnes?'

He pressed a finger to his lips. 'Shh. Don't tell anyone or I'll get chucked out of the big brother club.'

'You're such a goof.' And the best big brother any girl could ask for. Pausing at the threshold, she remembered something. 'Hey, Sam? Can you double-check the diary, I think there's a new guest arriving today? He said he'd stayed here before when I took the booking last week. A solo guy…Owen something.'

Sam froze with his roll halfway to his mouth. 'Coburn?'

'Yes, that's it.'

'Well, that'll be something to look forward to.'

His sarcastic tone confused her. Sam was just about the most laidback person she knew. It took a lot to rub him up the wrong way, but it sounded like whoever this Owen guy was, he'd managed it. 'Is there a problem?'

Sam shook his head. 'Not really, he's just a bit of pain in the arse. Last time he was here he was sniffing around Beth…' Her brother scowled. 'He'd better not hassle her about selling the emporium again, or I'll be having a quiet word with him.'

Worried now, Eliza frowned. 'Did I make a mistake in taking his booking? Neither of you have ever mentioned him to me.'

'No, I'm sure it'll be fine. He's a property developer interested in the bay for some reason. He made an offer to buy next door when Eleanor died.' Sam closed the distance between them and kissed her cheek. 'Don't fret about it. Go and get your head down. Mum and Dad can handle things downstairs, so I'll sort Owen Coburn out when he arrives and then I must get the lighting scheme for the restaurant finalised.'

Mention of Subterranean never failed to put a sparkle in his eyes, and she felt a frisson of excitement. 'How's it all going?'

Sam beamed. 'Fantastic. The main contractor is ready to go, I'm just waiting on the bank to approve the loan application and then we'll be full steam ahead.' His smile dimmed a little. 'I had to give them another set of projections. I'm not sure they get the concept. I really hope they don't try and water it down into something more mainstream as a condition.'

She'd been so caught up in her own little bubble, she'd had no idea that was even a possibility. 'Oh, bloody hell! That'll ruin the whole thing if they do. What do they want, some boring little bistro with red and white checked tablecloths?'

'Probably.' He shrugged. 'I'll cross that bridge if we come to it. I believe in the concept, and I have to hope and pray they will too.'

'Let me know if there's anything I can do, okay?' A huge yawn cracked her face. 'But maybe wait until my brain is functioning again.' She shuffled out, eyes already drooping.

The bacon roll was gone within a few bites, the remnants of her tea drained down to the dregs. It crossed her mind she should clean her teeth again, but a stomach full of warm food and drink was doing a grand job of making her drowsy. This time when her head touched the pillow she was out like a light.

With her tamed curls still damp from the shower tied back with a scrunchy, and wearing her oldest, most comfortable, yoga pants and a long T-shirt, Eliza ducked out the back of the pub with a shouted goodbye to her parents. She secured the gate behind her, then stopped short at the sight of a familiar black car in the alley way. A smiling Davey closed the boot, clutching a stack of cardboard trays. 'Well, that's good timing! As soon as I saw the order I knew you three must be having a girl's night in.'

'Hello, Davey, lovely to see you again.' Davey and his wife, Gina, ran one of the local takeaways. Their pizzas had the thinnest, crispiest bases and were always loaded down with toppings, not like the heavy, doughy things the big chains seemed to churn out. Her tummy gave an appreciate rumble as she adjusted the bag over her shoulder holding her overnight things and the bottle of wine her mum had thrust into her hands as she was leaving. 'Here, I'll take them.' She held out her hands.

'If you're sure you can manage? Shall I get the gate for you? Beth said on the phone that she'd unlock it for me.' Davey handed over the pizza boxes then scooted around her to push open the entrance to the back yard behind the emporium.

Ever since a vagrant had broken into the back yard and caused an accidental fire which nearly destroyed the shop, Beth had been paranoid about security. Using her elbow, Eliza pressed the buzzer for the intercom. 'I've got pizza and wine!' she called into the speaker when Beth answered.

'Oh, and here's a little something from me and Gina, I almost forgot.' Eliza turned to find Davey holding a white carrier bag.

The door to the emporium flew open and Beth grinned at her before her eyes skipped past to fix on the bag. 'Ooh, is that what I think it is?'

Davey's smile widened to reveal a set of dimples that hinted at the handsome young man Eliza recognised from one of the many photos that Gina had decorated the back wall of the take-away with. 'Gina's homemade tiramisu, and it's on the house before you say anything.'

Beth raised an eyebrow but didn't protest as she accepted the bag. It was an old argument, one they knew from experience they had no chance of winning. 'Well, thank you both.'

'Yes, you're very kind,' Eliza added.

Davey left with a wave, looking pleased as punch. Beth trailed him to the gate and locked it behind him. After securing the back door, she ushered Eliza upstairs. 'Libby's already here.'

Eliza headed straight for the living room to drop the pizzas on the coffee table. Libby bounced out of one of the armchairs to peck a kiss on her cheek, then sank back down and grabbed an already open bottle of wine. 'I started without you! Grab a glass, and hurry back or I'll scoff all this pizza too, I'm starving.'

It always amused her how anyone who worked in a fish and chip shop could be hungry all the time, surely dealing with food all day would put her off? Eliza pulled the bottle of wine out of her bag and placed it on a shelf in Beth's fridge. Then again, working in the pub hadn't lessened her admiration for a nice, dry white, had it? Grinning to herself, Eliza returned to the living room and claimed her usual spot on one end of the sofa, a bookend to Beth.

Libby took her glass, poured a generous measure and handed it back with a grin. 'So, Beth tells me you were whisked off by some dark, mysterious stranger yesterday morning.' She waggled her eyebrows.

Knowing she'd have to spill the beans, Eliza decided to make them stew for a few moments. She took a sip of her wine, then put her glass aside to tug the pizza boxes towards her. 'We should eat before this gets cold.' It was hard not to smirk at the two sets of stony glares fixed upon her. 'What?' Helping herself to a slice from the top box she settled back into her corner of the sofa. 'I spent the morning with a sexy, brooding farmer who kissed me. I don't get what the big deal is…'

If only she'd had a camera to hand because the stunned look on Libby's face was an absolute picture. Trying not to smile, Eliza nibbled at the slice of pizza in her hand. The silence lasted for a whole five seconds before Beth and Libby exploded into action. A barrage of questions flew from their lips, but she resolutely ignored them until she'd finished the slice.

She reached for her wine, only to have Beth snatch it away and lean back as far as she could to keep it out of Eliza's reach. 'No way! Not another drop until you tell us what you're talking about. I was only teasing you this morning, I can't believe you let him kiss you—you barely know the man!'

Libby perched on the edge of her chair, nodding like one of those little plastic dogs people put on the parcel shelf of their cars. 'Exactly, exactly! God, Eliza, what if he's a serial killer?' She gulped a mouthful of wine then waved the glass around. 'Or, even worse, what if he wears budgie smugglers when he's on the beach?'

Eliza snorted. 'You're being ridiculous. He's a nice guy. We had a look around the farm, he kissed me and we both decided it was a huge mistake. There was plenty of time for him to bump me off if that was his plan.' She'd meant the last as a joke, expected her friends to laugh, but they both just stared at her. A seed of resentment formed in her middle. She knew telling them about the kiss, about her confusion over her attraction to Jack when things were still so raw after Martin, would be awkward so she'd tried to make light of it. You'd think she'd told them she'd been rolling in a haystack with him! When Beth had been sneaking around kissing Sam it had been a different story—Eliza had been expected to be excited for her. Not that she and Jack were sneaking around—or planning on anymore kisses.

Feeling annoyed, she stood and marched into the kitchen to fetch a fresh glass and poured herself some wine from the bottle in the fridge. When she returned to the living room, Beth and Libby were whispering furiously, their foreheads almost touching. Eliza leaned against the door frame. 'Something the two of you want to share?'

Beth at least had the decency to look guilty as she glanced up. 'We're just worried about you, that's all.'

Libby tucked her feet up underneath herself then tugged the baggy front of her jumper down over her knees. 'I was only messing about earlier, I didn't really expect anything to have happened between you two…'

'Why not?' God, why was she being so contrary? Hadn't she already decided the kiss was a mistake? Eliza tried to get a grip on the unusual flare of temper.

Tugging at a loose thread on the hem of her jumper, Libby

huffed out a breath to blow her peacock blue fringe out of her eyes. 'Why do you think?'

Furious now, Eliza gulped at her wine. 'So, this is about Martin? You hypocrite! Who was practically turning cartwheels of joy along the prom over the fact I'd left him? And now you're worried because I might be moving on? I was miserable for months, *years*, for Christ's sake! What if I did decide I wanted to pursue things with Jack, would it be too much to expect you to support me? Don't I deserve a little bit of something in my life that might make me happy?'

Beth shot to her feet. 'Of course you do!' Hurrying over, she flung her arms around Eliza. Still angry, she stood stiffly in her friend's embrace. Beth pulled back a little to meet her eyes. 'I want you to be happy, we both do, but what if this is a just a rebound? A reaction to all the stress and strain you've been under? We don't want you to get hurt, that's all.'

She knew they were right, but she was still so pissed off at them for stealing her thunder, for spoiling the joke she'd been expecting them to laugh over all evening. 'Like I said, we decided it was a mistake. It was a stupid kiss, nothing more, and we've decided to just be friends.' Knowing she was over-reacting, Eliza tried to shake off her ridiculous mood. Cocking one hand on her hip, she flicked her hair back over one shoulder. 'Besides, so what if I am on the rebound? You've seen Jack! Who wouldn't want to rebound into six feet of hard-bodied farmer?'

'She's got a point, B,' Libby chipped in. 'I can think of worse ways for her to get over being married to that wanker. I wouldn't mind rebounding into Jack myself a few times. Now, sit down you two, before this pizza gets cold.'

And just like that, the tension between the three of them vanished and they were all laughing. Eliza leaned her head against Beth's shoulder and they exchanged a quick squeeze before resuming their seats on the sofa. When they each had a fresh slice of pizza in their hands, Eliza looked between the two of them.

'Listen, I'm not going to go and make a fool of myself over Jack, okay? But just for a moment he made me feel beautiful and wanted, and I haven't had that in such a long time.'

A little frown creased Beth's forehead, but she didn't say anything, just gave a quick nod. Libby wasn't so easily cowed though. 'If he's that good a kisser, maybe you *should* think about rebounding into him.'

Eliza let her mind drift back to that moment in the processing shed, to the heat and light that had radiated from her lips to every molecule in her body. 'It's a tempting prospect, but it'd only end in tears.' She took another sip of her wine. 'He comes across all big and gruff, but there's this vulnerability about him once you dig a little deeper. We're not rushing into anything. I told him about Martin, and he's got his own issues so we're just going to be friends.'

Thinking about what she'd just said, Eliza let out a groan. She wasn't ready, and from the little glimpses she'd got of Jack's current situation he certainly wasn't ready. And yet there was no denying the strength of their attraction. Just talking about him was making her want to see him again, to find out if that little spark between them had been an aberration or a hint of what the future could have in store for her. 'Oh, Lord, I'm not fooling anybody with that, am I?' *Least of all herself.* 'I'm not saying never, I'm just saying not right now and so is he. It's not like either of us is going anywhere.'

Beth mimed zipping her lips closed while Libby settled for shaking her head slowly as she stuffed half a slice of pizza in her mouth. With a sigh, Eliza snagged a piece of garlic bread and chewed thoughtfully. Despite her little flash of anger, she was grateful that she had people around her who cared about what happened in her life, who didn't want to see her get hurt. But, then again, she'd tried so hard to be careful and sensible and look how that had turned out.

Maybe she should just stop worrying so damn much about

everything. Things with Jack might develop into something later down the line, they might not, but she couldn't let fear of getting hurt again rule her life. If she didn't seize every opportunity to live the most fulfilling life she could then what had been the point of turning everything upside down? She might as well have stayed with Martin. Pep talk over, she let herself relax back into the deep cushions of the sofa. 'Right, enough of that for now, let's talk about something else.'

'Like what?' This was from Libby.

Eliza shrugged. 'Oh, I don't know…tell us what's going on with you, Libs.'

Libby curled her upper lip and added another good glug of wine to her glass. 'Nothing to tell. I get up, I fry chips, I serve 'em and then I go to bed. No brooding farmers, no blue-eyed boy next door falling over himself to tell me he loves me. Not a bloody sausage unless you count the ones dipped in batter.'

'Kinky,' Beth murmured, almost causing Eliza to snort wine out of her nose.

'Oh, B, that's disgusting!' Libby sounded properly outraged which only made Eliza giggle more. She laughed so hard her hand shook, spilling wine onto her yoga pants.

'Now look what you made me do!' She lifted her leg and bent over to suck the wine from the cotton material and it was Beth's turn to giggle. 'What? It's not like I'm going to let it go to waste now, is it?'

'Apparently not.' Libby still had her nose stuck in the air as though disgusted with the both of them, but laughter glimmered in her eyes.

Eliza turned to Beth. 'And what about you? Everything here going okay? Sam was moping about like a lost puppy at the prospect of sleeping at home tonight.'

Beth rolled her eyes. 'I'm sure he'll cope, it's not like we live in each other's pockets.'

Eliza exchanged a knowing glance with Libby. 'Of course not.'

'I can't think of the last time I saw the pair of you together,' added Libby in her driest tone.

'Oh, shut up, you two.' Laughing, Beth poked out her tongue. 'I love spending time with Sam, but it's great to have a girls' night for a change.' Her eyes widened in worry. 'You won't tell him I said that, though, will you?'

'Your secret's safe with me.' Eliza crossed her heart. 'Besides, it sounds like he'll have his hands full dealing with our new arrival this evening. From the way Sam was talking about him, he sounds a bit of a nightmare. Although you probably know better than me because Sam said this Owen guy tried to buy this place not too long ago.'

It was Libby's turn to choke. 'Oh, bloody hell, don't tell me he's back, that's all I need!'

Her outburst startled Eliza. 'Do you know him too, Libs?'

'I could rather wish I didn't, rude sod. He's all right to look at, but that's the only good thing about him.' She tugged her jumper further over her knees, a dark scowl marring the pretty elfin features of her face. There was a story there, and Eliza might've started digging had Beth not spoken and distracted her.

'I wonder why he's back? If he thinks I might have changed my mind about the emporium, then he's wasting his time.' Beth folded her arms across her chest.

'Don't worry. Sam was already breathing fire at the prospect of that so I'm sure he'll have put him straight before he's finished checking in.'

'Well if he doesn't, I certainly will if I see him.' Beth reached for the remote. 'Right, let's see what Netflix has to offer us, shall we?'

Eliza cleared away the empty boxes into the kitchen and returned balancing three plates with a slice of tiramisu on each, and the bottle of wine she'd previously opened tucked under her arm. She dished out the plates while Beth scrolled through the film menu and argued with Libby about what to watch. 'I don't know why you're arguing,' Eliza said around a mouthful of delicious, creamy cake. 'You know we'll end up watching *Pitch Perfect*.'

'Oh, good call!' Beth checked her watch. 'If we get on with it we can fit in one of the sequels too.'

They knew the film almost off by heart, but that was what made it special. As she settled down to enjoy the mix of music and comedy her phone vibrated on the arm of the sofa where she'd set it down earlier. Expecting it to be either one of her parents, or Sam, she couldn't help but smile at the sight of Jack's name on the screen. She clicked open the message.

I had a really nice time yesterday. J x He'd sent her a kiss. That had to mean something, because he didn't strike her as the kind of guy who was naturally demonstrative.

She quickly tapped out a reply. *Me too x Thanks for tour.*

The phone vibrated a few seconds later. *My pleasure. Bastian's pining for you, so we're going to swing past the pub when I take him for a walk Saturday evening*

Her heart did a little flip-flop in her chest. *I'll be sure to save him a spot at the bar*

Glancing up, she noticed the room was silent—the figures on the TV screen frozen in mid-action. Heat filled her cheeks and she cast a sheepish look towards her friends who were both grinning at her. 'Jack might pop into the pub Saturday night.'

Libby rubbed her hands together, her expression gleeful. 'Right then, that's our weekend entertainment sorted, right B?'

Beth nodded. 'Oh, yes. It's been *ages* since I caught up with your folks, Eliza, a little get together in The Siren sounds perfect.'

Groaning, Eliza grabbed a cushion and buried her face in it. *What on earth had possessed her to say anything?* Poor Jack, she just hoped they didn't give him too much of a grilling. 'I hate you both, so much.'

The gales of laughter which greeted her declaration didn't help one bit.

Chapter Ten

Jack reached the end of the row and switched off the rotovator with a sigh and a stretch. After raising the subject with Eliza, he'd decided to seize the bull by the horns and mentioned to his mum about wanting to diversify the farm into other fragrance-producing crops. To his delight, she'd been full of enthusiasm for the idea. With the next few days expected to be quiet, he'd pulled their old rotovator out of the back of the shed to clear and dig over the abandoned vegetable patch.

The physical work was also helping him take his mind off his impulsive decision to text Eliza the previous evening. He'd regretted it the moment he'd hit the send button, worrying what he'd intended to be a friendly message might be misconstrued. Especially after that bloody kiss! He didn't know what had come over him to be honest and had filed it away as a moment of madness. Now if only he could stop thinking about it every damn minute of the day.

'You're making good progress.'

Jack turned to find his mum approaching with a mug in her hands. Accepting the coffee with a grateful smile, he took a quick sip before replying. 'The soil's in pretty good nick—better than I expected.' He nodded over to the growing pile of gnarly old carrots, parsnips and other root vegetables the machine had churned up. 'There's enough there to make some soup.'

His mum wrinkled her nose. 'I'm not sure I'd feed them to pigs, never mind humans. Maybe we should stick to what the Tesco's delivery man brings.' She shook her head. 'What would your dad think if he could hear us now? Ordering from the supermarket is about as far from our dream of self-sufficiency as you can get.'

'Come on, Mum, don't be like that. We've all done our best since losing him and now Jason. Something had to give, and I'll be damned if you should feel guilty over a bit of internet shopping.' He glanced down at the churned over soil at his feet. Perhaps he should've been more sensitive about digging up what had once been his dad's pride and joy, but he couldn't imagine he'd want them to leave it fallow forever. 'I didn't mean to upset you, Mum, we can reinstate the garden if you'd prefer?'

She gifted him with the sweetest smile. 'Don't apologise, darling, I'm being silly and sentimental that's all. Besides, you're right, we don't have the time to keep a plot this size up and I really like your plan for the roses. It's good to see you changing things up around here.' Her features clouded as she raised a hand to shield her eyes from the sun. 'I don't ever want you to feel like you have to keep the farm going for me, I hope you understand that.'

'Oh, Mum.' The guilt in her voice hurt his heart. Jack drained his coffee to give himself a moment to find the right words. 'I'm not Jason. I know that you and dad wanted to give us the best life possible when you moved us down here, and I couldn't have asked for more than you guys gave me.' Crouching down he gathered a handful of the rich brown soil and let it trickle through his fingers. 'Farming is in me, blood and bone, and I cannot imagine wanting to do anything else with my life. I get what you're saying, but I need you to know I'm not acting under any kind of obligation, okay?'

She nodded, her eyes a little misty. 'Okay.'

Jack pushed to his feet once more. 'When the time comes, I'll give Noah the choice to follow whatever path he wants which is one of the reasons I want to keep him at school. He needs to know there's a whole world beyond the gates of the farm.' But there had to be a way to give him the best of the experiences Jack had had growing up without him feeling stifled. He'd never forget the excitement the first time his dad had let him steer the tractor for himself, or all the practical lessons his mum had passed on as they'd gone on nature rambles around the farm. 'There's that small plot of land behind the old cottage. We could turn it into a kitchen garden if you like. It'd do Noah good to learn that food doesn't just come from a few clicks with the mouse and with the school holidays coming up we could do with something to keep him occupied.'

Excitement replaced the last of the sadness on his mum's face as she listened to his idea. 'It wouldn't have to be anything too ambitious,' she said. 'A few carrots and potatoes, maybe a frame of runner beans.'

Jack nodded. 'Exactly. Maybe even some sunflowers. Noah's getting old enough now to take a little bit of responsibility. We can get him his own set of gardening tools and a watering can, make him the head gardener.' He could just picture him puttering around in his wellies. 'Let's talk to him about it over the weekend.' Thinking about that, he remembered his plans. 'I'm going down the pub Saturday evening if you're all right to watch Noah for a couple of hours?'

His mum beamed at him. 'I'm glad to hear it. It's about time.'

Jack raised an eyebrow. 'About time for what?'

'You know what I'm talking about. Eliza's a lovely girl.'

Wow, he wasn't the only one getting ahead of himself. Jack held up a hand. 'Steady on, Mum. We've spent the sum total of one morning together, don't make plans to buy a hat just yet. Besides, I've got enough on my plate without getting involved with anyone and Eliza's not long separated from her husband. We're friends, nothing more.'

She fixed the same look on him that had made him squirm since he'd been a little boy. 'I know what you're like Jack William Gilbert—always looking for problems that aren't there. You've always been the same, worrying over doing the right thing so much that you end up missing out.'

You could always rely on his mum to cut to the chase. She had a point, too, which didn't make it any easier to hear. 'It's not the right time, okay?'

Reaching up, she rubbed a soothing hand on his upper arm. 'Life's messy, darling. There's never really a right time for doing anything. You can plot and plan to your heart's content, think you've got it all mapped out perfectly and life will pull the bloody rug right out from under your feet. Did I tell you I had a boyfriend when I first met your dad?'

The abrupt shift in topic confused him, but when he looked down at his mum her eyes had lost focus, like she was seeing a moment in the past. 'I never knew much about how you two met,' he admitted.

A dreamy smiled played about her lips. 'He was a friend of a friend. We met at a party and got chatting. It was like we'd known each other all our lives. Nothing happened that evening, there wasn't even a hint from him that he was interested in me in that way, but I broke up with my boyfriend the next day. We'd been quite serious, and I honestly thought I had my future all planned out until your dad wandered into that kitchen for a beer.' Her smile widened. 'We bumped into each other at a bar a couple of weeks later—although I found out later he'd set that up through our friends—and that was it. We were inseparable from that day on.'

'That's a lovely story, Mum, but what's it got to do with me?' He knew he was being obtuse, but he really didn't want to get into it with her about his love life—or lack of it. His eyes roamed over the part-dug ground in front of him. Time for a change of subject. 'How's the research been getting on this morning, any luck?' His mum had taken it upon herself to get on the laptop and find out the best type of roses for his new project.

The look she gave him made it clear the topic of Eliza wasn't over, though she let it go for now. 'Great! I've put been putting together a spreadsheet with links as well as prices. I should have it all together for when you come in for your lunch.'

'Sounds good. I'm also going to make an appointment with the wholesaler, see what he thinks about us diversifying—' His mobile rang, cutting Jack off mid-thought. 'Hello?'

'Oh, Mr Gilbert, thank goodness. I tried the house phone, but there was no answer.'

'We're both outside, sorry who is this?' The slightly breathless voice sounded familiar, but he couldn't quite place it.

'Sorry! It's Mrs Taylor from the school. Noah's a bit upset… nothing serious, but I wanted to let you know.'

Jack put a hand on his mum's arm to keep her beside him as he tried to stay calm. 'What's happened, is he hurt?'

'Oh, no! Nothing like that, there was just a bit of a mix-up over something with one of the other boys that's all.'

'Just tell me what the problem is—actually, no, I'm coming now, so you can explain it when I get there. I'll be about five minutes.' He hung up over her blathering protests. Why phone to tell him, and then make it sound like no big deal?

'What's wrong?' His mum had turned pale as milk.

'Noah's not hurt, but something's upset him. I'm going down there.' He was already moving towards the farmhouse to get his keys, heedless of the mud on his boots.

'Of course.' His mum trailed him back to the front door. 'Will you ring me when you can?'

'Yes.' He brushed a quick kiss on her cheek. 'Try not to fret.' It was a pointless comment, his gut was tied in knots already, so goodness only knew how she was feeling.

The drive to school passed in a blur, and it was only after Jack pulled on the handbrake in one of the visitor's parking spaces that he realised he had no recall of the journey. *Had he even stopped at the traffic lights at the Chapel Street junction?* Gripping the steering wheel, he battled the urge to throw himself out of the Land Rover and storm into the building. Noah needed him to be calm, to not make whatever the problem was worse. He closed his eyes, counted to ten and huffed out a breath.

Feeling more in control, he climbed out and strode towards the redbrick building. Built between the wars, it had a sturdy, slightly foreboding look to it, but inside was bright and colourful with noticeboards covered in awards for good behaviour and examples of the children's work. A dark ridged mat covered the space between the outer and inner doors. Jack paused to wipe his boots, realised it was a futile gesture as they were caked in mud and he toed them off with a curse for not taking the time to change them at home.

The tiles in the quiet corridor were slippery beneath his thick work socks, forcing him to check his stride or risk falling on his arse. Thankfully, it wasn't far to the main office, and he half-skidded through the door, startling Mandy, the school secretary in the process.

'Oh, Mr Gilbert! I didn't hear you coming.'

He wiggled his feet on the carpet. 'Sorry, I was working outside when I got the call and forgot to change my boots.'

She glanced down at his socks with a smile. 'Oh, you didn't need to worry about that. Noah's in with Mrs Taylor, I'll let her know you're here.' She picked up the phone, but he was already moving across the little office towards the closed door.

He knocked, but didn't wait, and had the door open before Mandy had finished saying his name. Mrs Taylor stood behind her desk, the phone at her ear as she stared at him, but he barely spared her a glance—all his attention was for the little figure huddled on a beige two-seater sofa which formed part of an informal seating area against the opposite wall. 'Noah?'

A whirlwind blur of red-and-grey uniform flew across the room towards him and Jack crouched down to catch the boy up in his arms. 'Uncle Jack!' The rest of what Noah tried to say was choked off in heaving sobs which cut Jack to the bone.

Moving carefully, he carried Noah back to the sofa and sank down into the sagging cushions. Noah crawled into his lap and buried his face in Jack's chest. Holding him close, Jack fixed a cold stare on Mrs Taylor and shook his head when she made a move to join them. She subsided into her chair, and Jack's anger was mollified slightly by her contrite expression.

Pressing a kiss to the top of Noah's head, Jack gave him a squeeze. 'I'm here, bud, Uncle Jack's here now, it's all right. Shh, now.' He let him cry for a minute, muttering gently that it would be okay, that Jack wouldn't let anyone hurt him, his heart twisting to know it wasn't true.

Noah's breathing calmed, the sobs dying away to sniffles and Jack urged him to sit up a bit. Casting around, Jack spotted a box of tissues on the coffee table in front of him. He leaned forward, bracing Noah with a firm hand on his back while he made a grab for the tissues. Noah managed a little giggle as they settled back on the sofa with a thump and he took a handful of tissues from the box.

'Have a good blow, it'll make you feel better.' They exchanged a grin when Noah made a high-pitched squawking noise as he blew his nose. 'Are you ready to tell me what's made you sad?'

Noah's face crumpled. 'I can't play football because I haven't got a daddy anymore.'

*What the fu...*Jack swallowed the curse on his lips. 'What do you mean you can't play football?' He frowned over the top of Noah's head at Mrs Taylor then looked back down at his nephew.

'Michael said I can't play football because Daddy's dead.' Noah flung his arms around Jack's neck once more and he hugged the boy close.

'There's been a terrible misunderstanding…' Mrs Taylor rounded her desk to take a seat in the armchair across from them 'The school's taking part in the national "Fit and Fun" campaign and we thought it would be a nice idea to get some parents involved. We're organising a fathers and sons football competition down on the beach next weekend…' Her voice trailed off.

'And you didn't stop to think how this might affect one of your pupils who'd recently suffered a bereavement?' It took all his effort to keep from shouting, but Noah was upset enough as it was. Jesus, what the hell had they been thinking?

Mrs Taylor blanched. 'I know, it's inexcusable not to have discussed it with you first. It didn't seem like a problem though because Noah was excited about asking you to do it with him.'

Jack wasn't sure his poor heart could take much more of a battering. He sucked in a breath, his hands stroking up and down Noah's back as he tried not to hug him too tight. 'So why all the tears?'

The headteacher sighed. 'I'm afraid one of the other boys in class took exception and said something unkind to Noah. I'll be having a talk with him afterwards but seeing to Noah was my first priority.'

It looked like she wanted to say something more, so Jack loosened his hold on Noah. 'Hey, buddy, why don't you pop next door and see Mandy? Ask her if she'll help you wash your face and maybe get you a glass of water? You don't want to get a sore throat.'

Noah slipped down from his lap. 'You'll be here?'

'I won't move from this spot, I just want to talk to Mrs Taylor for a minute and then you can come home with me if that's what you want.'

'Okay.'

He watched Noah trot out of the room, then rounded on Mrs Taylor. 'What the hell's going on?'

She rubbed her hands on the thighs of her trousers. 'I'm not sure I can say anything without breaking a confidence.'

'Bollocks!' Jack snapped his lips shut, took a breath and started again. 'Sorry for swearing, but you must see this from my point of view, if one of the boy's is picking on Noah, I want to know why and I want it stopped right this minute!'

Mrs Taylor nodded. 'The boy in question doesn't enjoy a lot of home support. I think he wanted to stop Noah from joining in with the football so he wouldn't be the only one who didn't go.'

Jack paused to let what she was saying sink in. 'So this boy's dad won't take him on Sunday?'

'It's highly unlikely.' She crossed her legs and sat back in her seat. 'It's still absolutely no excuse for him to upset Noah, but I don't think he said it to be cruel. I'll make sure he understands and apologises.'

What a bloody mess. Jack had to admit as angry as he was about Noah, he didn't envy Mrs Taylor her job having to juggle with dozens of tiny emotional timebombs every day. 'If the kid's having a hard time, let's not make it any worse for him, okay?'

Her sense of relief was palpable. 'Thank you, Mr Gilbert. That's very understanding of you. I hope you will be able to bring Noah along next Sunday, it's clear the two of you have a very strong bond.'

'If he still wants to do it, then I'll make the time for him, of course. Do you have something with all the details on it?'

'Yes, I have a flyer somewhere…it's a bit short notice but a couple of the other dads put the idea together and we decided to support them.'

Standing, Jack accepted the piece of paper. He gave it a quick glance over then folded it up and stuck it in his back pocket. A soft tap came on the open door and he looked up to see Noah standing there, with his hand tucked into Mandy's. His face was washed, and apart from a little redness around his eyes he looked much better. 'All right?'

Noah nodded. 'Mandy had some orange and pineapple squash and it was yummy.'

Jack smiled to himself. If only all problems were so easily resolved. 'I don't think we have any of that—you can tell Nanna about it when we get home, so she can put some on the shopping list if you like?'

'Can I tell her about it tonight? It's nearly breaktime and then we have drawing. It's my favourite lesson.'

God above, the kid was going to kill him with his brave little soul. 'Of course, buddy. Come and give me a hug and then you can go out and play with your friends. I'll be here to pick you up after school, all right?'

Noah hugged him tight for a minute then stepped back. He glanced down then up at Jack with a giggle. 'You forgot your shoes, Uncle Jack!'

Jack wriggled his toes. 'I had to leave my boots by the door because they were covered in mud. I've been digging up the vegetable patch because Nanna and I are going to plant some roses there. You know how we make oil from the lavender? Well, we can do the same with roses too.'

'And they will look pretty! Nanna likes pretty flowers.' Noah took his hand. 'I'll show you the way back if you like?'

Jack bit his lip against a smile. 'That would be very helpful, thank you, Noah.' He nodded to Mrs Taylor, then Mandy. 'I'll be off then. Give me a call if there are any more problems.'

'Yes, of course.' Mrs Taylor shook his free hand then stepped out of the way to let them passed.

'I'll send you a quick email with the details of that orange squash, shall I?' Mandy asked as she walked with them the couple of paces to the outer office door.

'Cheers, Mandy, you're a star.' She blushed bright red and scurried back behind her desk.

Hand in hand, Jack and Noah wandered towards the exit, pausing beside the board which showed Noah's class's achievements. It was obvious from the wide array of names and some of the more spurious prizes mentioned that the teacher worked hard to give everyone a fair mention.

Noah pointed out his star for being the best helper for the previous week, pride shining bright on his face. Jack squeezed his hand. 'Well, I reckon that deserves a treat. What say we stop on the way home and you can choose a new comic? We could get some flowers for Nanna as well.'

'Yes, please!'

The bell rang, and the sound of chairs scraping came from the classroom next to them. 'That's breaktime, then? I'd better be off.' A stream of children came flowing down the corridor, sweeping Noah up in their midst and Jack let him go with a smile.

Digging his phone out of his pocket, he rang his mum with an update as he shoved his feet into his boots. She sounded as relieved as he now felt, and they agreed to talk it over when he got home. Jack checked the screen out of habit before putting it away and saw the text message icon. He scrolled to his messages as he made his way across the playground, trying to dodge zooming, laughing children as he went.

The girls want to meet you so we're having a bit of a get-together in the pub tomorrow. I hope you don't mind. Sam's arranging a distraction x

Jack considered Eliza's message, wondering what she'd said to them last night to warrant them wanting to meet him. It had to be a good thing, right? Or maybe they were worried about whether he was good enough for their friend. He gave himself a mental slap. There wasn't anything going on between them for anyone to be worried about. *More's the pity.* He texted her back quickly. *Looking forward to it x*

He climbed into the Land Rover. If he tried hard enough, he might even convince himself he meant meeting her friends rather than getting the chance to spend time with Eliza again.

Chapter Eleven

'Sam? Have you seen the Aspirin?' Clutching her head, Eliza all but staggered towards the kitchen. Having woken early, she'd had the foolish idea of squeezing in a couple of hours at her sewing machine before things got busy. Her hangover had kicked in halfway up the back stairs. She stopped in her tracks at the sight of her brother all but facing off with an unfamiliar man. 'Oh, sorry, I didn't realise you had company.'

Sam flicked her a strained smile. 'Hey, Sis. This is Mr Coburn, he's up and about early.'

She could understand his irritation. The family and guest sections of the upper floors of the pub were clearly demarcated, and most visitors respected those boundaries. *Most*, but not all it seemed.

Owen tucked his hands in the front pockets of a pair of crisp chinos and leaned one hip against the table, looking every inch like he owned the bloody place. His hair was cropped close to his head, and his casual stance did nothing to lessen the impact of him on Eliza's poor addled brain. The man breathed confidence from every pore, no wonder he had poor Libby at sixes and sevens.

The corner of his mouth twisted up in something

approximating a smile. 'I waited in the breakfast room, but when there was no one about I decided to try and track down a cup of coffee.'

Confidence? Arrogance more like! It was on the tip of her tongue to point out all guest rooms were supplied with a kettle and supplies to make hot drinks, when Sam opted to take the high road and crossed the kitchen to flip on the coffee machine. Whoever was last up always set it up before going to bed, so it would only be a matter of minutes before it brewed.

Moving next to the fridge, Sam opened the door and removed a carton of juice. 'Orange, that's your preference if I remember rightly?'

Owen nodded. 'Yes, thank you.' He half-turned towards the table which was littered with blueprints and paperwork. 'I was nosing around while I was waiting. This looks interesting, I'd like to know more about it.'

Finding the frank admission disarming, Eliza decided he might deserve the benefit of the doubt after all. She watched as Sam approached the table and handed one of the glasses of juice to Owen before rifling through the papers to find the master design sketches. 'I'm going to convert the skittle alley beneath the pub into an exclusive restaurant.' He nudged the drawings over, giving Owen tacit permission to look through them. 'Well, as soon as the bloody bank pulls their finger out, I will be.'

Owen hummed a sympathetic noise of agreement as he flicked through the papers before him. 'That's always the fun part of any project—getting the investors to buy into your vision.' He pulled out a chair and sat. His hand hovered over the ring binder file Sam was using to manage the project, then paused. 'May I?'

The banging in Eliza's head wasn't getting any better so she left them to it and hunted for the old biscuit tin they used as a first aid kit. Hugging a packet of painkillers to her chest, Eliza returned the tin to the cupboard then poured her own glass of juice. She drained half of it before washing down a couple of pills with the rest. The rich smell of fresh coffee filled the room, combining with the hit of hydration from the juice to make her feel marginally more human. 'I'll fix us some coffee, shall I?' Belatedly remembering Owen was supposed to be a guest, she rustled up a smile. 'Did you want anything to eat yet?'

Nose-deep in a spreadsheet, Owen gave an absent nod. 'A slice of toast for now. I'm not in any rush this morning so I'm happy to wait for a few more people to stir before you start cooking. I can't seem to lie in, even when I'm not working.'

Sam stood up. 'I'm on duty, Sis. Grab a seat and I'll sort this out.'

Grateful, Eliza slunk into a seat at the kitchen table

Whilst Owen studied columns of numbers, Sam pottered around pouring the coffee and sticking four slices of bread in the large toaster. 'I remembered you were an early riser from last time,' her brother said to Owen. 'My girlfriend kicked me out for a girls' night with Eliza here and their other best friend, so I didn't sleep well myself.'

Accepting the coffee, Owen took a gulp of the hot liquid and sighed. 'God, I'm useless without caffeine. Those instant sachet things are all right at other times, but I need something decent to get my brain working first thing.' He took another drink then set the mug down. 'Your girlfriend's the one who owns that junk shop next door, right? I remember her warning me about you when I asked her for a drink.'

All thoughts of Eliza's hangover fled as she stared slack-jawed at Owen. God, he really had a price on himself! And from the scowl Sam was throwing at him, that smug grin was about to get knocked right off his face. 'Don't let Beth hear you call it a junk shop or she'll bite your face off, she loves every inch of the emporium.'

Owen raised an eyebrow. 'Feisty, is she? I would've thought face-biting would be more the style of that weird friend of yours—the one with the mad hair.'

There was something in his tone which caught her attention. A slyness to the way Owen had slipped a mention of Libby into the conversation, and coupled with her friend's odd reaction to him the previous night…Eliza sat back in her chair, beginning to enjoy herself. 'Libby? She's been doing her hair like that since we were only thirteen or fourteen. Our teacher sent her home , and everyone expected Mick, her dad, to punish her, but he marched straight up to the school and gave the head a right earful.'

After placing the coffee and toast on the table, Sam resumed his seat and smiled at the memory. 'I remember that! Those two are a formidable partnership, have been since Libs lost her mum. They run the chippy along the prom—you should try it one night; best fish and chips in the county.'

Owen's knife clattered onto his plate as though it'd slipped out of his fingers. 'You've got to be bloody kidding me.'

'About what?'

Owen blinked, appearing startled by the question. Sam watched him open and close his mouth a couple of times before Owen shrugged. 'I just meant it's a surprising recommendation from someone who trained at Le Cordon Bleu.'

'Well, it's the truth. Mick and Libby are like family to us, have been since the girls all made friends together at school. It's one of the perks of growing up in a small town like this, everyone kind of adopts each other.'

The colour drained from Owen's face and he pushed abruptly to his feet. 'I need to go. Thanks for the coffee and the toast.' And with that, he was gone.

Funny sod. Eliza turned to meet Sam's equally bemused gaze. 'What was that all about?'

He shrugged. 'Dunno—' He halted as Owen suddenly reappeared at the door.

'I forgot the plans.' Owen gestured towards the table then moved to gather everything up. 'I'll have a look and let you know later what I think.' He was gone again before either of them could say anything.

'He not here yet then?' Libby said as she bounced up to the bar, her blue and green hair still wet from what must've been a quick shower and change.

'Not yet, but there's a lot of work to do on the farm so it's not exactly a nine-to-five job.' Eliza tried to ignore the butterflies in her stomach as she fished a bottle of white wine out of the fridge behind her. 'You having a large one?'

'Does the Pope shit in the woods?' Libby grinned.

'Charming as ever, I see.' Owen's deep drawl made them both jump. Without the haze of a hangover clouding her judgement, Eliza could see he really was one of the most attractive men she'd ever met. Though with such a severe crewcut and a tattoo she'd not seen earlier covering his upper arm from the edge of his T-shirt sleeve to his elbow, he was definitely not her type.

'You didn't fall under a bus then? That's a pity.' Libby's rapid-fire retort was followed by a deliberate turn of her back to the man. 'If you're going to let any old riff-raff in here, Eliza, I might have to start drinking somewhere else.' *Curiouser and curiouser*. He might not be Eliza's type, but he was exactly the kind of trouble to catch her best friend's eye. So why all the hostility between them? Eliza would have to have a quiet word with Beth later and see if she could shed any light on things.

Owen shook his head at Libby's snippy comment and placed a ten-pound note on the bar. 'A pint of lager, and I'll buy your friend a drink if you slip some arsenic in it for me.'

Eliza couldn't stifle a giggle, earning herself a wink from Owen and a scowl from Libby. She slid the note back towards him. 'It's on the house. Sam's grabbed a table over there in the corner.' She nodded behind Owen as she placed his pint in front of him.

Owen raised his glass. 'Cheers, and thanks.' He strode across the pub to where Sam and Beth were sitting at a table beneath the window.

'What the bloody hell is that all about?' Libby demanded. "*It's on the house.*' God, you were practically drooling.'

Too intrigued to wait and quiz Beth later, Eliza checked around her then nodded Libby into the corner between the bar and the door leading to the private, family area. When her friend slouched over, Eliza leaned close. 'What's the problem? You've barely exchanged more than two words with the guy and yet there's all this animosity between you. Has he done something to hurt you?'

Libby shrugged, the single shoulder lift a decidedly sulky gesture. 'He's a stuck-up git, that's all. Why are you and Sam so bloody chummy with him all of a sudden?'

Eliza frowned. It sounded a poor excuse for so much tension between two relative strangers. 'Because he's looking over the plans for the restaurant. Having someone with his experience involved in the project can only strengthen Sam's position, and he might even agree to invest because the bank have been dragging their heels apparently. You know how important this is to Sam—to Beth as well. This is their future in the balance. Owen told Sam he was still on the lookout for projects situated here in the bay to invest in.' She took Libby's hand. 'If he's bad news then we need to warn Sam.'

Libby bristled for a moment before shaking her head. 'Ignore me, he just winds me up for some reason. I wonder why he's so fixated on our little town though, you can't get much further from the glamour of London than Lavender Bay.'

'Maybe that's the point, who knows? Sam and I thought a friendly drink would help grease the wheels a bit.' And, if she was being honest with herself, she'd hoped adding Owen to the group would take some of the pressure off Jack.

She knew her friends had been mostly messing around when they'd decided to put him under the microscope tonight, but she didn't want them to give Jack the wrong impression. The deep frown half-hidden by Libby's floppy fringe worried Eliza however, as did the clear animosity between the pair. Libby got on with just about everyone. From Pops and his pals up at the Baycrest retirement home, to little kids who were always fascinated by her bright hair, people gravitated towards Libby. She might dress like a thundercloud, but she was just about the sunniest soul in the whole of Lavender Bay. 'If you really don't like him then I don't want to spoil your evening. We can probably just leave him and Sam to chat…'

'If it means that much to Sam then I can put up with Mr Full Of Himself for a few hours,' Libby grumbled, though her tone was much less antagonistic. 'But I'm not going to kiss up to him, so don't expect me to.'

Eliza gave her a quick hug. 'I'm not asking you to, just don't shank him with a wooden spork from the chippy, all right?' They both snorted at the idea and just like that, Libby's bad mood evaporated.

A customer at the bar caught Eliza's eye and raised his empty glass. She nodded to show she'd seen him and pointed Libby over to an empty stool. 'Sit here, and I'll be right back. You can keep me company until Jack shows up.'

After a sudden influx of orders, it was a good five minutes before Eliza made her way back to where Libby was perched, by which time Beth had abandoned Sam and Owen to their business discussions and joined them at the bar. 'How's it going?' Eliza asked.

Beth raised her eyebrows. 'Surprisingly well, I left them drooling over tile samples.'

'Do you think Owen will get involved with the restaurant?' Libby's question was a study in polite neutrality, though there was no hiding the flash of fire in her eyes. There was definitely more to all of this than she was letting on.

'They haven't got that far, although Owen seemed to think he could get Sam a much better deal on some of his quotes so even if he stops at that it'll be a bonus,' Beth said.

Eliza took a sip of her drink. 'He seems all right, you know? Arrogant, but who can blame him when he looks like that?' She couldn't help dangling that little bit of bait under Libby's nose.

Libby made a rude noise but didn't add anything further unfortunately. She turned sideways on the stool and rested her arm on the bar, leaning slightly towards Eliza. 'So, where's this sexy farmer of yours, I hope he's not going to stand you up?'

'I don't know.' The admission came out on a sigh. 'I sent him a text warning him you guys were going to be here. He said he was looking forward to meeting everyone, but maybe he changed his mind.'

Libby's face fell. 'Oh, bloody hell, why didn't you say something? We'll bugger off, won't we, B?' She turned to Beth who nodded.

'Absolutely. We can either join the guys or go next door to the flat. Send him a text and tell him we'll leave you in peace.'

'No, no! Don't be daft, it's not like a date or anything. Honestly, I should never have said anything to you two about him!' Eliza cringed, they'd really got the wrong end of the stick.

'I hope you're not talking about me?'

Just the sound of Jack's deep voice was enough to send a shiver up her spine. *Oh hell, she was really in trouble*. Feeling suddenly awkward, Eliza turned to him with an apologetic smile. 'We were, actually. I was just saying I was worried the threat of meeting these two might have put you off.'

When he laughed, all white teeth and sparkling eyes Eliza's knees gave a wobble. From the starry-eyed expressions on her friends' faces, it looked like she wasn't the only one feeling the effects of it. Maybe it was just a hormonal attraction and she was reading too much into the effect he was having on her.

Jack glanced down at his feet, then back up. 'I couldn't let Bastian down now, could I? He's been looking forward to seeing you all day.' He bent at the waist to unhook the dog's lead and Eliza found herself almost knocked sideways as several pounds of enthusiastic Labrador bounced through the open hatch at the side of the bar.

'Oof! Hello, gorgeous boy.' She scrubbed the dog behind his ears sending his tongue lolling in ecstasy.

Within seconds both Beth and Libby had crouched down to join her, the three of them making a huge fuss of Bastian who wagged his tail and took it all as his due. After a few moments, Eliza glanced up to see Jack watching them with a rueful smile. Straightening up, she left her friends to fuss over the dog and came to stand close at Jack's side. He'd teamed a pair of dark grey cargo shorts with a jade-green polo shirt which did something amazing to the green flecks in his warm hazel eyes. 'It's good to see you, again. What can I get you to drink?'

'I'll have a pint, please.' His gaze flicked to where Bastian was holding court then back to her. 'Do I get a scratch behind the ears too?'

She grinned, delighted at his silly teasing. 'And a treat if you're very good.' She'd meant it as a joke, a reference to a dog biscuit type treat, but his pupils flared as though he'd read something else into it. She'd have to watch what she said around him or she'd be giving him the wrong impression again. *Or the right one.*

Feeling flustered, and more than a little exposed with her friends in such close proximity, Eliza slipped along the bar towards the beer taps. 'Lager, that's what you like, right?'

The corner of Jack's mouth quirked up. 'Amongst other things.' *Oh, bloody hell, he was flirting with her*!

Face on fire, she made the mistake of turning away and caught sight of the Cheshire cat gallery behind her. Beth fanned her face whilst Libby gave her a double thumbs-up, both entirely unrepentant that they would be in full view of Jack should he be looking in their direction. Muttering under breath about 'bloody men' and 'bloody so-called friends', Eliza fixed her eyes resolutely on the pumps in front of her and concentrated on pulling the slowest pint of her life.

Inevitably, she got caught up with other customers, but a quick glance across showed Jack apparently at ease with his hands in his pockets as he chatted to Beth and Libby. By the time she made her way back, Sam and Owen had left their table—both clutching empty glasses—and were greeting Jack.

Eliza watched as Libby made a casual move to place her own empty glass on the bar which just happened to put her on the farthest edge of the little group away from Owen. Eliza took the glass and swapped it for a clean one. 'Do you want another?'

Libby checked her watch, then sighed. 'Yes, but no. I've still got to give dad a hand with the late rush in a bit so no more booze for me.'

Eliza switched out the wine glass for a high-ball and poured her friend a glass of sparking water. She added a curly straw and placed a slice of orange with a cocktail umbrella sticking out of it on the rim of the glass. Libby laughed when she saw it. 'Aww, thanks.'

Having sorted out refills for the others, Eliza managed to catch Sam's eye. She raised her eyebrows and was encouraged at the little nod he gave her in return. Things were going well, it seemed.

Something warm and wet stropped her hand, and she looked down into a pair of appealing brown eyes. 'Oh, I forgot to get a drink for you!' She grabbed one of the metal dog bowls they kept underneath the bar and hurriedly filled it at the sink. Bastian slurped at the water, then rested his head against her knee, leaving a wet patch on the folds of her long cotton skirt in the process. 'Gee thanks.' She nudged him gently away, only for the dog to return a couple of seconds later.

'I told you he was pining for you.' Jack had circled the group to stand closest to her, unwittingly placing Libby directly beside Owen in the process. Eliza tried to catch Libby's eye, but her friend seemed lost in her own world, her posture stiff, her gaze locked on the contents on her glass. 'Problem?' Jack's question was soft enough to be discreet.

'Bit of a personality clash,' Eliza confided.

'Ah.' Without further prompting, Jack slid easily across the group to position himself next to Libby. Standing sideways on to her, his broad body acted as an effective shield between Libby and Owen. Heart soaring at his thoughtful intervention, Eliza moved closer in time to hear him speak. 'So, what's the verdict? Do I pass inspection?'

Eyes sparkling, Libby looked more like her usual self than she had almost all evening. Casting a considering look up and down Jack's length she tapped her lip. 'Hmm. The jury's still out, but I have reason to believe you can expect a favourable verdict.'

Laughing, Jack toasted her with his pint and took a drink. 'I'm pleased to hear it. If there's anything I can do to tip the scales in my favour, be sure to let me know.'

'Flowers should do the trick.'

'Libby!' Eliza couldn't help her shocked laugh. 'Leave the poor man alone.'

Jack waved her off. 'Don't queer my pitch, I think I'm close to winning her over.' He smiled down at Libby. 'So, these flowers… are they for you, or for Eliza?'

Libby grinned. 'Both of us, I reckon, just to be on the safe side.'

'Oh God, behave!' Shaking her head, Eliza began stacking dirty glasses in the dishwasher beneath the bar, dismissing his silly banter as nothing more than that. Of course he wouldn't be buying her flowers. At least he didn't seem to mind being thrown in at the deep end with her friends and looked to really be enjoying himself.

Daydreaming, Eliza didn't notice her mum approaching until she reached past her to add another couple of dirty glasses to the dishwasher. 'Hello, lovey, how's it all going?'

Wiping her hands on a tea towel, Eliza let her gaze wander over the busy bar. Everyone seemed to be having a good time, a few customers had even spilled out onto the promenade in front of the pub. She checked the time and decided they could have a few minutes more in the cooler air before she'd have to start herding them back inside. The last thing they needed was complaints of noise or for the pub to get a reputation for rowdiness, but as long as they had the front door shut before half-nine, she reckoned it would be okay. 'It's a good night, Mum. No problems to speak of…touch wood.' She tapped her temple.

'Well, your dad's settled for the evening and there was nothing on the telly, so I thought I'd give you a hand. Why don't you grab a break while there's a bit of a lull. I can keep an eye on the place.'

'Are you sure?'

Annie patted her arm. 'Of course I am, and your dad and I have had a bit of a chat and we're going to ask Josh to increase his hours so you can concentrate on getting your new venture up and running. He's been a great asset to the place since Sam took him on and it's about time we rewarded him for all his hard work.'

Blindsided, Eliza had to blink hard against a sudden sting behind her eyes. 'That's amazing, you can't understand how much that means to me.'

'I think I can, lovey, and it's good to see you finally doing something you've got a passion for. Now go and see your friends.' She eyed Eliza with a speculative grin. 'Or, even better, grab that lovely tall farmer and sneak him out into the backyard for a smooch or two.'

'*Mum*!' Eliza covered her eyes with her hands, shaking her head at the same time. 'Don't you start as well!'

'Don't you "Mum" me, young lady. I'm not too old to remember what it's like, and it's obvious to anyone with eyes in their head that you've taken a fancy to him, and he's hardly taken his eyes off you since he walked through the door.' She flicked the tea towel in Eliza's direction.

What was wrong with everybody trying to push the two of them together? 'It's too soon, Mum. I like Jack, but I can't go stumbling into another relationship when I still haven't sorted out the mess of my first.' She'd still not heard a word from Martin, and it was starting to really worry her. There was no denying her attraction to Jack though, and the vibes she'd been getting from him suggested he was feeling it too. 'I don't know what to do for the best.'

Folding her arms, her mum gave her a steady look. 'You don't have to spend the rest of your life punishing yourself over things not working out with Martin, that's all I'm saying. Now, shoo!'

Eliza skipped back to avoid the end of the tea towel her mum had flicked at her, almost bumping into her brother who'd come behind the bar. 'Steady on, Sis.' He righted her with a hand on her shoulder. 'Hey, have you seen the keys for downstairs? I want to show Owen around.'

She pointed at the ring of keys hanging from a hook she'd nailed into the back wall after losing them too many times to count. 'At this time? Wouldn't you be better off waiting until the morning?'

'No time like the present. He's got some suggestions about the lighting and it's easier to go down and have a look rather than traipsing upstairs for the plans. Besides, the others want a tour.'

It looked like she wouldn't be able to follow through on her mum's suggestion and invite Jack out into the yard even if she wanted to. It would be nice to take a breather before things wound up towards last orders, and he had made the effort to walk down and see her. If they were alone, she could find a way to talk to him about how confused she felt, see if there really could be something between them in spite of what they'd both said to the contrary. Dejected, she followed Sam around to the other side of the bar.

'What's up?' Jack touched his little finger to hers, the s+mall connection enough to brighten her spirits in an instant.

'Oh, nothing really, I hear Sam's giving you all a guided tour downstairs.'

He shrugged. 'You looked busy, so I was going to tag along. I've got enough plans of my own whirling around in my head, so I've not been paying too much attention to the finer details. I supposed they'd feel the same way if I started discussing the oil yields of different rose species with them.'

'Oh.' Maybe he hadn't been having as much of a good time as it seemed. 'Are you fed up? I'm sorry it's been so busy.'

He shook his head. 'Not at all. I like the sound of the restaurant, but I'm more interested in sampling the finished product. I only meant we all have our own work obsessions and that doesn't always translate well to others.'

Now or never, Eliza. 'Well, if you're not bothered seeing a dusty old skittle alley, perhaps I can steal you away for a bit of fresh air. I'm on my break.'

Jack grinned. 'That's the best news I've heard all night. Steal away.'

With a quick glance at the others, Eliza took Jack by the hand and led him through the swing door and across the small, square hall. Bastian trotted at their heels, tail wagging at the opportunity to explore somewhere new. After pausing to flip one of the switches on the wall, Eliza led them out into the blessed cooler air of the rear yard.

She'd left the main spotlights off, but there was enough glow from the sconces high on the wall above them to illuminate most of the area. The dog abandoned them to pad around the yard, sniffing at every nook, cranny and corner, whilst Eliza leaned back against the cold bricks of the wall with a sigh. 'That's nice,' she said enjoying the silence.

Jack stood next to her, close enough for their arms to touch. Heat from his body soaked into her through the thin cotton of her sleeve. Gathering her courage, she inched her hand across the rough surface of the bricks until she could capture his hand with hers. He squeezed back, and she closed her eyes for a moment to savour the rightness of the way their fingers intertwined. 'We agreed anything more than friends would be too complicated.'

His thumb played gently over her knuckles in a distracting rhythm. 'We did.' His tone was non-committal.

The shadows pressed around them, the sound of Bastian's snuffles muted by the thundering of her pulse in her ears. 'We've both got too much going on in our lives. It's the only sensible option.'

'It is.' Keeping hold of her fingers, Jack placed himself directly in front of her. His free hand slid beneath the thick mass of hair at her neck to massage her nape.

Eliza's lashes fluttered closed once more as his strong, clever fingers loosened a knot she hadn't been aware of. 'I'm not feeling very sensible.'

'Me either,' he murmured. They stood in silence, their bodies pressed together from shoulder to hip, but there was no urgency between them, just a sweet, gentle appreciation of being close to one another. Eliza settled her hands at Jack's waist, liking the solidity of his flesh beneath her fingers. Honed by those long hours of manual labour, there was nothing soft about him, and yet she felt completely at ease.

Some men of his stature used their size to intimidate, to take up more than their fair share of the space around them, but she didn't get that sense from him. He was careful with her, in a way that she knew she'd only have to make the slightest movement, or say a single word, and he'd step away without complaint.

Safe.

She felt completely safe with him, and there was a headiness that came with that knowledge, a willingness on her own part to be bolder in her actions than she might otherwise have been. Curling her hands tighter and lower to cover the top of the waistband of his jeans, she lifted her head to meet his eyes. 'Kiss me.'

'This must be the treat you promised me,' he said, making her smile so her mouth was already half open when he lowered his to meet it.

Chapter Twelve

Time seemed to slow down as the world contracted to him and her and the soft night breeze cooling his shirt where it clung to his back. The pub had been packed, and the press of bodies had combined with the lingering heat of the day and his own nervousness to dampen the skin at the base of his spine.

For all his earlier good intentions, he'd fretted the entire walk down from the farm to the pub. It was already clear to him from the few conversations they'd had that Eliza's friends were incredibly important to her, and he'd never found it easy to make a good first impression. And with every step that had taken him closer it had also become clear to him that was exactly what he wanted to do. He wanted Eliza's friends to like him, wanted her to like him because for all their mutual protestations he couldn't stop thinking about her.

From the second he'd stepped into the pub and caught sight of her gorgeous smile the nerves had evaporated, and he'd found himself at ease. As much fun as he'd been having chatting with the others, it didn't compare to this though. The sweet welcome of her open lips, the way her body slotted effortless against his—in spite of the difference in their heights—like she was made to stand there in the shelter of his frame, all combined to make his heart pound and his head spin with a thousand and one dreams it was far too soon to be weaving.

That same heated connection he'd felt the first time they'd kissed roared back to life. Part of him wanted to pour fuel on the flames, but it was neither the time nor the place to consider all the delicious things he suddenly wanted to do to her. He settled instead for slow and easy, peppering her mouth with teasing pecks and the occasional soft glide of their tongues.

Her hands tightened at his waist, pulling him closer in a way that threatened to scatter all his good intentions. He pulled back with a gasp. 'We're in the yard of your parents' pub with about fifty people not more than a dozen feet away.'

Her eyes flared in the soft glow of the overhead lights. 'So, we're back to being sensible?'

'For now.' He let her hear the regret in his voice.

'You're no fun.' She sighed, then straightened up against the wall, creating space between them. 'Actually, you're a lot of fun, but you're also right unfortunately.' She curled her fingers through his and drew their clasped hands into the space between their bodies. 'Why don't you tell me about your day?'

Jack opened his mouth to tell her about the call from the school, then froze. In his desire to protect Noah he'd made no mention of him to Eliza yesterday, figuring they had plenty of time to see if their relationship was going anywhere before he had to consider the two of them meeting. But the way she made him feel, the sheer rightness he felt every time he was anywhere near her meant only one thing—he was in this for the long haul. He'd never believed in love at first sight, he still didn't, but there was no denying there could be something special between them, and he'd be doing them both a disservice if he didn't acknowledge it.

'Come and sit down a minute.' He led Eliza over to the back steps and sank down next to the fence, angling his body into the corner.

She stood over him, the long curls of her hair hanging forward to shadow her face. 'Is something wrong?'

'No, not at all, I just need to think a minute about what I need to say.' Jack patted the step beside him and she sat. Turning her hand over, he massaged her palm with his thumb, marvelling at the softness there in contrast with the callouses and stubby nails of his own hand. He drew her hand up to his mouth and kissed it. 'I like you, Eliza. I know we're only just taking our very first steps together, but I want to get it right. I'm not trying to hurry things along between us, but I need to acknowledge this…' He waved his free hand around as he fumbled for the right word. Damn, he was a bloody farmer not a wordsmith. 'This…'

'Potential?'

'Yes!' Relief flooded him at her apparent understanding. 'That's exactly it. I've always been a casual guy, when it comes to relationships, but whatever it is I'm feeling for you, Eliza, it isn't that.'

She rested her arm across his bent knee, leaning her weight into him. 'Me, either.' She sighed. 'I've still got a lot of baggage to sort out…'

The satin curls of her hair teased his cheek, and he turned his head to draw in the sweet scent of her fresh shampoo. She'd given him the perfect opening so it was time to make it clear what she would be taking on. 'I don't know if you know this, but when Jason died he left behind a son.'

Straightening up, she turned to face him. 'Oh, that's so sad. He can't be very old?'

Jack shook his head. 'Noah's six. His mum's not been in the picture since he was a baby. Jason asked me to be Noah's guardian in the event anything happened to him.' Reaching out he touched a gentle hand to her cheek. 'I have a son. It's not something I would have ever asked for because of the way it came about, but for now and the foreseeable future, Noah has to be my number one priority.'

'I see.' She remained silent for a long moment. 'So there's more than just us at stake in all this.'

'Yes.' He didn't want to hurt her feelings, but he needed to be clear. 'I don't want to introduce the two of you yet. He's been through so much turmoil, I need him to find his feet, to know he can place his absolute trust in me before I bring someone else into his life. With the best will in the world, things between us might not come to anything, but I also didn't want to *not* tell you about him because that wouldn't be fair to you either.' God, that might have been the most words he'd said to anyone in one go in his life, and he still wasn't sure he'd managed to convey what he was feeling. He scrubbed a hand at the back of his neck, wishing like hell that for once life could be uncomplicated for five minutes at a time.

Lifting her arm from his knee, Eliza wiggled closer until she was tucked in against him with her back resting against his raised leg. She rested her head on his chest and cradled their clasped hands in her lap. 'Thank you for telling me about Noah. I completely understand that you need to protect him. It's something I'm going to have to think about as well. You already know things between me and Martin are unresolved—not that there's any circumstances under which I'd want to get back with him—but it will still take time to extricate myself from our marriage.' Lifting her head to gaze up at him, her mouth curled up at one corner in a wry smile. 'Meeting someone else so soon was never in my plans, and meeting someone else with a small child in tow…'

Disappointment settled in his gut like a heavy weight. Noah was going to be a deal-breaker for her. He didn't blame her, but that didn't stop it hurting like hell. 'I get it. I'm just glad we had this talk before either of us got too involved.' He needed to get out of there, but when he made a move to dislodge Eliza she curled her arms around his waist and held on.

'Wait a minute, that's not what I said.' Keeping her hands locked behind his back, she turned her face up to meet his eyes. 'Shrugging and saying that it's fine would be as wrong for both of us as if you hadn't brought the subject of Noah up at all, surely you can see that?'

Jack forced himself to sit back, though it was hard to let go of the tension in his limbs. She had a point, a bloody good point. 'You're right.' His previous thought surfaced again. 'God, this adulting shit is hard work.'

Eliza laughed as she pressed a kiss to the underside of his jaw. 'Isn't it just?' She went silent for a few moments, then loosened her arms to sit back and stare at him. 'Now I get why you were asking me about circumstances putting me in the position of having a child when we were discussing why I didn't want to have a baby with Martin.'

What else could he do but nod? 'Yeah, Noah was definitely on my mind then.' A surge of possessive love swept through him. 'He's a good kid, Eliza. A *great* kid, and I adore him. I won't ever not choose him, you know?'

She nodded. 'Whatever happens, I won't ever put you in a position where you'd have to make a choice. I'd like us to keep seeing each other, and I'm not averse to you coming with an added bonus, it's just a lot to take on board.'

An added bonus. He really liked her choice of wording, and it summed up the kind of person he already believed her to be, someone with a generous heart who would always see the best in a situation. 'I want to keep seeing you too, very much.'

'Good. We just need to keep being as honest with each other as possible, and try not to get too ahead of ourselves.' She settled back against his chest. 'You were going to tell me about your day…'

Jack rested his chin on the top of her head, holding her in the circle of his arms as he explained about his sudden dash to the school that morning. 'Thankfully, Noah seemed right as rain when I picked him up this afternoon. We had a good talk over glasses of milk and some of his Nanna's homemade rock cakes.'

'Man to man?' He could hear the smile in her voice.

'That's right. I asked him about this other kid, Michael, and from what Noah said they normally get on pretty well together. I think the headteacher was right, that the boy lashed out because he didn't want to be the only one missing out on the football.'

'Poor kid, it must be horrible to miss out on stuff. Beth's mum was always a bit like that, which is one of the reasons we became so close. Mum and Dad always made an effort to include her in our family stuff, so she didn't feel left out. I think that's partly why Sam's so protective of her, too. When her mum remarried she made it clear Beth was a spanner in the works which is why Eleanor, the old lady who used to run the emporium, took Beth in. She left the place to Beth when she died in January, that's how come she moved back here.'

Jack thought about it. They might have been more insular than some other families, but his folks had always made sure he and Jason felt wanted and loved and treasured. 'I wonder if I should have a word with a couple of the other dads, see if we can work out a way to include Michael without him feeling like the odd one out.'

'When is it, next Sunday?' Eliza sat up. 'Why don't you have a word with Sam? He's a big kid at heart and I'm sure he'd love a muck around on the beach. I'll check the rota, and make sure he's not working.'

It was a nice idea, but…

'I couldn't impose like that, I hardly know Sam.'

Taking his face in her hands, Eliza pressed a kiss to his lips. 'Ah, Jack. You really don't understand what us Barneses are like. We come as a package deal. This would be no different to Dad and Pops helping out with your tractor—everybody gets something out of it.'

He still wasn't sure, but she looked so certain it was hard to do anything other than nod in agreement. 'Okay, I'll mention it to him and see what he says.' The overhead light glinted off the face of his watch. They'd been out there almost the full twenty minutes of her break. He hadn't meant for things to get heavy between them, but he was glad he'd told her about Noah, even if he'd rather have been doing other things, like kissing the little spot beneath her ear that made her breath catch in her throat. 'It's almost half-past, do you need to get back to work?'

To his delight, Eliza tugged his head down. 'Mum can spare me for a few minutes more.'

When he deposited a slightly rumpled Eliza back behind the bar, Jack saw the others had returned from their trip downstairs to the skittle alley and had commandeered a table in the corner. Having accepting a bottle of alcohol-free beer from Eliza with a wink, he wandered over and took a seat next to Sam.

Sam glanced up from the sketch he was scribbling on the back of a napkin and grinned. 'There you are, we thought we might have to send out a search party.'

Jack sipped his beer. 'Yeah, sorry I missed the tour, a better offer came up.'

The others laughed, apart from Sam who grimaced. 'Mate, stop, that's my sister you're talking about.'

Jack shrugged, not feeling the remotest bit apologetic. 'Anyway, there's something I'd like to have a quick word with you about if you've got time?'

When Sam nodded, Jack outlined the situation with Noah and the football match. To their credit, they all seemed to take the news about his responsibility for his nephew well, although Jack didn't miss the pointed look Beth and Libby shared with each other. 'I was talking to Eliza about it, and she thought you might be willing to help out on the day, so I could get Noah to invite Michael along as well.'

'You'll have to be careful how you do it. If that kid's sensitive about stuff at home, he won't like feeling like a charity case.' Owen's mouth had set in a grim line, and from the set of his shoulders it looked to Jack like he was talking from experience.

'Okay. What would you suggest?'

Owen glanced away, then back, discomfort radiating off him in waves. 'If you single him out, that's as bad as him not going at all. He probably gets a hard enough time as it is, don't give the other kids any more ammunition to use against him.' Owen took a long draft from his glass, then crossed his arms on the table to lean forwards. 'Speak to the teacher, tell her you've got a couple of mates who'd love to get involved only they don't have boys of their own. If this Michael thinks he's doing us a favour so we get to join in, then it makes him look better. Kids need all the pride we can give them.'

'But if it's next weekend, you won't be here!' Libby's interruption surprised Jack. He'd sensed the awkwardness between her and Owen, had even done his best to distract her earlier when he'd seen Eliza watching her friend with concern. He'd thought them all sitting together meant things had improved, but from the frown on her face…maybe not.

The tightness in Owen's frame melted away in an instant as he gave Libby a wide grin. 'Now that Sam and I are going into business together, you're going to be seeing a whole lot more of me about the bay.' She opened her mouth, but whatever her response might have been it got lost in Sam's whoop of joy. There was no mistaking the shock on her face though.

Not wanting to be caught staring at her, Jack turned his attention to the others.

'You're serious?' Sam asked Owen.

'Absolutely. We can hammer out the details over the next few days. I'll need to go back to London tomorrow night, but most of my current projects are well in hand so I can be back here next weekend. See if you can make an appointment with the bank manager for the Monday or Tuesday afterwards, we should have things sorted between us by then I reckon.'

They shook hands, Sam still beaming. 'Fantastic, that's really fantastic, I can't thank you enough.'

Owen laughed. 'You haven't tried working with me yet. But, seriously, mate, I should be thanking you. I've been wanting to invest in something down here for a while now, and this is gonna be a great opportunity for the both of us.'

Libby stood abruptly. 'I need to get back and give Dad a hand with the late evening rush. I'll see you later, B.'

Apparently oblivious to the laser glare Libby was drilling into his back, Owen stood up. 'I'll walk back with you. Sam was telling me earlier how you make the best fish and chips in the county. I missed dinner, so I'm starving.'

A muscle twitched in her cheek. 'Fine.' Turning on her heel, Libby marched towards the door.

Owen drained the last of his pint then stood up. 'See you guys later. Jack, nice to meet you.'

Shaking the hand he offered, Jack half-stood. 'You too.' He hesitated, then decided to go for it. The football thing had worked out great, and the worst Owen could do was say no. 'Hey, do you think you'd have time to do a bit of a consultation on the side for me? There's an old cottage up at the farm and I'd like some advice on doing it up for my mum. It's a bit of an old-fashioned layout—downstairs bathroom and all that, so there'd be some structural stuff which is well outside my comfort zone. I'd just like to know what I'm up against, you know?'

Owen grinned. 'I'd be happy to. We'll catch up at the football, yeah?'

'Fantastic, thanks, mate.' A warm glow suffused Jack; he might just get used to this asking-for-help lark.

With both Owen and Libby gone, Jack felt a little awkward. Sam was still grinning ear-to-ear as he whispered something to Beth which made her duck her head, but not quickly enough to hide her blush. *Definitely time to leave.* He stood. 'Look, I appreciate you offering to help out with this football thing. I'll talk to Noah and the school and get back to you, Sam, okay?'

'Yeah, no probs, mate.' Sam's response was distracted as he tugged Beth closer into his side.

'Well, I'd better go, see you later.' Glancing around for Bastian, he spotted the dog curled up by the end of the bar, tail thumping lazily as he watched Eliza move back and forth serving customers and clearing dirty glasses, Jack bent down and hooked the lead that had been hanging from his back pocket onto the Labrador's collar. 'Come on, fella, we've got a long day tomorrow.'

'Are you off?' Eliza bent to give Bastian a pat on the head, then sidled around the side of the bar until she was standing close enough for Jack to count every freckle dusting across her nose.

'I don't like to leave Noah for too long, he's been having a tough time of it, nightmares and stuff.'

Her brow crinkled in concern. 'Poor little guy.'

If they'd been alone, he would've picked up where they'd left off in the yard, but he wasn't one for making a public spectacle. He settled instead for brushing the back of her hand with his. 'Message me later when your shift is over, so I can say goodnight.'

A hint of colour highlighted her cheeks. 'All right.'

With a soft tug on Bastian's lead, and a quick wave to Beth and Sam, Jack began to make his way home. He'd barely made it to the end of the promenade when his phone began to ring. 'Mum? Is everything all right?'

'Not really.' His gut plummeted. Behind her worried whisper, he could hear the sound of sobbing. 'Noah woke up and panicked when he couldn't find you.'

Shit! 'I'm on my way home now. Can you put me on speakerphone?' Jack turned off the promenade and began to jog up the hill, letting out a good length on Bastian's lead as he did so to let the dog trot behind him. 'Noah? Noah, buddy, it's Uncle Jack, can you hear me?' He had to shout into his phone to make himself heard over the noisy crying.

'Y...you...w...w...weren't here.' The trembling voice of his nephew dissolved into tears once more.

'I know. I'm sorry, but I'm on my way right now. Hold on, buddy, I'm coming.' Guilt and anguish tearing him to shreds, Jack shoved his phone into his pocket and increased his pace until he was running flat-out through the quiet streets.

Chapter Thirteen

Eliza and her mum were setting up the bar ready for opening when a knock came at the front door. Casting a quick glance at the clock on the back wall, she frowned. Half-nine was too early for even the thirstiest of holiday-makers. Stretching on tiptoe, she released the top bolt and swung the door open to be greeted by a glorious mass of yellow, pink and purple flowers. 'Oh, my goodness, how beautiful!' The trio of golden sunflowers were surrounded by cerise roses, sugar-pink carnations and cascades of pink and purple stocks.

Emma, the owner of the local florist's beamed at her around the side of the bouquet. 'Morning, Eliza! Delivery for you.'

'For me?' With shaking fingers, she reached for the flowers then balanced them in the crook of her arm in order to retrieve the little white envelope tucked into the top. *Something to brighten your day and hopefully tip the scales in my favour. Jack xx*

'Wow, let me see!'

Turning sideways, Eliza showed off the flowers to her mum. 'Jack sent them. Aren't they lovely?' She ducked her head over them. 'And they smell incredible.'

Her mum reached out to trace the velvet texture of one of the roses. 'He's pulling out the stops, that's for sure.'

Feeling shy, Eliza glanced away and back to Emma. 'Thank you for these.' She spotted another, smaller bouquet of yellow, pink and orange gerberas standing in a box at Emma's feet. 'Oh, he didn't?'

Emma grinned. 'I've already dropped one of these off next door with Beth. Someone's definitely out to impress.' Bending over, she picked up the box. 'I'm sure Libby will be as thrilled as Beth was, and I'm a big fan of any man who woos a woman's friends as well. It's very good for business! See you later, ladies.'

Moving free of the door to allow her mum to close it, Eliza couldn't help but hug the flowers closer. 'I'd better go and put these in some water.' She caught her mum's eye and couldn't help a little giggle. 'I can't believe he bought me flowers.'

Her mum laughed with her. 'When you call him to say thank you, tell him your mum's partial to peonies.'

'Mum!'

After fussing around arranging the bouquet in a large vase she'd retrieved from the kitchen, Eliza set them carefully on her dressing table. She'd just stepped back to admire them when her phone started to ring. Checking the caller ID, she was already laughing when Libby's shriek of joy bellowed through the speaker. 'I can't believe he bought me flowers! Oh my God, Eliza if you don't grab him with both hands then I'm going to steal him out from under your nose.'

'Beth got some too, same as yours. I'll send you a picture of mine, hang on.' She took a quick snap of her bouquet and messaged it over to Libby. 'What do you think?'

'Gorgeous.' The word came out on a breathy sigh. 'And the flowers aren't half bad either.'

They giggled together like a pair of silly schoolgirls. 'Oh, Libby, what am I going to do? I'm trying so hard not to rush into anything, but he's making it very difficult.'

Laughter fading, Libby's voice turned soft and serious. 'Just follow your heart, that's all you can do.'

'I'm scared, Libs. Things with Martin developed over such a long period of time, I never really noticed the shift in gears from that first innocent love into something serious. This is like being on a roller coaster. I'm careening out of control and not sure if I like it or not.'

'At least you've got a certain sexy farmer to hang on to!' Libby's humour was back in full flow. 'You never know, it might end up being the best ride of your life.'

Or the worst. Squishing down the negative thought, Eliza promised to catch up with Libby later, then flopped down onto her bed. Tilting her head to one side so she could keep the flowers in view, she called Jack.

It rang a few times, and when he answered his voice carried a strange echo. 'Hello?'

'Jack? Oh, they're gorgeous, but you shouldn't have!'

'Just trying to tip the scales in the right direction, that's all.'

'That's all? Buying flowers for us all is going to do a bit more than tip the scales in your favour. I've already had Libby on the phone and she's ready to fight me for you.'

His laugh sounded almost metallic. 'Tell her I'm off the market. Or at least, I hope I am.' The last came in a husky murmur.

Her stomach gave a little flutter at the implication in his words. 'I'll tell her. Where are you, Jack? Your voice sounds funny.'

'I'm in the barn scrubbing out one of the distilling vats, trying to get everything ready before harvest.' A metallic clang was followed by a few scuffs. 'Is that better?'

His voice came through without interference. 'Much. So when do you think you'll start the harvest?'

'Probably another couple of weeks, yet. So, what's on the cards for you today?'

Eliza let her eyes stray from the flowers to the stack of bags and boxes in the corner of her room. 'I was going to set up a trestle table in the yard and make my first test batch of soap.' Now she had the essential oil from the farm, she was eager to get started. Even if the soap turned out okay it would take several weeks to cure properly before she could start giving out samples.

'Will you have enough room out there? You'd be more than welcome to bring your stuff up here and work at one of the benches. It's going to be another scorcher, so you might be more comfortable in the shade.'

He had a point. It would be quite a delicate process, and the more room she had to work in the better. 'If you wouldn't mind…?'

'I can't think of anything I'd like more. I'm fascinated to see how it all works, and I'd get to spend some of the day with you.' The warmth in his voice thrilled her all the way down to the tips of her toes.

'I have to finish off helping Mum and then get everything loaded in the car, so it'll probably be another hour before I can get there.' She did another quick calculation. 'Shall I put something together for lunch?'

'Perfect. There's an old copse near the north boundary, we can have a bit of picnic. There's plenty of shade and a great view out over the bay.'

Eliza bit her lip, then gathered a little courage. 'Sounds very romantic. I'll see you soon.'

Ah, the best laid plans, Eliza thought ruefully as she stared through her windscreen at the lashing rain after parking as close to the door of the barn as possible. A storm had come out of nowhere, rolling in from the sea in the few minutes it had taken her to drive from the pub up the hill to the farm.

'Come in before you get soaked.' Jack held open the door as Eliza made a mad dash with her first load of bags.

'Where on earth did that come from?' Eliza shivered, brushing away her wet fringe. 'It was fine when I left the bay.' The thin, long-sleeved T-shirt she'd paired with an old pair of jeans clung unpleasantly to her arms and she tugged at the damp material with a grimace. She dropped her bag on one of the benches then turned back towards the door. 'There's another load yet.'

'I'll give you a hand.' And before she could protest, he plunged out into the pouring rain with her.

Dripping wet and laughing, they dumped their loads on the bench next to her other bags. 'Hold on, let me get some towels.' Jack headed to a small room she hadn't noticed on her previous visit. He returned moments later with a dark-green hand towel and handed it to her. 'So much for our picnic.'

'It might blow over if we're lucky, there wasn't anything in the forecast,' Eliza said as she used the towel to squeeze the worst of the moisture out of her hair, hoping it wouldn't go too frizzy after the drenching. She hadn't banked on looking like a drowned rat thanks to a rogue thunderstorm.

Closing the distance between them, Jack took the towel from her hands and rubbed it gently over her damp curls. Eliza melted a little under his touch, welcoming the warmth he massaged into her scalp. He tossed the towel on the bench next to the one he'd used to dry off then folded his arms around her. 'It's good to see you, though this isn't exactly romantic.' He raised his eyes to the ceiling as the drumming of the rain on the corrugated roof echoed through the mostly empty space.

Eliza pressed her cheek into the broad muscles of his chest and sighed with happiness at the feel of his solid warmth against her. 'I don't care, I just needed this. Even for five minutes.'

'Me too.' His lips brushed the top of her head, her temple, then her cheekbone as she responded to the caress and raised her face. Jack claimed her mouth in a long slow kiss which curled her toes against the damp soles of her sandals. Lifting his head, he smiled down at her. 'I'll have to send you flowers regularly if this is my reward.'

Any lingering discomfort from her dash through the rain was soon forgotten as their mouths met and melded, parted to whisper soft kisses across each other's skin, then met once more.

When Jack broke their kiss, Eliza blinked her eyes open to check why he'd stopped and found herself squinting in the bright glare of the overhead lights. 'What's wrong?'

'Nothing.' He dipped his head to peck a kiss to the tip of her nose. 'But we've got work to do.'

'Spoilsport.' She pouted at him, earning a cheeky tap on her backside in return. 'Hey!'

With an unrepentant grin, Jack strolled towards the open hatch on one of the huge stainless steel vats then ducked inside. A dull clunk was swiftly followed by some very colourful language. 'Not a word from you!' His echoey warning had her stifling a giggle as she turned to the array of bags she'd brought with her.

Absorbed in the task of laying everything out exactly where she wanted it, Eliza didn't notice the storm still raging outside until a gust of cool air swept over her as Jack swung back the big double-doors. 'I remembered you mentioning needing lots of ventilation,' he said as he leaned on the bench next to her. 'Bloody hell, it looks like a chemistry lab.'

It did a bit. The key ingredient for converting the oil into soap was caustic soda which could cause some nasty burns if not handled correctly. As well as wearing long sleeves and jeans to protect her skin, Eliza had protective gloves, goggles and a mask to prevent inhaling any fumes. 'You'd better keep well back,' she cautioned.

'Okay. Will it be too distracting to talk me through it?'

'I don't think so.' Waiting until Jack had moved well away, Eliza drew a set of scales towards her and carefully measured out the correct amount of dry soda crystals then set them to one side. She placed a large glass jug on the scales, reset them to zero, and poured out distilled water from a large plastic bottle in accordance with the recipe she'd researched and written up in clear, bold print. 'It has to be distilled to avoid the caustic soda reacting with any impurities.'

Moving the scales out of the way, she tugged the mask up from where she'd hung it around her neck. 'This is the dodgy bit.' Taking as much care as possible, she poured the soda crystals into the water. It turned instantly opaque, and a thin steam rose from the surface as the soda reacted and heated the water in moments. 'Wow, that stinks.'

'You're not kidding.' Jack took a sidestep closer to the open door.

Using a silicone spatula from a cooking set she'd found cheap on the internet, Eliza stirred the contents of the jug. 'I have to wait until it goes clear again so I know all the soda has dissolved.' She touched a tentative hand to the side of the jug. 'It's really giving off some heat.'

'I don't remember chemistry being this much fun at school.' Stripping off the paper face mask with relief, she glanced up to find Jack had moved closer once more now the fumes had dissipated. 'What's next?'

She turned the recipe sheet around towards him. 'Can you measure out the correct amount of olive oil and add it to the larger jug?'

'Sure.' He raised his eyebrows at the large generic supermarket bottle of oil. 'Mum uses this for cooking.' He twisted off the cap with an easy flick of his wrist. 'What are you going to do in the meantime?'

Reaching for a smaller bottle of sweet almond oil, she poured a tiny amount into a glass beaker. 'I'm going to prepare the colouring and the fragrance. Once we start mixing the soap I won't have time to fiddle around so I want this ready to pour straight in.'

'Makes sense.' He passed the recipe sheet back to her, then watched with gaze intent as she spooned a small amount of colouring into the almond oil and picked up a tiny electric whisk. 'What the heck is that?'

Eliza grinned at him. 'I saw someone recommend it in one of

the videos I watched. It's what baristas use to froth up hot milk. It helps to blend everything smoothly…' She whizzed the mixture into a smooth paste. 'And now the magic ingredient.' With a careful hand, she added the lavender essential oil Jack had given her. The heady scent of the oil filled her senses and she leaned closer to draw in a lungful and let the calming property of the fragrance soothe her nervousness. 'Right, there should be a thermometer around here somewhere?'

'Here.'

Taking the device from Jack, she checked the soda and water mixture. 'I think we're about ready.' With great concentration, she poured the soda and water over the back of the plastic spatula she'd placed in the olive oil to avoid creating air bubbles. The oil turned cloudy as she stirred the mixture in lazy circles to blend evenly. Once satisfied, she reached for a hand-held blender and began the painstaking process of pulsing, stirring and blending until the contents of the jug thickened enough to leave small traces on the surface.

'So far, so good.' She allowed herself a small smile when her eyes met Jack's. 'Can you pour that in for me, please?' Using her elbow, she pointed at the beaker with the dyed and scented almond oil.

Jack moved around to her side of the bench. 'Like this?' He tipped the contents of the beaker slowly into the jug.

'Perfect.' A few more pulses with the mixer and the thickening liquid turned a delicate shade of purple. 'Time to add it to the moulds.' She'd bought a selection of different silicone moulds. Most were individually shaped into hearts and flowers, and there was one plain rectangle which had come with a set of rectangular dividers. Trying not to shake, she poured the soap mixture into each of the small shapes before draining the rest into the large mould.

Setting the jug aside, she paused to brush her fringe out of her eyes, surprised to find it damp with perspiration. 'Almost there.' She pressed the divider into the thickening soap then covered each container with a thick piece of cardboard. 'I need to keep these insulated for about twenty-four hours.'

'That's fine. No one else will come in here but us. I'll make sure the door's locked against inquisitive small boys and nosy dogs.' Jack laid out one of the thick towels she'd brought with her. Eliza transferred each container onto it then tucked a second towel over the top and around the sides. 'And that's it!' She stripped off her gloves then knuckled the base of her back with a sigh.

'And it'll be ready tomorrow?' Jack sounded sceptical.

'Lord, no.' It should have set enough to remove it from the moulds, but then I'll have to put it away to cure for several weeks.

'That long?'

She nodded. 'It's not the kind of thing to take up if you're into instant gratification.'

A wicked glint shone in his eyes. 'The best things in life are worth waiting for.' Her cheeks heated at the promise in those words. 'Are you ready to take a break?'

When she nodded, he took her hand and led her into the small kitchenette where they helped themselves to cold drinks from the fridge. The sparkling water soothed her parched throat and Eliza let herself relax back against the counter. 'I really enjoyed that. I kept waiting for something to go horribly wrong, but it went okay. Hopefully, once I get the hang of it, it won't take quite so long and I'll be able to increase the size of the batches.'

'It wouldn't take too much to scale it up.' His thoughtful tone had her turning towards him and his hazel eyes were so expressive she could almost see the cogs in his brain working.

'Hey now, don't be getting any ideas about poaching my business from me when I've barely even got going.' She was teasing—mostly.

Jack held up his hands. 'I wouldn't dream of it. It's clear how important this is to you, Eliza, there's no way I'd try and steal your thunder.' Reaching for her, he tugged her closer with one hand, 'I was thinking more in terms of a long-term collaboration.'

The flirtatious gleam was back in his eyes. 'Oh, really?'

'Mmm.' With his free hand, he placed his phone on the counter and fiddled with the screen. The opening bars of 'One Day Like This' by Elbow filled the air. 'Now, let's open negotiations, shall we?'

'I love this song.' Delighted by his choice, Eliza stepped into the circle of Jack's arms.

'Me too.' They began to move, the barest of shuffles, a sweet, slow dance to express the feelings it was still too soon to say. Soft light spilling through the open door, the mellow voice of the lead singer and the steady rhythm of the rain on the roof combined to block out everything beyond the walls of the barn until it felt to Eliza like nothing existed beyond the warm cocoon of their swaying embrace.

Chapter Fourteen

'Not too late, you two, okay?' Jack could tell by the round of giggles which greeted his call from just outside Noah's bedroom door that he was on a hiding to nothing, but he had to at least pretend he was in control of the situation. Noah's class teacher had welcomed the idea of a couple of extra bodies to help out at the beach football, and she'd made discreet enquiries with Michael's mother, Kelly. It turned out the boy was the eldest of four—including twins who were under a year old—and his father was pulling extra hours as a taxi driver after his hours had been cut at his regular job. During a very pleasant phone call with Kelly, Jack had offered to take Michael for the weekend and been embarrassed by her tearfully grateful acceptance.

The two boys had spent Saturday running semi-wild around the farm with a panting Bastian in tow. His mum had come up trumps with a homemade pizza lesson which had proven a huge success with both the boys, but particularly Michael, and Jack had made a mental note to pair him with Sam to see if it was an interest that could be nurtured.

Another round of giggles ensued from the two boys who were now ensconced in Noah's room in a giant makeshift bed Jack had made by dragging Noah's mattress onto the floor and placing it next to one from the spare room. With his mum's help, they'd covered the two with a king sized fitted sheet and added a mountain of quilts, pillows and cushions to create a part-bed, part-den configuration the boys had been thrilled with. He and Jason has always loved to camp out on the living room floor, so this was an homage to those fond memories. With a bittersweet ache in his chest, Jack pulled the door half-closed and left them to it.

'How are they?' his mum asked after Jack flopped down on the opposite end of the sofa to her. Bastian settled next to him, his head pushed into Jack's lap demanding ear-scratches.

Jack reached for the bottle of beer she'd placed on the side table ready for him and took a deep draft. The cold, bitter brew hit all the right spots and he closed his eyes in brief appreciation. 'All right, I doubt there'll be much sleeping going on, but it's just so good to hear Noah laughing.' A lump formed in his throat, and he scrubbed his fingers through Bastian's fur until the burn behind the back of his eyes faded.

'I'm glad Michael's mum packed extra clothing for him, they've been through two outfits already.' Sally smiled, fondly. 'I'll run everything through the washer and dryer on Sunday night so it's all clean for her.' She shook her head. 'I had enough on my plate with two of you, I don't know how she can manage four!'

Jack rolled his head to the side to smile at her. 'I'm glad I'll have Sam and Owen to help me corral them tomorrow, they're a real pair of dynamos.'

His mum nodded. 'You and Jason were exactly the same at that age.' She took a sip from the glass of wine beside her. 'I thought I'd come into town with you tomorrow. It's been ages since I had a good browse around, and most of the shops will be open. I can watch a bit of the football too, maybe drop into the pub for a drink…'

'The pub, eh?' Bloody hell, she was about as subtle as a juggernaut.

She gave him a not-so innocent shrug. 'It'd be rude of me to be in the bay and not pop in and say hello to Eliza.'

'Of course.' Knowing there was no point in saying anything once she'd made up her mind, Jack turned his attention to the TV. It was some talent competition, though he couldn't work out which one. Not that it mattered, they all seemed to follow a similar format—over-confident contestants, sneering judges, and the occasional knock-out performance.

His eyes glazed as his thoughts strayed, as ever, to Eliza. Their impromptu date in the barn had been one of the most intimate experiences of his life, though they'd done no more than kiss and slow-dance together. If anyone had asked him, he'd have said he wasn't a dancing kind of guy, but for Eliza...a slow smile stretched his cheeks. For Eliza, he'd be all that and more.

Watching her work, seeing the excitement in her grow as she'd mixed and stirred those basic ingredients into something beautiful had filled him with pleasure. He wanted her new venture to succeed, and though he hadn't mentioned it when she'd popped back to collect her soaps the next day, he could see a day when their combined careers blended into something they could build a future on. He didn't want to jump the gun and risk spooking her, but in the secret recesses of his heart he was busily building dreams of them running the farm together.

Sunday dawned bright and clear, the temperature already nudging the high teens when Jack stepped out into the backyard with a cup of coffee. The boys had still been whispering when he'd turned in last night, but had been dead to the world when he'd peeked around the door a few minutes earlier. The bed-den looked like a whirlwind had hit it leaving behind a tangle of boyish limbs, quilts, and one smug-looking chocolate Lab. Bastian had thumped his tail once at Jack's glare but hadn't abandoned his prime spot in between the two boys. Once the weekend was over, there would have to be some ground rules laid down regarding dogs and beds. Again.

He lingered over his coffee, enjoying the peace and quiet before what promised to be a long, hectic day. It might be his last chance to play hooky for a while, though, so he was determined to make the most of it. Noah wasn't the only one who would benefit from some fun new memories. The new rose plants were being delivered tomorrow. Jack reckoned he had one week, two at most before the lavender would be ready to harvest so the coming few days would be the only chance to get the roses planted. After that, it would be final checks on the distillery, and many anxious hours pacing the rows out in the fields watching for the perfect moment to begin cutting.

Claws skittered on tile, and he turned towards the open kitchen door in time to see Bastian trot over to his bowl where Jack had tipped a few biscuits whilst making his coffee. Jack ignored the dog in favour of the tousled, nervous looking boy standing barefoot opposite him. He offered Michael a reassuring smile. 'Good morning, did you sleep well?'

Michael nodded. 'Noah's still sleeping.'

'That's all right, we're not in any hurry this morning.' The boy looked nervous, as though he wasn't sure if it was okay for him to be there. Conscious of his size, Jack moved slowly and easily through the kitchen to put his cup next to the kettle. He switched it on then turned to rest his back against the counter. The position allowed him to bend his knees a bit so he didn't tower quite so much over the small boy. 'Would you like something to drink?'

Michael licked his lips, eyes darting from side to side. 'Yes, please.'

'Why don't you take a seat, and I'll see what we have.' Jack steered the boy towards the kitchen table and got him settled in one of the chairs, then opened the fridge. 'Right then, sir. On today's menu we have orange juice, milk, orange juice, water, orange juice, beer, coffee, or—' he glanced back over his shoulder and waggled his eyebrows at Michael '—orange juice.'

'You're silly,' Michael giggled, clearly delighted at Jack's teasing. 'Orange, please.'

'An excellent choice if I may say so, sir.' Jack made a big show of folding a tea towel then draping it over his arm like a waiter. He found a clean glass, placed it before the boy with a flourish, then poured some juice into it. With a sweeping bow, he backed away from the table to more giggles.

Having made himself another cup of coffee, Jack took his own seat at the table opposite Michael. 'Are you enjoying yourself this weekend?'

Michael nodded. 'Yes. There's lots of room here, and you didn't get cross when I got dirty yesterday.'

Knowing he needed to tread carefully, Jack took a sip of coffee to give him time to ponder his answer. It must be tough for the kid with three younger siblings, and he could only imagine how much washing they generated on a daily basis. 'Things are a bit different here because we live on a working farm. I spend a lot of time working in the fields, so dirty clothes are a way of life for us. I'm also lucky because I work right here, at home, so it's much easier for me to help out with things like the washing and ironing. I bet your mum has her hands full looking after all of you and with your daddy out at work all day.'

The boy looked solemn. 'He works at night sometimes too, and at the weekend.'

'Because he loves you all, and he's trying very hard to give you everything you need. I bet he misses you.'

'I miss him.'

Jack's heart ached, and he rubbed a hand across his chest as though he could ease the weight of the pain in those three sad words. He racked his brain for something that might help. He wasn't a technical whizz, but he could use his smartphone well enough. 'Why don't we make a video for your daddy today? We can send it to him and then you two can watch it together. Do you think he'd like that?'

To Jack's relief, Michael grinned. 'I can score a goal for him!'

'What a great idea, I bet he'll love that.' Deciding to steer the conversation back to safer topics, Jack pushed his chair back. 'I don't know about you, but I'm starving. Let's go and wake Noah up, and then we can have breakfast.'

'Slow down, you two!' Juggling a cold box, a rucksack stuffed with a blanket and a change of clothes for each of the boys, and Bastian's lead, Jack walked as quickly along the promenade as he could.

'Noah James Gilbert, you stop right there!' The sprinting boys froze on the spot, as did half the grown men on the prom at his mother's strident tones.

'Jesus, Mum, you scared *me* half to death, never mind Noah.'

His mum blew on her nails before buffing them on the front of her pretty peach sleeveless blouse. 'Still got it,' she said. 'Seriously, Jack, you need to be firmer with him sometimes or he'll run you ragged.' He knew she was right, but he hated to raise his voice to Noah. He watched as the two boys slunk back towards them, faces a picture of contrition and he had to admire how effective the right tone was.

He watched as she crouched before Noah and Michael. 'There are a lot of people around today, so I am trusting you both to be big boys and make sure you always stay close to either Uncle Jack or his friends, okay?'

'Yes, Nanna.'

'Yes, Mrs Gilbert.'

Jack gnawed on his lip to hide a smile as his mum patted both boys on the cheek and straightened up. 'Right, let's find a nice spot on the beach and get settled.' She took each one by the hand and Jack followed after as she headed down the steps towards the beach.

'Is that your mum? She's terrifying.' Jack turned to find Sam grinning at him, Owen a step behind. They were both clad in long casual shorts and T-shirts, same as him.

'Here, make yourself useful, will you?' Jack thrust the cold box at Sam. 'And as I recall, your mum can give mine a run for her money.'

Sam laughed as they jogged down the steps. 'Don't remind me! We must make sure they never meet, or they'll be plotting world domination within the first half hour.'

'Too late. Mum's decided to *pop in* to the pub later and see Eliza.' Jack rolled his eyes.

'We're doomed, then, mate.' Sam grinned. 'All mums are the same, right, Owen?'

'I wouldn't know.' Owen shouldered past the two of them then strode across the beach to where Jack's mum stood with the boys.

Jack watched as he knelt on one knee before Noah and offered his hand to shake, before doing the same to Michael. 'What the hell was that about?'

Sam met his eyes. 'Nothing good, I bet. He was kind of touchy the other night when we were talking about Michael's situation. There's a story there, for sure, but I'm not sure Owen's the kind of guy who'll share it.'

'Probably not,' Jack agreed. He'd have to be a bit more careful about what he said around him though. He knew from bitter experience that a stray remark could screw up your whole day.

It took a matter of moments to get themselves settled, and the blanket spread out on the sand. Up and down their little stretch of the beach other groups were doing the same and Jack exchanged nods and waves with parents he recognised from the school run. His mum surveyed their efforts and nodded in satisfaction. 'Right, if you're all sorted out, I'm going to go and do a bit of shopping.'

'Make sure you mention my name in the emporium, Mrs Gilbert, and the owner will give you a special discount,' Sam said with a grin.

'Oh really? Well, aren't you a handy young man to know?' She beamed at Sam.

Jack gave his shoulder a playful shove. 'Don't be giving your girlfriend's profits away.'

'Beth loves me, she won't mind.' Sam suddenly didn't look altogether sure about it though. He held out his arm to Jack's mum. 'I'll take you up there and introduce you. It's going to be hot today, so I might nip back to the pub and grab a couple of sun umbrellas.' He aimed his second comment at Jack.

'Sounds good. I'm going to go and get us signed in.' He pointed to where Noah's teacher stood a few feet away, clutching a clip-board. 'See you in a minute.'

To Jack's surprise, Noah slipped his hand in his, obviously intent on going with him. He glanced over at Owen, who waved him on. 'Michael and I will be fine, won't we, mate? We can work out our winning tactics.'

The pair were soon knelt down, heads together as Owen sketched stick figures in the sand. Bastian had claimed the blanket while no one was paying attention and didn't look in any danger of moving. With Noah beside him, Jack began to walk.

'Uncle Jack?' Noah tugged on his hand, forcing Jack to stop midway between their blanket and the group gathering around the teacher.

'Yes, buddy?'

Big hazel eyes stared up at him. 'Do you have a girlfriend?' The earnest question blindsided Jack and he scrambled for how best to answer.

In the end, he took the coward's way out, hoping to deflect his nephew. 'What made you ask that?'

Noah shrugged. 'I don't know. Sam has a girlfriend and it makes him happy. I thought if you had a girlfriend then you would be happy too.'

Out of the mouths of babes. Honestly, this sweet little lad would be the absolute death of him. Jack crouched down until they were eye to eye. 'I'm already happy, buddy. I have you, and Nanna and Bastian. We're happy together, right?'

Noah nodded. 'Yes. But, if you had a girlfriend then you could have a baby and I could have a little brother or sister. Michael has a brother *and* two sisters.'

There he was trying to keep everything on an even keel, and Noah was busy weaving dreams that would turn all their lives upside down. Jack swallowed. 'I don't think babies are going to happen for a long time yet, buddy.'

Noah's face fell like Jack had told he'd never be able to have ice cream again. Damn it, he was making a real mess of this. It would have been easier to laugh off the comment, but he hated to do that. He'd promised himself he would be honest with Noah to the best of what he thought a child his age could cope with.

He put his arm around Noah's shoulder and pulled him into a hug. 'I do have a new friend. Her name is Eliza, and she makes me happy, but we're still getting to know each other.' Jack pressed a kiss to the boy's temple. 'You are the most important thing in the world to me, buddy, and I need to make sure that Eliza and I can be friends for a long, long time to come before I bring her into your life too. Do you understand what I'm saying?'

Noah squinted up at him, a deep furrow between his brows. He was so expressive, Jack could almost see the little cogs whirring in his brain. 'I think so. She's your girlfriend now, but she might not be forever?'

'Exactly. You're such a smart boy.' Jack gave him another hug.

Noah hugged him back. 'If Eliza does become your forever girlfriend will you have a baby then?'

Jack swallowed a laugh. 'I don't know, maybe?' He and Eliza were so far away from even broaching this subject, hell, Jack wasn't ready to even entertain the idea of having a kid. He glanced down at Noah and amended the thought to *another kid*.

'Okay then.' Noah gave him the gift of his sweet smile then skipped away across the sand towards his teacher. Jack could only shake his head and follow him. Life was so much simpler when viewed through the eyes of a little boy. If you were lucky enough, you had adults in your life who you could trust to take care of you and keep the bad things at bay. Whatever it took, whatever sacrifices he might have to make, Jack was determined never to betray Noah's trust in him.

'Bloody hell, I'm getting too old for this.' Sam collapsed onto his knees on the blanket then rolled onto his back beneath the shade of one of the two large umbrellas he'd stuck into the sand.

'Me too.' Jack flipped the lid open on the cold box and drew out a couple of bottles of water, threw one to Sam and opened the other. 'I don't know how Owen can keep going.' The round robin matches had been concluded, and everyone was taking a break before the finals. Well, almost everyone.

Using one elbow to prop himself up, Sam watched Owen racing down towards the surf, two screeching boys and one barking dog in tow. 'He doesn't even look winded, bastard.' The insult was said with a hint of admiration, maybe even a hint of affection.

'He's all right, isn't he?' If Jack was honest, Owen was more than all right. Noah could be a little wary around new people, but he'd taken to the tough-looking man with alacrity. And Michael looked at him like he was some kind of superhero. The adoration appeared to be entirely mutual; Owen had endless patience around the two boys, taking time to explain things and showering them with praise for the smallest achievements.

Sam pushed himself upright, propping his elbows on his knees, his water bottle dangling down between two fingers. 'I like him a lot. He's got some great ideas about the restaurant, and I feel so much more confident about the whole thing now he's in my corner. I'll be glad when the meeting with the bank is over tomorrow, I just want the place to be finished so I can get on with the bit I love—feeding people.'

Jack nodded, keeping his eyes trained on the activity down by the water. He watched Noah like a hawk, ready to jump up at the first sign of trouble, but he needn't have worried. Owen kept the two boys contained without spoiling their fun as they splashed around. Any time one or the other of them looked like he might take a step deeper, Owen was there herding them back to the shore like a huge sheepdog. 'I bet you can't wait. I feel like that about the harvest, we're so close now and I know it'll be a nightmare few days, but I just want to crack on with it.'

'Eliza said she might head over and see how it all works. She's really getting into her new business thanks to the oils and stuff you gave her.' Sam gave him a sideways glance. 'It feels like I'm getting my little sister back, and I think you have something to do with that.'

Feeling a little awkward, Jack pulled at a loose thread on the blanket. 'She's amazing in her own right, and I don't think that has much to do with me.' Worried he'd given too much away with the intensity he could hear in his own voice, he forced himself to lie back on his elbows, trying to at least *look* relaxed. 'Is this where you give me the big brother speech and threaten to punch me if I break her heart?'

Sam slid his sunglasses down his nose and stared over the top of them at him. 'Do I need to?'

'Absolutely not.' Jack would cut his own heart out first, before intentionally hurting Eliza. 'We're playing it carefully around Noah for the time being, but not because I'm stringing her along or anything.'

Sam grinned. 'Didn't think so. I will offer you one bit of advice though…don't lie to yourself about your feelings. I tried to do that when I started seeing Beth, told myself it was just a bit of fun.' He laughed. 'I don't know who I was trying to kid because I was head over heels for her from the first time I kissed her.' Expression growing serious, Sam leaned over to clap Jack on the shoulder. 'There's so much crap in this life—hell, you don't need me to tell you that—we have to grab onto every bit of happiness we can.'

Jack gulped around a lump in his throat. He'd never talked to another guy about stuff like this other than Jason, and the loss of him slammed into Jack leaving him winded. Keeping his eyes fixed on the activity on the shoreline, he raised a hand when Noah turned to look up the beach.

The little boy ran through the sand towards him, Bastian at his heels, and threw himself into Jack's lap with a grin. 'You're soaked,' Jack managed to fight the words out.

Noah looked up at him, all ruddy cheeks and smiles. 'Bastian knocked me over!'

'Did he?' Jack wagged a stern finger at the Labrador. 'Bad dog.' Bastian lolled out his tongue in his doggy smile then shook himself vigorously, spraying them with the salty water soaked into his coat.

Jack ducked his head, but too late to miss the worst of the spray and he grimaced at the liberal coating of wet-dog smell that clung to his T-shirt along with the briny tang of sea water. 'Ugh, Bastian, you stink!' he told the unrepentant dog. 'You're getting a bath the minute we get home.' Turning to Noah, Jack gave him a sniff and wrinkled his nose. 'You too, smelly boy.'

Noah cackled with delight as he leaned into Jack. 'You three, smelly man!'

Sam tried and failed to smother a laugh. Jack met his eyes and soon the two of them were sniggering worse than Noah and Michael had been the night before. Noah knelt up between Jack's legs and threw his arms around Jack's neck. 'I'm having the best day!'

Jack's heart flip-flopped in his chest as he curled his arms around his nephew and hugged him close. 'Me too, buddy. Me too.'

Chapter Fifteen

Having just about crawled out of the hot shower on her hands and knees, Eliza made it as far as her bed and flopped onto her back still wrapped in a towel. Scooting around until she lay sideways across the bed, she raised her aching legs to prop them up against the wall. The pub had been mayhem after the beach football tournament with families deciding to extend their afternoon's fun into a couple of drinks and a bite to eat. Sam and Owen had shared a quick pint before going their separate ways—her brother to see Beth, and Owen to his room with a bottle of beer and a sandwich he'd persuaded Eliza to make with one of his charming smiles.

There'd been no sign of Jack and she'd tried very hard not to be bothered by that. Logic said he and his mum needed to get the boys home for dinner, and it would've broken their agreement to wait before she met Noah, but still…when she'd looked around at the smiling families and listened to half a dozen stories about the fun everyone had had on the beach, there'd been a definite feeling of missing out.

'Don't sulk Elizabeth Anne Barnes, it's unbecoming,' she said aloud in her best imitation of her mother, then rolled her eyes at herself. She pressed her sore toes against the cool plaster wall and contemplated the chipped polish on their nails. She really ought to redo them, but the thought of moving, never mind bending over to paint them, made her want to groan.

Her phone buzzed, and she flung out one arm to fumble for it. When she saw Jack's name on the display her bad mood vanished. 'Hello.'

'Hey, it's not too late to call is it?'

His warm, deep voice curled around her like a hug. 'Not at all. I've just finished my shift and had a shower. If I can scrounge up enough energy I might even make it underneath my quilt.'

'I wish I was there to tuck you in.'

The thought of him doing just that, or even better slipping in beside her, sent a delicious shiver through her. 'Me too.'

'Unfortunately, I'm hiding in my room from two sugar-filled monsters and the world's most disobedient dog.' She laughed at the despair in his voice.

'Are they giving you a hard time? If it's any consolation I don't think you're the only parent suffering. There were a lot of tears and tantrums when people who'd brought their kids into the pub after the football tried to take them home later.'

He was quiet for a moment, then said, 'I'm sorry I didn't bring the boys in, but it'd been a long afternoon. I told Noah about you, though.'

Her breath caught in her throat at his unexpected announcement. 'Was he okay about it?'

A soft chuckle in her ear. 'More than happy, he wants me to have a girlfriend, so I can be as happy as Sam. He was also angling for a little brother or sister, but I told him that was a long way off in the future.' Another laugh. 'God, the things he comes out with, he knocks me for six. I had no idea what to say.' He took a deep breath. 'It's terrifying, Eliza. I'm so worried I'm going to get everything wrong and mess him up. Jason always made it seem so easy.'

She couldn't imagine what it must've been like having to take on so much responsibility under such difficult circumstances—just the thought of anything happening to Sam was enough to bring tears stinging her eyes. 'You must miss him terribly.' Silence stretched between them. The sound of Jack's breath rasping over the phone was the only clue they hadn't been cut off. Eliza closed her eyes. He was ten minutes and a million miles away and she wasn't sure how to reach for him. 'I'm here, Jack. For as long as you need it.'

'Please.' A single choked word and her heart broke for him.

'Put your phone on speaker then lie down on your side,' she said. Scrolling quickly through the playlist on her phone, she found the track they'd danced to in the barn and selected it. She turned on her side and set the phone on the pillow beside her. As the soft strings of the intro started, she said, 'I'm right here, my darling.' An hour and a dozen songs later, they finally whispered their goodnights to each other.

Two weeks later, Eliza checked her reflection in the bathroom mirror, added a dash of pale pink lipstick and tousled her hair one last time, before giving herself a reassuring nod. Harvest was due to start in the morning, and although she was sure there were a million and one things Jack should've been doing instead, she'd dropped everything when he'd called and asked her to switch shifts and spend the evening with him.

They'd both been flat out, and their schedules had conspired against them to make spending time together impossible. When her head wasn't buried in research for her soap-making, she was behind the bar or bent over her sewing machine. The test garments she'd made for Beth to sell had flown off the shelves and she was struggling to keep up with demand.

School had broken up and between the farm and keeping Noah occupied, Jack barely had five minutes to think. He'd called her every night though, and after chatting about their days they'd played their favourite songs to each other. She began to live for those precious moments at the end of each day, but there was a bittersweet-ness to them.

Gathering her handbag and keys from the kitchen table, she said goodbye to her parents and hurried down the back stairs where she bumped into Sam. 'Oh, hey, I was just grabbing an extra box of crisps from the cellar—I don't know what's with everyone this evening but we're going through them like wildfire.' Sam paused and raised an eyebrow. 'You're looking very glam, Sis. Tell Jack he'd better be on his best behaviour.'

Eliza gave him a little twirl to show off the way the knee-length skirt of her dress flared out and laughed. 'Not a bloody chance.' They'd not laid eyes on each other since their dance in the barn and the need to touch him, to put her hands on him and know he was real had begun to itch beneath her skin.

Her brother pulled a face like he'd swallowed something nasty. 'I shouldn't have said anything because now I need to bleach my brain for just thinking about the two of you…' He shuddered then flapped his hands at her in a shooing motion. 'Get out of here.' Grinning at the discomforted look on his face, she obeyed.

She steered the little hatchback along the track leading to the farmhouse, then around the curve of the gravel driveway to park next to where Jack was waiting. The evening sun burnished his dark hair and made the crisp white short-sleeved shirt he'd paired with black jeans glow against the tanned skin of his arms. A shiver ran through her at the glimpse of sculpted bicep showing below his sleeve, the length of muscular thigh displayed by the close fit of his jeans. So much strength and power honed by years of hard work, and yet he never failed to touch her with anything other than gentleness.

Instead of opening the door, he bent at the waist to rest his elbows on the open window and smiled in at her. 'Hey, I hope you don't mind but there's a small change of plan.'

Her heart sank at the thought he might be cancelling on her again, but she did her best not to show it. 'There's nothing wrong, is there?'

'Not at all, there's just someone here who really wants to meet you.' He nodded towards the front door.

With a glance back over her shoulder, Eliza spotted a small dark haired boy hovering on the doorstep. Surprised, she turned back to Jack. 'I thought we'd all agreed it was better to wait…' Jack had told her about his chat with Noah on the beach and she'd been greatly relieved to know he seemed okay with the idea of her and Jack at least.

He shrugged. 'Yeah, I know, but I told him we were going out tonight and he hasn't stopped pestering me since. Maybe it's better this way, rather than making such a big deal of it.' He gave her a lopsided grin. 'You know I'm making this all up as I go along.'

Oh, boy. When he smiled at her like that, she was powerless to resist him. A deep thread of tenderness curled through her. He was trying so very hard to do the right thing by Noah. 'Well, all right, if you're sure.' Eliza undid her belt and popped open her door, trying to ignore the sudden swoop of butterflies in her stomach. It was foolish to be nervous, but it felt like a lot was riding on the next few minutes.

Jack appeared at her side, took her hand and helped her out of the car. He leaned close, smile gleaming as brightly as his white shirt. 'You look stunning.' His hand brushed the base of her spine, just a fraction above the curve of her bottom. 'Absolutely gorgeous.'

His words—and the span of his fingers at her back—gave her the little injection of confidence she needed. Smiling, she let Jack steer her across the gravel to the front door. He dropped into a crouch, bringing his eyeline on the same level as his nephew's, and her heart gave another little flutter at the way he was so careful and conscious of his size around not just her, but Noah too. 'Hey, buddy, this is my friend Eliza.'

Huge hazel eyes, just like Jack's, seemed to fill the little boy's face as he stared up at her. The smile on his face turned tentative and she couldn't help but notice the way he inched closer to the protective cradle of Jack's body. 'Hello.'

She didn't have as far to crouch as Jack, so Eliza bent at the waist and offered her hand. 'Hello, Noah. I've heard lots of lovely things about you from your Uncle Jack, so I've been looking forward to meeting you.'

Noah glanced towards Jack, received a quick nod of encouragement and then closed his small fingers around hers. 'Is Sam your brother? He's funny.'

When he didn't release her fingers, she turned her hand to cup his. 'That's right. He's my big brother which means he gets a bit bossy sometimes, but he's very good at looking after me.'

Noah gave her his mini-me version of Jack's lopsided smile and it was all she could do not to clutch the wall for support. These two would have her tumbling head over heels in love with the both of them if she wasn't careful. 'Uncle Jack said if you become his forever girlfriend you might have a baby, and then I can be a big brother too.' He puffed out his little chest. 'I'd be very good at it.'

Jack's jaw dropped, followed by a rush of colour to his cheeks and a desperate whisper of '*Noah*!' His expression was such a picture of abject horror it was all Eliza could do not to laugh.

Completely undeterred, Noah still had his eyes on her, and there was such eagerness and longing glowing in them it sobered her in an instant. Reaching out, she cupped his cheek. 'I'm sure you'd be a wonderful big brother, sweetheart, just like your daddy was to Uncle Jack.'

He smiled that shy, sweet smile and leaned against Jack's shoulder. 'My daddy was the best.'

'Yes, he sure was.' Jack's husky whisper drew her gaze and their eyes locked. 'Thank you.' He mouthed the words before turning his head to kiss Noah's temple, and the boy squirmed closer for a hug.

And there it was.

She'd assumed the moment her heart surrendered there would be a fanfare of trumpets, or an explosion of fireworks. Some epic gesture from Jack she could weave into a story to tell their children and grandchildren. But there was no lightning bolt—only a quiet, calm surety settling over her that she had found her place in the world at last. She had so much love to give, and she would give it all to this wonderful, lonely man and the heartbroken little boy in his arms.

Their drive to the multiplex on the outskirts of the nearest big town was quiet. Eliza left the radio on an easy-listening station which filled the car with old favourites and classic tunes she hummed along to. The atmosphere between them wasn't strained, but she wasn't quite ready to admit to Jack how she was feeling, and he seemed lost in his own thoughts. The car park was busy, and she had to crawl along the packed lanes of cars for fear of hitting one of the many groups of pedestrians who seemed to lose all sense of self-preservation in places like this.

'Over there.' The relief which filled her when Jack pointed to a free space near the end of the row melted away when she saw how close the people carrier on the left was parked to the white line 'I'll hop out,' he said, and did so.

She waited for him to do the typical man thing and take his place at the back of the space to guide her in, but instead he tucked his hands in his pockets and wandered down the aisle a few paces. If she hadn't already been smitten with him, that might well have sealed the deal. Forcing herself to pay attention to the task at hand, she edged the hatchback into the tight space and wriggled out of her side of the car.

Jack took her hand and they strolled towards the neon lights illuminating the cluster of bars and chain restaurants sprawled throughout the complex in front of the cinema. 'We've got time for a quick drink, if you'd like one?' he said, pausing outside the nearest bar. When she nodded, he tugged open the door.

A mass of people filled the entrance lobby and a barrage of noise from the packed bar beyond them swept over Jack and Eliza on a wave of thumping music and a head-spinning mix of perfume, alcohol, fried food and sweat. They'd never make it as far as the front of the queue before the film started. 'Maybe not,' Eliza offered.

Jack nodded swiftly in agreement and let the door go, cutting them off from the noise and smells. 'If it's this busy, we should probably go and buy our tickets while we can.'

The cinema was blessedly quieter, and cooler thanks to the powerful blast of the air conditioning units above the door. They made their way to the sales counter, pausing to verify the correct screen for their film. It had been ages since she'd been to the pictures, and even longer for Jack, so neither of them had had much of a clue about the latest films. They'd settled on a comedy which had been at the top of the charts for a couple of weeks, in the hopes it would be less busy than a brand new release.

Eliza hung back whilst Jack bought their tickets, letting her eyes roam over the dimly-lit foyer. The carpet felt sticky beneath the soles of her wedged sandals, and she decided it was best not to think about the gallons of coke, popcorn and other less savoury things that had likely been trodden into it over the years. The concession counter at the back of the foyer caught her attention, and she called to Jack who was closing in on the front of the queue. 'Shall I get us a drink? He cast a smile and a thumb's up over his shoulder, before turning back when the server spoke to him.

By the time Jack had secured the tickets and joined her, Eliza was standing to one side of the counter clutching a near-bucket sized soft drink which was already sweating condensation from the half a ton of ice inside it. 'The larger size was only 30p more,' she said with a rueful smile when Jack raised an eyebrow at the enormous cup.

He swapped it for the tickets, then took her other hand. 'Well, at least we won't run the risk of dehydration.'

Chapter Sixteen

Thankfully, the bored-looking kid dressed in an oversized black T-shirt and a baseball cap bearing the cinema chain's logo glanced at their tickets and pronounced the screen open. Hand in hand, they wandered along the corridor lined with garish posters advertising films Jack had never heard of and had even less inclination to see. It had been his idea to see Eliza that evening, and though nothing could spoil the thrill which jolted him every time her lovely curves brushed against his side, his mind was full of the day to come.

His friends and neighbours from the surrounding farms were lined up to arrive at first light. Most were family owned and run, same as them, and with each growing different crops their harvest times fell in different weeks, so they rotated their combined labour through the peak weeks of the summer. It was a damn sight cheaper than hiring in temporary field workers, and for Jack at least, it gave him a sense of security that the others all knew exactly what they were doing.

The Grosso was the first to ripen and would hopefully all be harvested within half a day. Once the plants were cut, a small team of ladies from town would spend the following few days sorting, bunching and hanging the lavender to dry and the shed would ring with their laughter and chatter. The bulk of the remaining crop—the Old English—looked like it'd be ready the following week from his inspection that afternoon. Harvesting that would take longer, but once it was in the shed, Jack could handle the task of transferring it into the enormous vats himself with the assistance of a couple of the herdsmen from a local dairy farm. They fit their hours with him around milking time, and welcomed the extra money he put in their pocket at holiday time.

Jack blinked and realised they'd come to a stop outside a large set of double-doors. Eliza was watching him with a half-smile on her lips. 'Everything all right? I think I lost you there for a moment.'

'Sorry.' He raised her hand to press a kiss to it. 'I was miles away.'

'Knee-deep in your fields, I'll bet.' There was no censure in her tone, but his conscience still gave a guilty twinge. The evening had been his idea after all.

'You have my undivided attention from now, I promise,' Jack said as he held open one of the doors for her.

'You'd better spare a little for the film, too,' she teased.

They found their seats in the mostly empty screen. The enormous cup of soda was too big to fit in the holder on his armrest, so Jack placed it on the floor by his feet then wiped his freezing, wet hand on the leg of his jeans. Seeing what he'd done, Eliza pulled a face. 'Sorry, I should have paid more attention when I was ordering it.'

'Forget about it.' Jack lifted his arm. 'Come here.' With a smile, she propped her arm on the rest between them and leaned into his hold. He curled his other arm across his body and linked their hands together. 'That's better. I've been thinking about this all day.'

Eliza tilted her head up. 'Me too.'

Jack cast a surreptitious glance around the room. They were tucked discreetly on the far end of the aisle near the wall and the few people scattered around weren't paying any attention to them—either intent on their own conversations or staring at their phones. It wasn't the ideal place, but it was private enough. 'I've got something for you.' He fumbled in the pocket of his jeans then drew out the surprise he'd been working on for her.

Eliza's eyes lit up as he placed the small object wrapped in tissue paper in her palm. 'What is it?'

'Open it and find out.' It was something and nothing, an idea which had come to him when he'd watched her using different moulds to shape her soap.

He held his breath while she carefully peeled open the paper. 'Oh, *Jack*.'

The bruised thumb and the cut on his palm he'd sustained whilst carving the square of wood were more than worth it for the way she said his name. 'It's so you can stamp your logo into your soaps, the same way you've been stitching it onto the clothes you make. It's all about branding, right?'

Her gaze glittered, even in the relative gloom of the screening room. 'I don't know what to say. It's perfect! It must've taken you hours to carve.'

You'd think he'd given her a diamond ring or an expensive designer piece by her reaction, but then his Eliza wasn't one for the material things. Thrilled at her obvious joy over the little stamp, Jack ducked his head and pressed his mouth to hers, relishing the sweet yielding as she opened for him. All his worries about the morning melted away in the tender heat of their kiss.

He lost track of time, lost track of everything but the warm press of lips and tongues until something thudded into the back of his seat. Surprised had him jerking back from Eliza, and he turned his head to see a pair of women about his mum's age fussing with cardigans, bags and a large tub of popcorn before finally settling into the seats behind them.

'Oh, don't mind us, dear,' the woman directly behind him said, with a wink.

Her companion nudged her arm. 'In our day the back row was reserved for that kind of thing, wasn't it, Janice?'

With his face feeling like it was on fire, Jack offered the pair an apologetic smile then turned back to find Eliza shaking with suppressed laughter. He slunk down in his seat as far as possible, not easy with legs as long as his, and tried to pretend he wasn't there. Thankfully, the house lights went down, sparing his blushes, and music began to blast from the surround-sound speakers.

They made it through an interminable round of adverts, trailers and jokey warning films asking patrons to switch off their phones. From the myriad glowing squares he could see, it was clear the last had little-to-no impact on most of the audience. The BBFC notice filled the screen and the noise around the room hushed to the odd cough and the rustle of sweet wrappers. Jack squeezed Eliza's hand and focused on the opening credits.

He made it about thirty minutes into the film before admitting to himself they'd made a terrible mistake. It was awful. Jack had never considered himself uptight before, but the parade of penis jokes and rank misogyny on the screen made Noah's fart jokes appear sophisticated in comparison. His knees were also starting to ache from being scrunched in one position for too long.

With a sigh, he shifted around in his seat then bent down to retrieve their drink. He nudged Eliza and offered her the drink; she shook her head. One sip and he winced, wishing he hadn't bothered. The ice had melted, leaving a watered-down sickly syrup that in no way resembled the top brand soda it claimed to be. He dumped the cup back on the floor, then settled back in his seat.

Eliza rested her head on his shoulder and he glanced down to see her staring up at him. 'This is the worst film I've ever seen in my life,' she whispered.

Oh, thank God! 'Me, too. Do you want to get out of here?' There was a narrow aisle between his seat and the wall, meaning they wouldn't have to clamber across everyone else to escape.

Taking her hand, he ducked out of his seat and they fumbled their way down the stairs to the bottom section of the seating. He paused to check there was nothing vital happening on the screen, then strode out into the wide cross-aisle towards the exit. A couple of murmurs reached his ears, but he kept walking, keeping Eliza close beside him until they rounded the edge of the seating and into the dark corridor leading to the exit.

With a quick shove of his shoulder against the door, they stumbled out of the darkness and paused to blink in the harsh overhead lights. Eliza clung to his arm, laughing and shaking her head. 'Oh, that was awful! That bit with the dog…'

Jack shuddered. 'Don't remind me, please! I can't believe everyone else was laughing so hard.'

'Maybe it's us? Maybe there's something wrong with us that we didn't find it funny.' Eliza shrugged.

'If we're wrong because of that, I can live with it,' Jack said as he hooked an arm around her shoulders and they began to stroll towards the main exit. They hit the pavement outside and he paused to survey the other entertainments on offer. From what he could see, all the restaurants looked full, and they'd already agreed to eat before going out anyway. So that left one or other of the bars, or the ten-pin bowling alley. None of it appealed, but he'd promised Eliza a proper date night. 'What else do you want to do?'

'I don't mind, you can choose.' Eliza didn't sound any more enthusiastic about any of it than he felt.

All he wanted was to go somewhere quiet and just be with her. 'There's a really nice spot on the way back to the farm, we could just park up under the stars and listen to the sea.'

She snuggled into his side, her arm curling around his waist. 'Sounds perfect.'

'Just over there, on the right.' Jack pointed across Eliza to indicate the large passing area to the side of the road. It was wide enough to accommodate a tractor and trailer, but there was so little traffic on the private road, he'd only ever used it as somewhere to sit and enjoy his lunch, or chill out at the end of a busy day. Eliza steered her car into the space, parking at a right angle to the road so they faced out over the town towards the sea beyond.

Jack lowered his window fully, letting the warm evening breeze drift in. Eliza did likewise, turned off the radio and placed her phone on the centre of the dashboard between them. The warm, sultry tones of a female singer he'd never heard of filled the car. 'Playing songs to you is much nicer when we're actually in the same place.'

He couldn't agree more. Unhooking his belt, he turned sideways as Eliza twisted up onto her seat so she could lean across the handbrake towards him. Their lips met, and Jack slid his hands into the soft river of her curls, drawing her closer. She jolted against something. 'Ow.'

Jack sat back and watched Eliza rub her knee. Frustration rose in him. He was thirty bloody years old, what the hell were they doing fooling around in the front seat of a car? It was fruitless to be annoyed, though. They couldn't go back to the farm without disturbing his mum, and possibly Noah, which would put a definite kibosh on anything remotely romantic. The pub would be even worse, between Eliza's family and any guests who were staying.

His eyes roved over the soft street lights of the town below them. It was high season, so the guesthouses and hotels would likely be full, and it felt a bit seedy to even think about sneaking her down into one. He sighed; they'd have to make the best of what they had. *If he pushed his seat back, maybe…*

'Come around to my side of the car,' he said as he opened the passenger door wide.

Eliza did as he said, waiting outside until he'd rolled his seat back as far as it would go, then tilted the back down about halfway. He patted his lap. 'Sit sideways so your legs can hang out the door.'

She turned her back to him, then sank down across his thighs. 'You're full of good ideas.' Her voice was a soft murmur as she leaned her head against his chest and he curled an arm around her back to support her.

'Needs must, and all that.' Jack pressed a kiss to the top of her head, then closed his eyes and let his head fall back against the seat.

The music wove a spell around them, and the warm air carried the tangy-sweet scent of saltwater and lavender to wrap them in the scents of home and hearth. Totally relaxed for the first time since she'd arrived on his doorstep, Jack catalogued the feel of her in his arms. The weight of her head on his shoulder, the way her hair tickled against his cheek. The lush curve of her breast resting on his forearm where he encircled her. The press of her hip against his groin. She felt good, *right*, like she belonged there.

He drifted, not asleep, but not altogether conscious when something warm and wet touched the underside of his chin. He stirred into full wakefulness as the touch came again—Eliza's tongue tracing the side of his neck between his jaw and his ear. A groan rose in his throat which he quickly stifled, not wanting to do anything that might distract her. Her tongue flickered again, and then her lips closed over the pulse point in his neck and she sucked lightly.

Head swimming, he let his hand glide over the sweep of curves from her breast to her thighs, the silky material of her dress beneath his fingers adding another sensation to those already whirling through him. 'Touch me.' She breathed the words against his throat and his hand was already skimming halfway under the skirt of her dress when he gripped her thigh and wrangled himself back under control.

'We don't have to do this…when I suggested we come up here, it wasn't because I expected anything from you.' He wanted to touch her, God, he'd wanted to since the first moment their mouths had fused. The need to touch her, to glide his hand higher and feel her come apart burned like a breath held too long. But, he didn't *expect* to touch her unless she absolutely wanted it.

Eliza sat back and raised her hands to cup his face. With the rays of the setting sun haloing around her, it was hard to make out her expression, but the press of her fingers was as compelling as her tone. 'I want this, Jack. I want *you*, right here, right now.'

He swallowed the last word in a searing kiss, using his lips, his tongue, and then his hands to show her all the things he felt, but didn't have the words to say. She met him press for press, stroke for stroke, until her dress was a silken tangle on the back-seat and his shirt was lost somewhere on the ground outside the open car door.

Eliza ended up perched across his thighs, the lace of her bra rasping his chest as her breath came in little pants. Her nimble fingers busied at his waistband, tugging the button and then the zip. Jack sucked in a breath as her knuckles brushed against him and he had to brace her weight, so she could lift up enough to help him wriggle his jeans down. 'Wait, in my wallet…' He managed to grind out the words with what little bit of his brain still functioned enough for rational thought.

Thankfully, she understood his meaning, found it in his pocket and retrieved the condom tucked into a spare credit card slot. As she rustled the wrapper, Jack reached down beside him, hunted for, then found the handle to lower the back of his seat as far as it would go. And then there was no more room for thought because her hands were on him, sheathing him, guiding him, then sliding up his chest to grip his shoulders as she settled the heat of her around him.

The close confines of the car limited their movements, turning the act of their union into an exquisite slow dance of shifting muscles and rolling hips. In those slow, heated moments as the sun slipped below the waves in a final blaze of pink, purple and red, all the words he thought he didn't have came spilling off his tongue in a litany of praise, encouragement and love. 'So sweet…

so damn sexy.' And later. 'God, you're beautiful, my darling.' And as they wound each other higher than he'd ever dreamed possible—'I love you, Eliza, love you so much.'

After, they sprawled together in a tangle of twisted clothing and limbs, sweat cooling on their skin in the soft breeze. The music from her phone had cut out at some point, leaving only the sounds of the night. A soft rustle of a nocturnal animal in the hedgerow lining the road, the rhythmic, otherworldly cry of an owl, and beneath it all the susurration of waves breaking on the shore of the bay far below them. Eliza stirred against his chest. 'It's getting late.'

'Mmm.' Still sated, it was about all he could manage as a response.

Her fingers traced patterns through the smattering of hair on his upper chest. 'You've got a long day tomorrow, if it would help you out then I could take Noah for a few hours. I need to prep the bar in the morning, but I'm sure Dad would be happy to keep him occupied and then I can take him for an afternoon picnic on the beach.'

It was on the tip of his tongue to refuse, worried about taking advantage of her generosity and dumping Noah off on people he didn't really know didn't seem fair on the boy. Before he could say anything, Eliza rested a finger against his lips. 'You don't have to do everything alone, Jack. I know you want to protect Noah, but I think it's important for me to spend some time with him.'

His need for control warred with the sheer practicalities of trying to look after Noah. 'I just want to give him the same care and attention Jason did. He always made it seem so effortless.'

Eliza rested her head against his cheek. 'He had you and your mum to help him. Without him, you've got all that extra work and one less pair of hands.'

'I never thought about it that way.' He'd been so intent on being the perfect replacement for Jason, he'd lost sight of the fact they'd all worked as a team to raise Noah. And that team was missing a key player. 'Well, he did ask to meet you tonight…'

'And we'll only be a few minutes away. If anything happens, or if Noah decides he's had enough I'll bring him straight back home.' She cupped his cheek. 'I'm here, Jack.'

'I know.' And it meant more to him than he could possibly say.

A yawn cracked her jaw and she snuggled sleepily against him. 'We should really make a move…'

Capturing her fingers, he lifted them to his mouth for a kiss before placing their clasped hands back on his chest. 'Five more minutes, beauty. Just let me hold you like this for five more minutes.'

Once they let the real world back in, they'd be caught up once more in their tangles of responsibility. The farm would be controlled chaos for the rest of the month, and finding time to be alone together would be a challenge. So while he had her here in his arms, he would make the moment last for as long as he could.

Chapter Seventeen

'Smug.' Libby's pronouncement made Eliza pause in the act of restocking one of the fridges behind the bar and glance up at her friend. And in doing so, she forgot what Libby had said as her latest look startled her again. Eliza thought she'd seen every possible combination of hairstyle from her, but this morning's new look was something else again. The left-hand side had been bleached and dyed canary yellow, whilst the right glowed fluorescent pink. She reminded Eliza of one of those rhubarb-and-custard penny sweets she'd loved as a child.

Libby's wild hair had been a part of her for so long that it rarely gave those close to her pause for thought. And, until today, Eliza would have sworn that Libby changed her look for no other person than herself. She studied the halo of gelled spikes around her friend's face with a frown. For the first time, it seemed to Eliza she was deliberately trying to provoke a reaction. *From who, though?*

A bag of crisps from the box Libby was emptying into a large basket for display on the bar came sailing through the air towards Eliza. She ducked just in time. 'What was that for?'

'You're staring.' There was a distinctive challenge in Libby's tone.

Refusing to take the bait—no matter how juicy—Eliza returned to her task of filling the fridge. 'I wasn't staring, I just didn't understand what you said.'

There was a moment's pause when Eliza worried Libby would call her out on the fib, but the tension lifted as she cocked her head and grinned. 'I was trying to decide what word best described the look on your face, and finally settled on smug.' Abandoning the crisps, Libby squatted down beside her. 'Come on then, dish the dirt.'

Eliza stuck her head in the fridge under the guise of retrieving a fallen bottle at the back of the shelf. The cool blast of air did little to dull the heat rising on her face. 'There isn't anything to dish,' she muttered.

'Have a word with yourself,' Libby scoffed. 'You and farmer hotty had a date last night and now you're floating around on at least cloud nine, if not ten. That means *dirt*.' There was no mistaking the lascivious emphasis she placed on the last word.

The effervescence which had been bubbling inside her since the previous night bubbled out in a sudden rush. 'Oh, Libby! You have no idea…I mean, *I* had no idea.'

Libby's eyebrows climbed up nearly to her hairline. 'But, you were married all those years…oh…*oh*!' A knowing grin spread across her face.

'Exactly, oh!' Eliza hugged herself. 'And, he told me he loved me.'

'He did? Oh my God!' Libby screeched. 'It's always the quiet ones!' She clapped her hands together.

'Shh, keep your voice down!' Eliza cast a worried glance towards the ceiling. 'Noah's upstairs with my dad, remember. The last thing I want is him asking any awkward questions.'

Libby looked contrite for a moment then spoke in a stage whisper. 'Hold on a minute, did he say it while you were…' She made an obscene gesture with her fingers that made Eliza gasp. 'Because if he did, you know that doesn't count right?'

Libby might have had a point, there had definitely been something of the heat in the moment in Jack's urgently whispered words, but she hadn't been there. Hadn't felt the connection between them which had transcended more than the physical. 'Believe me, it counted.'

The pair of them collapsed onto the floor, trying unsuccessfully to smother their giggles. Eliza laughed until the tears rolled down her cheeks. They were so caught up in the moment, neither heard the approaching footsteps of Sam and Owen coming up from the skittle alley below. A heavy knock on the wooden bar startled them into silence.

'What are you two cackling about?' Owen might have addressed the question to both of them, but his attention was solely fixed on Libby.

Any man in his right mind would've beat a hasty retreat at the evil glare Libby fixed on Owen as she stood to face off with him, but he was either a fool or ridiculously brave. Possibly both. 'Nothing you'd know anything about, *believe me.*' Libby cast a long scornful glare up and down Owen's tall frame.

'You keep telling yourself that, darling, but we both know better.' Far from being quelled, Owen appeared delighted at goading a response from her. The smile he gave her was free and easy, the epitome of a man confident in every aspect of his life. 'I like what you've done with your hair, by the way.' He turned his back to Libby, and looked to Sam. 'I'm ready for that cup of tea now.'

'Sure thing.' Sam waved Owen towards the door which led upstairs. 'After you.' Eliza caught his eye and they exchanged a look. After all their years growing up together they'd developed their own entirely silent language and it was clear her brother had no more idea of what was up between Libby and Owen than she did.

The door swung shut behind them, and Libby turned to face Eliza, her jaw clenched so tight a muscle twitched in her cheek. 'Oh, God, I hate him so much.'

Rising to her feet, Eliza put her arms around Libby. 'He's a wind-up merchant, Libs. He only does it to get a rise out of you. I know it's hard, but if you can ignore him, he'll soon get bored.' She decided against pointing out that Libby was behaving just as badly. They were best friends, so Eliza's loyalty fell firmly on Libby's side—even when she might deserve a good shake.

Libby rested her head on Eliza's shoulder and groaned. 'I know, I know, he's just so…' Whatever he was, she couldn't seem to find the word to describe him.

Eliza gave her one final squeeze. 'Come on, let's get these fridges loaded so I can spend some time with Noah. I'll even treat you to a bag of crisps.'

Her friend laughed as they broke apart. 'Cheese and onion?'

'Only if you're very good.'

Libby snorted. 'No chance of that!' The wicked gleam resurfaced in her eyes. 'And no chance for you either, after last night.' She knelt to open the flaps on a carton of wine bottles. 'Right, I want all the gory details…'

'Now, are you sure you've got everything?' She watched Jack rifle through the colourful backpack his mum had bought Noah to help him ferry all his bits and pieces between the farm and the pub. They'd been shuttling him and Bastian back and forth for the past week, and he seemed to be settling nicely into the routine of everything. He really was the dearest little soul and every moment she spent with him endeared him to her a little more.

'Yes, Uncle Jack. I'm helping Mr B do his work this morning and then Eliza and I are going rock-pooling after our lunch.'

'If you're going to be out in the sun, don't forget to wear your hat.' Eliza had picked up a bright blue baseball cap which had a flap hanging down from the back to protect the vulnerable skin on Noah's neck. It also served as a great marker for spotting him on the busy beach, or when he skipped ahead of them on the promenade.

'I won't forget.'

'All right then.' Jack gave him a quick kiss on the cheek, then led him out to the car where she waited for them. He helped Noah strap himself into the back seat, then patted his knee. 'Be a good boy for Eliza, and Mr and Mrs B.'

'Yes, Uncle Jack.' There was definitely a singsong quality to Noah's tone which made Eliza want to laugh. She turned away before he could see her grinning.

'Cheeky monkey. I'll be down to pick you up in time for tea.' Jack tweaked his nose, then closed the car door. Turning, he almost bumped into Eliza standing behind him, and he drew her into his arms. 'You'll call me if there's any problems?'

'Yes, Uncle Jack,' she mimicked Noah.

'And you're a cheeky monkey, too.' He swooped in for a kiss hot enough to turn her knees to water. 'Now I know where he's getting it from.'

Her laughter faded as he tightened his arms in reflex around her waist. 'We're like ships that pass in the night.'

'There's time enough.' It had become their daily mantra. He pressed their foreheads together. 'Are you working tonight?'

She shook her head. 'The relief manager is pulling some extra shifts because he wants to save up enough money to take his girlfriend away for the weekend.'

'Lucky sod,' Jack grumbled. 'We're starting the cut on the Old English today, which means I get to spend the bulk of the day with a pitchfork in hand transferring the lavender from the trailer to the vats.'

He'd already explained the steam extraction process which would produce the essential oil, and it would be brutal work. Her back ached in sympathy. 'Rather you than me.'

His hands settled in her favourite place—the indent of her waist just above the swell of her hips. When he held her like this she felt like her body had been shaped just for him. 'Why don't you come back with us when I collect Noah later? You could stay over, and I can take you home in the morning. I need you in my arms again.' Eliza felt her breath catch in her throat at the heat in his gaze. She wanted that too, needed it like oxygen. 'Don't be getting any ideas, though,' he added. 'Rubbing some Deep Heat into my back is likely as hot as things will get.'

Laughing, she linked her arms around his neck. 'If you ask nicely, I might scrub it for you first when you have your bath.'

'Mmm.' He moaned against her cheek. 'I'll be thinking about that all day.'

'And that's my cue to leave.' One last quick kiss and then she was sliding into the car.

'All set, passenger?' she asked as she clipped on her seatbelt.

Noah raised his hand in salute. 'All set, driver.' They grinned at each other. It was a silly little routine they'd fallen into from the first morning she'd picked him up. With a final wave to Jack they were off.

The steady whir of the sewing machine never failed to lure Eliza into a trance as she worked. Everything disappeared into the background as she hemmed and finished the half-dozen cotton sundresses she'd promised to drop off with Beth. With the high-pressure system showing no signs of moving on, the bay was roasting under the heat of the summer sun, and her cool, floaty designs were proving popular with visitors and locals alike.

She was just stitching her logo onto the last dress when a knock sounded on her half-open bedroom door and two heads poked around the corner. Their matching grins did something funny to her insides. As much fun as she'd been having spending time with Noah, he'd developed a very special bond with her dad. His seemingly endless patience and the boy's natural curiosity for all things mechanical were a match made in heaven. In the past week, they'd taken apart everything from one of Noah's toy cars to an old carriage clock which had decorated the mantelpiece for as long as Eliza could remember.

'Hello, double-trouble! What have you been up to this morning?'

'We've been counting, haven't we, Mr B?' Noah tilted his head up to stare at Paul—a look of sheer adoration on his face.

'That we have, Noah-lad.' He ruffled the boy's hair then looked across at Eliza. 'He's been such a good assistant, I've promised him some money to buy an ice cream later.'

'Wow, that's great!' Standing up, Eliza stretched out her back. 'Well, I'm finished here so how about we drop these off next door with Beth and then we can hit the beach?'

Ten minutes later, with sunhats on and every inch of bare skin slathered in factor-50 sun cream, Eliza held open the door of the emporium and ushered Noah inside. 'Why don't you check out the nets over there in the corner and I'll have a quick word with Beth? We'll need a bucket and spade, too.'

As he skipped off, she twisted round the clothes hangers she had draped over her shoulder and held them out to Beth. 'Here you go.'

'Fantastic. Oh, I love these colours, and this material is so soft!'

Eliza had picked up a roll of brushed cotton decorated with bright, tropical flowers. 'There's some left, I can put together something for you, if you'd like?' The colours would look fabulous against Beth's summer tan and dark brown hair.

Her friend smiled in pleasure. 'That would be fab. How about one of those cover-ups you made last time? I was going to keep one back, but the last one sold this morning.' The over-sized tops were little more than two squares of fabric sewn together with loose draping sleeves, perfect for throwing on and off during a day on the beach.

'Deal.' Eliza glanced over at Noah to check he was happily occupied. 'I need to tell you something.'

Beth's brows drew together. 'Of course. There's nothing wrong, is there?'

'Quite the opposite.' The past few days with Noah had gone

so well that it had given Eliza the confidence to believe there really was a long-term future for her and Jack. And in order to be able to have that, it was time to get serious about sorting her life out. Despairing over Martin's continued silence, she needed to understand her options. 'I've made an appointment to see Mr Symonds tomorrow.' The local solicitor had helped Beth navigate her inheritance from Eleanor, including the emporium.

'Oh?' Comprehension dawned on Beth's face. 'Oh!' She looked between Eliza and Noah who was still happily browsing. 'You're really serious about this, then?'

Eliza nodded. 'I adore Jack; I adore them both.' And even if the worst happened and things didn't work out between them, she couldn't ever see herself going back to Martin. Being with someone who valued her own achievements as much as his own had only served to highlight how little Martin had done to encourage her. 'Whatever happens, my future's here in the bay.'

'Who would've thought this time last year that we'd both find ourselves back here again?' Beth sniffed, then gave a little laugh as he dabbed at her eyes. 'Bloody hormones, who'd be a woman?' Straightening up, she clapped her hands together. 'Right, so tell me what adventures you two are going on today.'

Grateful that Beth had changed the subject before the pair of them started watering like a pair of pots, Eliza turned her attention to Noah. 'We're going rock-pooling, aren't we, darling?'

'Yes!' He ran over to her, a bright green net on a pole in one hand, a red bucket and spade which banged against his knee with every step in the other. 'Are these all right?'

'I think they'll be perfect. Put them on the counter so Beth can ring them up for us.'

He lifted them up, but Beth waved him away. 'They're on the house. A present from me and Sam.'

Noah's eyes lit up. 'Thank you!' He turned to Eliza. 'Can we go now?'

Heart full, she adjusted the bright cap on his head. 'Of course we can, but no running on the prom, okay? It's very busy out there so I need you to stay with me.' She mouthed a quick 'thank you' to Beth, and noticed tears glimmering in her eyes again.

Beth gave her a wobbly smile. 'Don't mind me, I cried when Sam brought me a cup of tea this morning. Poor thing, he knows I get like this every month, but it still freaks him out. Anyway, give me a call after your appointment tomorrow and let me know how you get on,' she murmured before giving Noah a wave. 'Have fun you guys!'

They spent the next couple of hours scrambling over the lowest levels of the rocks which covered the top end of the beach. The knees of her lightweight trousers were soaked through from kneeling on the damp, mossy stones and Noah had had to take off his sandals after his foot had slipped into one of the pools. By the end of their explorations, the little red bucket contained a selection of shells, seaweed and even a couple of small crabs. 'Time to put everything back where we found it.'

Noah pouted. 'But I wanted to show Uncle Jack and Nanna what we found.' He'd been very good, but there was a definite mutinous air about him.

'We've got plenty of photos. Come on now.' She held out a hand to lead him back to one of the larger pools.

'But—'

'Please, Noah. No more arguments.' She tried to keep her voice soft, but his head and shoulders dropped as though she'd read him the riot act. He was so good most of the time that it would be easy to let him get away with it on the few occasions he balked her, but spoiling him wouldn't do either of them any good. Crouching down, she ducked below the brim of his cap to catch his eyes. 'Hey.' She kept her voice as soft as possible.

His eyes flicked away then back to her. 'Hey.'

'I'm not trying to be mean, darling, but we can't take the crabs away from their home. If everyone who came and played here did that then soon there won't be anything left for other children to enjoy. Can you imagine what it would be like here if the pools were all empty?'

Noah poked the bucket with his toe. 'It wouldn't be as much fun.'

'Exactly.' She traced the back of his cheek with her knuckles. 'Come on, Noah, chin up. Let's put your friends back where they belong and then we can have that ice cream Mr B promised you.'

His face brightened, much to her relief and there were no more protests as Noah carefully lowered the bucket into the pool and let the crabs escape. When she held out her hand to lead him back down to the beach there was no hesitation on his part and they were soon perched side by side on the edge of the prom both clutching a '99' cone with a flake. As the creamy ice cream dripped down the side of the cone and over her fingers, Eliza sent up a little prayer of thanks. It seemed like they'd negotiated their way through their first tricky moment.

With every moment she spent with Noah, her admiration for Jack grew. He'd been thrown in at the deep end, and for all his protestations about making it up, the balanced nature of the little boy at her side was a testament to his hard work. She'd have to make sure she told Jack so later when she scrubbed his back.

Chapter Eighteen

The next week passed Eliza in a blur. With Sam entirely focused on the restaurant, the pub was absorbing all of her time, though not all of her attention. Her fingers itched with the need to go upstairs and check on her batch of soap for the millionth time. It looked fine, smelt even better, but if she tried to use one of the bars before they were fully cured it would only end in disappointment. She already had a dozen different recipes she wanted to try but until she could be sure she was on the right track they would have to wait. Her hand must have strayed to the phone in her pocket a dozen times before she stopped herself with a gentle reminder that Jack needed to focus all his energies on the harvest.

Noah was spending a few days with Michael, his mum having found a free activity workshop run by the local council, and Eliza missed her little shadow. Her dad was even worse, and the heat was playing havoc with his lungs so he'd been laid up in bed. With the hot spell showing no signs of letting up, when she wasn't rushing around the bar, she was stationed in front of a fan she'd placed next to the sewing machine in her room, doing her best to cool off.

Lunchtime had been manic with a constant stream of families desperate to seek some shade from the blistering heat of the noonday sun. When the crowds showed no sign of abating, Eliza took the decision to keep the doors open rather than take a break as she would normally do during the afternoon lull.

Her mum had taken over around half-four, after practically frog-marching Eliza upstairs to eat the bowl of soup and sandwich she'd prepared. A long, cool shower and change of clothes had given Eliza the second wind she needed to see her through the early evening crush. She wriggled her toes against the padded soles of her slip-on trainers. A few more hours and she'd be able to lie on her bed and give her poor swollen ankles a rest.

A roar of laughter rose from the impromptu locals vs. visitors darts match which had sprung up in the corner, and she wandered to that end of the bar to join in the banter. Having made sure everyone had a drink who wanted it, she turned her attention back to the main part of the room and stopped dead at the sight of a familiar figure in the open doorway. *Oh, bloody hell.*

With a sharp gesture towards her mum who was already moving to head him off, Eliza rounded the edge of the bar on an intercept path to the door. 'What are you doing here?'

Martin glanced over her shoulder, made a move like he wanted to step further into the pub then checked himself when she held her ground. 'Hello, Eliza.' His eyes roved over her. 'You look well.'

The note of surprise in his voice did little to soothe her nerves or the sick feeling rising in her stomach. 'You can't just show up here out of the blue, what were you thinking?'

He gave her his best hang-dog expression. 'In your emails you kept saying we needed to talk.' *Those emails he'd chosen to ignore for weeks now.* When she opened her mouth to tell him she had nothing to say to him, he hurried on. 'I need to talk, please. I didn't come here to fight with you, I promise. Can we just go in the back for a minute?'

No chance. There was no place for him anymore in the private spaces of her life, and that included any part of her home. 'We can talk outside, but it'll have to be quick because you can see how busy we are.' Eliza looked over to her mum. 'Can you cover for me a minute?'

'Yes, love.' Annie raised an eyebrow at Martin but gave him no other acknowledgement as she passed them on her way to the bar.

Eliza bit her lip as the ingratiating smile fell from her soon-to-be-ex-husband's face. He'd always been a suck-up when it came to her parents. In her younger days, she'd found it charming the way he'd tried so hard to get on with them. It was only later she'd understood it to be another part of his manipulation tactics. She gestured once more to the door and followed him outside.

The promenade was busy with late evening strollers enjoying the last of the sunshine. The interminable heat had cooled somewhat, helped by a breeze coming in off the sea. Dog walkers ambled along the shoreline, as the final few families trudged off the beach laden with windbreakers, cold boxes and inflatable lilos.

Weaving her way through the crowd of pub patrons leaning against the outside wall, Eliza folded her arms and strode to the railing lining the opposite side of the promenade where they would be far enough away from the drinkers to afford a modicum of privacy. Leaning with her back against the metal rails, she faced Martin. 'Five minutes, and then I'll have to get back inside.'

'I booked a flight back as soon as I got your last email.' After seeing the solicitor on Monday, she'd written to Martin and advised him it was time to seek his own legal advice.

'But you must have known this was coming.' She tried to keep the exasperation from her voice. Fighting with him was the last thing she wanted as Mr Symonds had made it clear she would need Martin's cooperation if she wanted to extricate herself from their marriage any time soon. Without a claim of adultery, and with them not having lived apart for long enough, the only legal grounds she had was if she could get him to agree to a petition for unreasonable behaviour.

Wringing his hands, he stared past her out towards the water.

'I thought you'd come back. I wanted to give you some space to think about things, but I always assumed once you'd had a break and sorted out your head—or whatever—that you'd come back to me.'

Guilt sliced through her at the pain in his words. 'That's not going to happen, Martin. I'm sorry, but you need to accept that it's over.'

'But I didn't do anything wrong.' His voice trembled like he was on the edge of tears. 'All I ever did was try to love you, Eliza.'

Dumbfounded, Eliza stared at him. *Did he honestly believe that?* After what had happened in the airport, after all those decisions he'd made without consulting her, the years of prioritising what he wanted and never stopping to assume she might not want the same thing? 'That's not how it felt from my side, though, Martin. I was unhappy for a very long time, and you didn't seem interested in doing anything to remedy that.'

'Well you can't put all the blame on me.' The trembly voice slipped into something more petulant. 'You should have told me what you wanted instead of agreeing all the time. And now you want to make out like it's all my fault. That I've been the *unreasonable* one. Remember who left who at the airport, Eliza. You were the one that walked out—not me!'

This wasn't getting them anywhere. *And maybe he had a point.* If she'd stood her ground earlier, they might not be in this mess. But she hadn't, and they were. And now she'd met Jack and had a taste of what life could be like with him…

'The unreasonable behaviour thing is just a means to an end, Martin, it doesn't mean I'm blaming you. If it bothers you that much, you petition for divorce instead and we can come up with grounds for my unreasonable behaviour.' Her solicitor had recommended they work together to establish five or six incidents they could state in the petition to get it through the courts.

'But I don't want a divorce.' He ran his hands through his hair in a gesture of sheer frustration. 'I'm doing this all wrong. I love you so much, and these past weeks without you have been hell. I know I haven't shown you that often enough, that I've taken you for granted for far too long. I wanted Abu Dhabi to be a fresh start for us, hoped that a new place would give us a chance to fix things, but I was being an idiot. I wasn't trying to fix our problems, I was compounding them.'

Propping his foot on the railing behind them, he crossed his arms across his chest and sighed. 'I'll give up the job there, Eliza, if that's what you want. I'll even move back here to the bay. Just tell me what I need to do to make things right between us and I'll do it. Please give me one more chance.'

He sounded so heartfelt, so sincere, that a part of her heart ached for him. Why hadn't they had this conversation two years ago? Hell, even six months ago it might have made a difference. 'I've waited so long to hear you say these things, Martin—' The scuff of feet behind her distracted Eliza, but when she turned around there was no one in the vicinity. Still, she took his arm and led him further along the promenade. What she had to say to him next didn't need an audience.

Once they were well away from everyone else, she tried to let go of his hand, but Martin had other ideas. Keeping a tight grip on her fingers he pulled her forwards so she lost her balance and stumbled into his chest. To her horror, he lowered his face to hers as though coming in for a kiss.

'Martin, no.' Twisting away she evaded his mouth and managed to break free of his hold. 'What are you doing?'

Frowning in confusion, he reached for her hand again. 'But you said you'd been waiting to hear me say how much I need you.'

Oh, God. 'You didn't let me finish. Yes, I've waited a long time for you to say all those things, too long. There might have been a time when we could have picked up the pieces, but it's too late now. We want different things.'

'Don't say that.' Martin swiped a hand across his eyes. 'Don't you say that. I want whatever you want, Eliza, whatever you need to make you happy.'

The lump in her throat was the size of an egg as she uttered the four hardest words of her life. 'Then let me go.'

'You can't mean that.' He shook his head. 'You're just trying to punish me.'

That was the last thing she wanted. Once upon a time she might have, but now she just wanted this all to be over and done with. 'I don't love you anymore. I'm sorry, Martin, but it's over between us.'

'*Eliza!*'

The sound of his sobs burned in her ears every step she took back towards the pub. Tears soaking her own cheeks, she hurried through the bar with her head down and straight out the back. She didn't stop until she reached the shelter of her own room and fell onto the bed.

Burying her face in her pillow, Eliza wept. Not in despair, but in mourning. Martin would always be her first love. Her first of so many things; but not her last. Though she ached for what might have been, what could have been if they'd had the sense and maturity to communicate with each other better, she had no regrets. The very best of her past couldn't hold a candle to the promise of her future.

It was only as she finally drifted off to sleep that she realised Jack hadn't called to wish her goodnight.

Chapter Nineteen

'*I've waited so long to hear you say these things, Martin.*' Eliza's words haunted Jack all night. Having had a terrible day, he'd wanted nothing more than to spend a few minutes in her sweet, calming company. After a quick shower, he'd grabbed his keys and driven the few miles down to the bay. Leaving the car at the top of the promenade, he'd been enjoying the cooling breeze coming in off the sea as he strolled along when he spotted Eliza deep in conversation with a man he hadn't recognised.

Curious, he'd approached quietly just in time to hear the man beg for another chance and then Eliza had shattered Jack's heart into pieces. Unable to bear witness to their reunion for a moment longer, he'd turned on his heel and run like the hounds of hell were chasing his heels. He'd driven back to the farm on autopilot. Not knowing how to answer his mum's surprise enquiry at his early return, he'd headed straight upstairs and ignored her tentative knock at his door when she'd come up to bed.

Gritty-eyed, Jack avoided his reflection in the bathroom mirror as he cleaned his teeth the next morning. The door swung open and Noah bounced in already dressed in shorts and a striped T-shirt he'd managed to put on back to front. Jack crouched down. 'Here, let me help you with that. What are you doing up so early?'

Head buried under his top as Jack tried to help him wriggle his arms free, Noah answered, 'Eliza's taking me to see the sandcastles today.' *Shit*! In an attempt to provide entertainment for the tourists, the local traders' association had paid for a beach sculptor to visit. Today was the first day he'd be working, and Jack had forgotten all about it. 'There's been a change of plans, buddy, you'll have to stay here for the day. You can help Nanna in your new garden.'

Noah scowled. 'I don't want to. I want to see the sandcastles! Mr B said he'd help me build one afterwards.'

And this was exactly why Jack should have listened to his first instinct and kept Noah and Eliza apart. She could break Jack's heart if she wanted to, hell, it was his own fault for getting involved with a married woman, but hurting Noah wasn't bloody fair. 'Eliza and her folks are going to be busy for a while, so you won't be able to spend any more time with them.' It was a crappy excuse, but he needed some time to work out how to tell him the truth.

'But why?' The look of bewilderment on his nephew's face echoed the confusion in Jack's heart. 'Did I do something wrong?'

'Ah, no, buddy.' Jack gathered him into his arms. 'You didn't do anything wrong. Not one thing.'

Having managed to calm Noah down, Jack left him to wash his face while he tapped out a quick text to Eliza. *I'll be keeping Noah here with me.* Within a few seconds his phone began to ring. Gritting his teeth, he answered. 'What?'

'I just got your text, is everything all right?' Eliza sounded a little out of breath and Jack's mood turned ugly at the thought of what she might have been doing before she called.

'Given your change in circumstances, I assumed you'd have something better to do than babysit my kid,' he snapped.

'Change in circumstances, what on earth are you talking about, Jack? What's going on, you sound terrible.'

And who was to blame for that? 'I decided to drop by and see you last night and was just in time to catch that touching reunion between you and Martin.' He lowered his voice to a hiss. 'I might forgive you one day for what you've done to me, but I'll never forgive you for letting Noah down. *Never*.' He hung up, unable to say any more with the roaring pain inside him threatening to choke him. When the phone rang again, he rejected the call.

'Uncle Jack?'

Jack banged the back of his head against the wall hard enough to hurt as he stuffed everything down as far as it would go. 'Hey, buddy, ready for breakfast?'

Wary hazel eyes stared up at him. 'Who were you shouting at? Was that Eliza?'

Damn it, so much for giving himself some time to work out how to break the news. 'Eliza and I aren't friends anymore, Noah. I'm sorry.'

He reached for his nephew, but the boy ducked past him and ran down the landing. 'No! No, it's not fair!'

Jack reached the top of the stairs in time to see Noah dash past his mum. 'What's going on, what's all the shouting about?'

A wave of bleakness swept over him and he sank down on the top step. 'Eliza's husband showed up and they're getting back together.'

'*What*? Are you sure? I thought things were getting serious between the two of you.'

'I saw it with my own eyes, Mum.' A crash sounded from the kitchen and Jack jumped to his feet. 'Noah overhead us on the phone just now, and he's not taking it well.' He wasn't the only one.

His mum held up her hand. 'Leave him to me, love. You've enough on your plate. I was coming up to let you know Ben and Simon are here.' The two farmhands were there to help him load the cut lavender into the steam vats.

'Christ.' Jack scrubbed a hand over his face. 'Okay, you see to Noah and I'll get things started outside.' The harvest wouldn't wait for him to get his act together.

The morning flew past in a cloud of dust, tiny purple flowers and sweat. By the time Jack paused to gulp down a sandwich and a mug of tea, his mum reported they'd cut the whole north-east field and would likely get at least half of the north-west done before they stopped for the day. After draining the dregs of his cup, Jack handed it back to his mum. The muscles in his back had already started to nag so he rolled his shoulders before the break in constant movement caused them to seize up. By the end of the day he'd be feeling as crap on the outside as he did on the inside. 'How's Noah?'

She sighed. 'He was very upset. Once Mac got going with the cutting, I took him over to the garden but he wasn't very interested. He complained of a headache, so I let him go upstairs for a nap. He's slept right through lunch, but I didn't want to disturb him. Hopefully when he wakes up he'll be feeling a bit better.'

'Poor kid. I'll have to try and make it up to him somehow. This is all my fault.'

His mum shook her head. 'Don't blame yourself, love, these things happen in life and he'll bounce back soon enough. He's a lot more resilient than you give him credit for. I'm more worried about you.' There was more than a hint of moisture on her lashes.

'I'll be okay.' Jack forced out the lie. He wouldn't be okay, not for a bloody long time. He hooked an arm around his mum's shoulders and gave her a squeeze. 'I couldn't do this without you.'

The smile she gave him was watery. 'And you're a good boy. A good man, I should say. Your dad would be so proud if he could see you now.'

It was his turn to water a little. 'Behave yourself, Mum, or you'll have us both in floods. Look, I'd better get back to work.'

His mum reached up to pat his chest. 'All right, love, I'll leave you in peace. I've already put a lasagne in, and there's plenty of salad in the fridge to go with it. We can sit down for a proper family dinner and talk things out with Noah.'

'Cheers, Mum, you're a star.' Jack strode across the yard and was in the process of pulling his work gloves out of his back pocket when his phone rang. Seeing Eliza's name on the screen, all the fury he'd been swallowing down came roaring back to life. 'Can't you take a hint and just leave me the hell alone?'

'Oh God, Jack, there's been an accident!' Her breath panted in his ear as though she was running. 'It's Noah. You must come!'

'Noah? What the hell are you talking about. He's upstairs in his room…'

'No, he's not. He's out on the rocks!' The world stopped, or he kept moving, whatever it was Jack staggered as though out of sync with time. His vision narrowed, the edges going black as the wail of sirens filled his ears and he felt once more the heavy weight of the doctor's hand on his shoulder as he told him Jason was gone.

'Noah! No, darling, stay where you are, don't move!' Eliza's frantic cry snapped him back into reality.

'Where are you?' He spun on his heel, running flat out for the house.

'Top end of the beach, near the car park. Noah's hurt, I have to get down there. Please, Jack, hurry!' She was gone before he could reply.

'Keys, keys!' He thundered into the kitchen, startling his mum who was arms-deep in the washing-up bowl.

'They're on the dresser.' She nodded in that direction then reached for a tea towel. 'What is it, what's wrong?'

'Noah's had an accident on the beach. I don't know the details. I'll phone you when I get there.'

She trailed him to the door, white-faced with the same panic gripping his own stomach. 'Noah? But he's upstairs…' Her eyes widened in horror. 'Oh, Lord! I should've checked on him, but I thought it was best just to let him sleep.'

'Well, apparently he had other ideas. I've got to go.' He called the last over his shoulder as he sprinted for the Land Rover.

Please, God. Please, God. Like some kind of sick déjà vu, the same mantra he'd chanted on that awful drive to the hospital just a few short months ago after Jason's crash fell from his lips as he all but threw the heavy vehicle down the farm track and onto the winding streets of the town.

He made it as far as the car park closest to the promenade before his final shred of patience ran out behind an old woman trying to reverse into the narrowest of spaces. Forcing his way past her, he bumped up and over the curb at the bottom of the car park and abandoned the Land Rover on a patch of scruffy grass.

'You can't park there!' The uniformed attendant came bustling out of his little wooden shed as Jack ran past him out onto the promenade and began to frantically scan up and down the beach.

Eliza's description of her location had been vague—there were several patches of rocks along this part of the shore, but it was soon clear from the crowd gathering about halfway along the prom from him where the drama was. Ignoring the repeated complaints of the parking attendant, who'd followed him out of the car park, Jack broke into a run once more.

Reaching the outskirts of the people milling around by the steps, he shouldered his way through to the front and stopped dead in his tracks. Eliza was perched in a hollow between two high points on the rocks, one of her legs coated in blood. A white-faced Noah was cradled in her lap, with Bastian nosing at them both.

'Someone call an ambulance!' he shouted, as he ran down the steps.

'They're already on their way.' Jack waved a hand to acknowledge the information, his attention already on the slick stones in front of him. *What the hell had Noah been thinking*? He could hear him crying, hear Eliza speaking to him in soft voice, but they were too far for him to make out her words.

Crouching low, he began to crawl on hands and knees towards

the huddled pair. 'Shit!' A sharp edge grazed his hand, taking several layers of skin with it. Jack paused to check the small wound, belatedly remembering his work gloves were still in his pocket. He tugged them on, then resumed his climb.

'Be careful. That's where I slipped.' Eliza sounded shaky.

'Are you okay?' Jack made himself keep his eyes on the rocks and shale beneath his feet no matter how much his brain screamed at him to lift his head and check on them again. He reached the steepest part above them, and began to inch his way down the side. 'What the hell's going on?'

'I'm okay, but Noah says his arm hurts.' Jack slithered down the last couple of feet towards them, as Eliza pressed a kiss to Noah's head. Their eyes met over the crying boy, and he could see the stark fear in their green depths. 'He said he was coming to find me.'

Jack managed a tight nod. He wanted nothing more than to rip Noah from her arms and clutch him tight, but it would only scare the boy further. He settled a brief hand on the top of Noah's head. 'It's all right, buddy, I'm here.'

Bastian whined and nuzzled first Noah and then Jack. 'Come out the way, boy.' Jack eased the dog back.

Shouts came from the promenade. Jack glanced up to see Sam and Owen scrambling down towards them, he waved them back. 'It's bloody treacherous down here. Stay where you are!' He waited just long enough to be sure they did as they were told then turned back to Eliza. 'What the hell happened?'

'I don't know,' Eliza said. 'Someone came running into the pub, said there was an accident. I could hear Bastian barking like mad and then I saw…' She gulped in a deep breath. 'I saw Noah down here.'

'Swap places with me.' Jack needed to check Noah for himself. As they shuffled past each other, he did his best not to let their bodies touch. Being this close to her was fucking excruciating.

As Jack settled Noah in his lap, he remembered his mum and

grabbed his phone. She answered on the first ring. 'Jack?' The desperate worry in her voice cut him like a knife.

'It's all right, Mum. Noah's had a bit of a slip on the rocks and hurt his arm. I've got him.'

'Oh no, is he okay?'

Jack flicked his eyes towards Eliza, then away. 'Not sure yet. He's crying but talking okay. The paramedics are on their way.' A call came from behind him and he glanced around to see an ambulance pulling onto the promenade. 'They're here, Mum, so I'd better go. I'll call you in a bit when I know what's going on. Are you all right with everything there?'

'Yes, yes, don't even think about this place. I've got everything in hand. Call me when you can, sweetheart. Give Noah my love, and Jack…take care of yourself too, all right?'

Jack managed a smile. It didn't matter how old he got, she could make him feel like a little boy who just needed his mum to make it all better. 'I will, love you.'

He flicked a glance at Eliza. 'We need to get off these rocks.' Turning his attention to Noah, he softened his voice. 'Is it just your arm, buddy?'

Noah sniffled, then nodded. 'I fell on it and it hurts.'

'The ambulance is here now, and they'll fix you right up. Can you be a brave boy for me and stand up?' Jack braced and lifted Noah to his feet while Eliza supported his arm.

'Well done, Noah, you're doing so well.' The tenderness in Eliza's words shredded Jack in two. She would've made a wonderful mother for him—for those brothers and sisters Noah yearned for. No. There would be time enough to lick his wounds; his boy needed him and that was all he could think about right now.

Taking a deep breath to still his shakes, Jack took the delicate weight of Noah in his arms, doing his best not to jostle his arm. He whimpered. 'Sorry.'

Eliza moved up beside him. 'What can I do to help?'

He wanted to brush her off, to tell her he didn't need anything from her, but that would be just his pride talking. 'Can you keep Bastian out of the way?'

'Of course.' She bent to gather up the dog's lead then began to lead him back over the rocks. It was only then he noticed she was limping.

'Are you hurt?'

She turned, and he saw the front of her skirt was stained with blood. He'd been so fixated on Noah, and trying so damn hard not to look at her for more than a moment he'd forgotten she'd been hurt too. 'I cut my leg when I slipped, but I'm okay. It looks worse that it is.'

The need to comfort her overwhelmed him for a moment until he remembered it was no longer his place. A shard of pain sliced through his heart so sharp it threatened to fell him to his knees. 'Okay, be careful.'

'You too. I love you, Jack.' She turned away and began to inch her way back over the rocks.

Jack shuddered from head to foot, making Noah whimper again. 'Sorry, buddy. Shh, it's all right now, Uncle Jack's here.' The words of reassurance sounded hollow to his ears. *Uncle Jack's here, but he's got no bloody idea what he's doing.*

Chapter Twenty

Eliza tried her best to remain calm. The cut on her leg stung like hell, and wouldn't stop bleeding. She'd pressed a folded section of her skirt to it as instructed by Julie, the paramedic who'd met them at the end of the promenade, and waited patiently while the woman dealt with the difficult task of immobilising Noah's arm without causing him too much distress. Throughout it all, Jack sat beside her, stiff and monosyllabic unless he was talking to his nephew. Pressing her lips together so she wouldn't obey her heart's panicky demands to speak to him again, Eliza turned her attention to the crowd gathered around the ambulance. She wanted so desperately to explain what had happened between her and Martin, but now was neither the time nor the place. Once Noah had been seen to, hopefully Jack would calm down and she could clear up the mess between them.

Sam caught her eye and edged his way around the gathered group to crouch beside her. 'How are you doing, Sis?' He brushed back a strand of hair that kept blowing in her face.

'I'm okay.'

Sam squeezed her shoulder. 'I think they're going to start moving you guys soon. I heard the policemen saying they're going to move the crowd back in a minute so the ambulance can get through.

'Okay, thanks.' She touched Jack's arm, trying not to notice the infinitesimal twitch away from her touch. 'We'll be on the move soon, Sam says.'

'Good.' He ducked his head over Noah's. 'You hear that, buddy? We're going to get you to the hospital soon and get you all fixed up. You're being such a brave boy.'

Julie cleaned her hands, then pulled on a pair of thin gloves. 'Right, lovey,' she said to Eliza. 'Let's get your leg seen to.' Eliza let her cluck and fuss as she cleaned the wound, then wrapped it tight. Julie's constant stream of chatter flowed over her, and Eliza even found herself laughing a couple of times. The contrast between her gossipy, informal attitude and the swift, sure efficiency of her hands was marked, and it was clear to Eliza that even though Julie made her feel like she was the absolute centre of her attention, the woman knew everything that was going on around and behind them.

She finished with Eliza's leg and gave her a pat. 'You'll have to come along with us to the hospital. It's a deep cut and you'll need stitches—well, I say stitches, but they'll most likely glue it.'

'Okay, thanks.'

A sea of faces lined the edge of the railing to the left of the steps, and it was all she could do not to snap at them. What was it about the human psyche that made so many people treat potential tragedy as a spectator sport?

Her disgust at them vanished in a wave of warm hugs as her mum, Beth and Libby caught her up in their arms the moment she and Sam reached the top of the stairs. 'I'm okay, just a cut...Noah's got a broken arm, they think...' She tried her best to keep up with their flurry of questions, tried hard to focus on them and not on the man and boy at her back who held every inch of her heart.

'Oh, God, we were so worried. Are you sure you're okay?' Libby's skin was ghost-pale beneath her shocking hair, her eyes flicking past Eliza's shoulder to watch whatever was happening behind her.

'I'm okay, no need to fuss.'

A grumble rose from the crowd around them as the policemen began to herd them backwards. A handful of people started arguing, standing on tiptoes as they tried to see past the outstretched arms of the police. It was on the tip of her tongue to say something, but before she could, Libby started shouting.

'It's not a bloody soap opera, those are my friends down there, my family…' Her words choked off and it was Owen who dragged her into a hug. Libby fought with him for a second, before her arms wrapped tight around his waist and big ugly sobs broke free.

Eliza cast a glare at the crowd. A few shuffled their feet and looked away when her eyes fell on them, but the rest paid no notice—their attention glued to the drama on the rocks. 'Come on, love.' The paramedic urged her back in the direction of the ambulance.

'I'm really okay.' She wished he'd just leave her alone.

Implacable brown eyes met hers. 'You've had a shock. From the state of your skirt you've lost a bit of blood, so you're going to come and sit down and have a drink of water, and you're going to stay there until I say otherwise.'

God, she was being a brat, and making everyone's job that much harder. 'I'm sorry.'

The paramedic winked. 'You're all right, love. If I can handle the drunk tank on a Saturday night, I can manage you without any bother.'

She laughed. 'I bet you can. My folks run The Siren, the pub down the promenade so I have a good idea of what you're talking about. Not that we get much in the way of bother.' An idea occurred to her. 'In fact, next time you're all off shift you must come down for a drink—on the house.'

A genuine smile stretched his cheeks. 'That'll be smashing, love, cheers.' Eliza let the paramedic and his partner settle her on a fold-down seat in the ambulance. She accepted a bottle of water and took slow, steady sips as they instructed. The minutes seemed to drag on, and for every one that passed her anxiety ramped up a couple of notches. Desperate for distraction, she studied the inside of the vehicle, reading every notice, every label on the equipment, anything to keep the welling screams at bay.

There was a sudden flurry of activity outside, and—*thank, God*—Jack appeared with Noah in his arms and Julie one step behind them. 'Let me get out of the way.' Eliza was down and off the ramp, ignoring the frown from the male paramedic. Feeling useless, she hovered off to the side while Jack and the paramedics discussed getting Noah transported.

'Can I ride with him?' Jack asked. His expression was agonised, and Eliza wanted to do nothing more than reach out for him, but his entire focus was on Noah.

'Yes, of course, let's just get him settled and we'll be off.' The paramedic clapped his shoulder then followed his partner back up the ramp.

Eliza took her chance. 'Jack?'

He blinked at her almost like she was a stranger, then his face cleared. 'We'll be fine. Thanks for your help.' God, he sounded almost robotic.

Blind panic threatened to choke her and she cast around for a way to help, a way to stop him from dismissing her. 'Have you spoken to your mum yet?'

Fresh guilt darkened his hazel eyes, and she reached out for him as he fumbled for his phone. 'I called when we were down there. I promised to update her…'

Eliza placed her hand on his chest. 'Hey, stop now, you're doing the best you can. Let me call her, and she can come and meet you up at the hospital.'

He shook her off. 'She can't leave the farm unattended.' A scowl marred his face. '*Shit*, I've got the car.' Jack shoved his clenched hands into his hair looking for all the world like he was ready to pull it out from the roots. 'What a fucking mess.'

'Give me your keys. I'll call your mum and let her know what's going on and we'll sort everything out. You just focus on Noah.'

'I don't need your help,' he gritted out.

She swallowed hard against a surge of frustrated tears. This was all so bloody stupid. They could sort it all out within two minutes if she could only speak to him alone. 'Stop cutting your nose off to spite your face, Jack. If you don't want my help, at least let the others help you. Owen can take the Land Rover back to the farm and look after your mum, I'm sure Beth or Libby will go with him. I need Sam to drive me up to the hospital so I can get my leg stitched.'

Was that a flash of guilt in his eyes? Whatever, she was too tired to worry about it now. The shock and adrenaline were ebbing away, leaving her ready to drop.

'Fine.' He was moving towards the ambulance when she called his name. 'What?'

Eliza held out her hand. 'Keys.'

He dug them out of his pocket, tossed them to her and then he was being herded into the back of the ambulance. He paused halfway up the ramp. 'The dog? Where's Bastian?'

Eliza looked around, spotted Owen standing next to Libby, with the Labrador's lead wrapped around his wrist. 'Owen's got him, now go!' Jack hesitated, then ducked inside.

Clenching her fingers around the jagged edges of the keys, Eliza drew in a deep breath. She could do this. She just need to be like a shark and keep moving and she'd get through it. There'd be time enough later to go to pieces. She and Jack would sit down and talk, and everything would get back to normal. *Be a shark, not a jellyfish.* The ridiculous metaphor gave her the little boost she needed to face what she needed to do next.

Eliza limped over to where Sam and Beth stood with Libby and Owen. 'Can you drive me to the hospital?' she asked her brother.

He nodded. 'Of course.'

'Jesus Christ, did you see the terror on Jack's face? That's one of the many reasons I'm never having kids.' Owen was frowning at the departing ambulance. He shook himself, then turned towards her. 'What can I do? If you're going to be stuck up at the hospital, do you want me to help out behind the bar? I've never pulled a pint, but I can tidy up, keep the fridges stocked or whatever.'

Her spirits lifted another notch. Somehow, he'd gone from an arrogant stranger to an integral part of their little group. 'No, it's fine. Josh is working tonight so him and Mum can handle everything. Someone needs to retrieve Jack's Land Rover from the car park and take it back to the farm, though. It's their biggest harvest day so his mum is probably swamped'

'Consider it done. I'll stay up there as long as she needs me.' Owen tugged Bastian's lead. 'Let's get you home, eh, mate?'

Eliza handed him the keys. 'Thank you. Sam and I should be able to swing by and collect you on the way home from the hospital.'

He shrugged. 'Don't sweat it, I'll doss on the sofa if needed. Do you know Jack's reg number?'

She shook her head. 'It's black and probably covered in mud.'

'Like every other bloody Land Rover.' Owen grinned. 'I'll just point and press until one of them unlocks.'

Eliza watched him walk away. There was something about the set of his shoulders, the way he carried himself that made people instinctively move aside for him. She could do with borrowing a bit of his confidence right now.

He was maybe twenty feet away when Libby shouted. 'Hold up, I'll come with you,' and darted after him. Eliza watched Libby's pink and yellow head bob through the crowd for a moment then shrugged. She couldn't think about what had caused the sudden rapprochement between those two right now, there was too much else to sort out.

*

'I'll go and see the reception, see if I can find out how Noah is.' Eliza took a step forward before she stopped when Sam's arm blocked her.

'You are going to sit right here.' He steered her over to a row of plastic chairs. 'And you are going to wait for this nice triage nurse to see your leg.' Sam pointed at the spot of red showing through the bandage. 'I'll find out what's going on.'

Eliza subsided into the chair. 'You're so bloody bossy.'

'Big brother's prerogative. Behave.' He tugged one of her curls then strode away to the reception desk.

Two hours later, with the cut in her leg glued and re-wrapped, Eliza finally located the side room where Jack was perched by the side of Noah's bed. The boy's eyelids drooped, and the horrible pallor of his skin had faded somewhat. She tapped on the door frame. 'Hey.'

Jack glanced up, worry etched into thick grooves around his eyes. 'Hey.' He left Noah's bedside to lean against the wall next to her. 'How's your leg?'

'Okay. I might have a bit of a scar, but no lasting damage. How's Noah doing?'

Jack ran a hand through his hair. 'He's had an X-ray and some pain relief. They're coming any minute to fit a cast and then we're off to paediatrics. They've told me I can stay with him.' He glanced at the open door behind her. 'There must be a shop around here somewhere, so I'll try and find a toothbrush and stuff while they're plastering his arm.'

Eliza nudged the bag at her feet. 'Owen's been and gone with some stuff for you. I think your mum's adopted him, he was very happy about the prospect of lasagne for his dinner.'

That earned her the first smile she'd had from him all day. 'Mum's always happy if she's got someone to feed. Did he say how the harvest was going?'

'Everything seemed under control. I can call her with an update on Noah, and check?'

He shook his head. 'I'll speak to her.' His eyes strayed back to the small figure on the bed behind him then back to her. 'I need to get back to him.'

Unable to wait any longer, she took his hand. 'We need to talk, Jack.' He stared down at her hold like he might shake her off again, then all the fight seemed to go out of him. Taking a deep breath, she drew him outside the room.

Jack dropped her hand the moment they reached the corridor then propped himself against the wall with one shoulder. Eliza's gut lurched at the pain and sadness etched in his hazel eyes, in the grim lines bracketing his mouth. The harsh lights in the hallway made her tired eyes ache, the smell of disinfectant burned her nostrils. A pall hung in the air, as though all the collective pain, fear and loss experienced in the corridor had left a lingering presence.

Clenching her hands against the need to reach for his hand, she leaned against the wall beside him. 'It's not what you think between Martin and me, I don't know what you overheard but I sent him away. I've been to see a solicitor and I've made it clear to Martin that I want a divorce.'

'Don't.' Jack's voice was strained.

'Please, Jack, listen to me. I love you so much, Noah too. That's the future I want, nothing else.' She stretched on tiptoe to cup his face. 'Jack?'

Jack pressed his forehead to hers for a long minute. 'I love you too.' The elation filling her vanished when he spoke again. 'But I don't know how to do this. I don't know how I can take care of Noah, run the farm and be with you. It's just too much.'

'I know it's been hard, Jack, but we can work it out. Please, don't give up on us when we're only just getting started.' She reached for him, but he stepped back, shattering her dreams to pieces in the process.

'We tried that and look what happened. Because of our relationship, Noah got hurt. Jesus Christ, he might have bloody died!

I'm sorry I got the wrong end of the stick about you and Martin, but all this mess has made things clear to me. I have to put Noah first.' Jack closed his eyes for a brief second. When he opened them again, the finality in them was stark. 'Having it all isn't for people like us, Eliza. We have too many responsibilities.' He leaned forward to brush a bittersweet kiss over her lips. 'I'm so sorry, I wish things could be different.' And with that, he walked out of her life, closing the door of Noah's room behind him.

Eliza let everything roll over her. All the stress and strains of the day, the dull pain in her leg she'd been trying to ignore all afternoon, her disappointment with Jack for not being willing to fight for them. Fingers digging into the cold wall behind her, she let it come, didn't try to fight it. Tears came and went in a hot rush, and she let them flow.

It might have been five minutes later, might have been an hour, but Eliza finally steadied herself. She wiped the tears from her cheeks and straightened her spine. Jack might not be willing to fight for them, but she bloody well was.

Chapter Twenty-One

'Uncle Jack?'

Blinking away the gritty feeling in his eyes, Jack straightened up in the high-backed padded chair and winced at the kinks in his spine. The nurses had made up a pull-out bed for him, but he'd dozed off before managing to get in it. A soft lamp shining on the bedside table illuminated the pale skin of Noah's face. He was still nearly as white as the sheets cocooning him. 'I'm here, buddy. Do you want a drink?'

Noah nodded. Jack braced a hand behind his nephew's back with one hand, holding out a plastic cup with a straw in the other. The boy sipped a bit, then settled back against his pillow. 'Where's Eliza?'

'She had to go home and rest her leg.' The lie tasted ugly on his tongue, but Jack didn't have the energy for anything else.

'Will she be back tomorrow?' The hopefulness in his voice sliced Jack to the bone.

'I don't think so, buddy.' Damn. He should've stuck with his original instinct and not let them meet until he'd been sure of everything. He'd got the boy's hopes up—got his own bloody hopes up—and now he'd have to deal with the fallout.

'I didn't mean for her to get hurt.' Noah's voice lowered to a whisper.

Jack placed his hand on Noah's leg. 'Hey, it's not your fault, buddy. It was an accident. What were you doing down on the rocks?'

Face screwed up, Noah began to cry. 'I wanted to see the sandcastles. I didn't mean to let go of Bastian's lead. He ran away, and I tried to catch him. I'm sorry, I didn't mean to be naughty…' The rest of his words were lost in deep sobs.

Jesus. A fresh wave of guilt hit Jack as he bent over and gathered Noah gently in his arms, careful not to jostle his plastered arm where it rested on a pillow next to him. 'Shh. It's okay, buddy. Don't cry now.' Cursing himself for not taking better care of him, he held Noah, rocking him until the tears subsided and he quieted enough for Jack to lay him back on the pillow and tuck him back in.

He buried his face into the crisp white sheets and bit back a groan. He'd been an idiot, and a coward. Let his fear rule him. And it hadn't just been his fear over Noah, though God knew that had been crippling enough. When he'd seen that blood streaming down Eliza's leg, seen Sam and Owen ready to scramble over the rocks heedless of their own safety, he'd panicked about all the new people he suddenly had in his life to care for. More family meant more risk of something bad happening and his soul had rebelled against it.

And ending up back in this damn hospital where he'd had to stand at a little glass window and identify Jason's pale lifeless body just a few months ago had been the final straw. Eliza had stood there and offered her heart to him, and he'd pushed her away unable to stand the stink of disinfectant, the rush of painful memories and the sight of her blood so bright against the white cotton of her skirt.

'Bloody idiot.'

'You did a swear, Uncle Jack.' Noah's shocked tone made him realise he'd spoken aloud.

Jack raised his head. 'Don't tell Nanna, okay?'

'Okay, I promise.' Noah crooked his little finger for Jack to hook his around and they shook on it.

'Go to sleep now, buddy, or the nurses might not let me take you home tomorrow.' He smoothed the sheets over Noah's body, then held his hand until he slept. With a sigh, he tumbled onto the pull-out bed, not bothering to do more than toe off his boots. He needed to take his own advice and sleep. Tomorrow would be another long day, and when it was over he would need to track down Eliza and do whatever it took to persuade her to give him a second chance. Hopefully, he'd have better luck than Martin.

Jack tugged on his seatbelt to give him enough room to lean forwards between the front seats. 'Just over the top of this hill, and you should see the farmhouse.'

The taxi driver nodded. 'All right, mate. And just park in front?'

'Yeah, anywhere on the driveway will be great.' He settled back in his seat. Noah nuzzled into his arm. He'd been clingy since waking up. Jack didn't mind, he was feeling pretty bloody clingy himself that morning.

Doubts racked him. He'd failed at the first hurdle, made all those promises and balked the moment things got difficult. If Eliza told him to sling his hook, who could blame her?

'Behind this little hatchback, yeah?' The taxi driver asked.

Hatchback? Jack shook off his blues to stare out the window, a sudden rush of hope stealing the breath from his lungs. Behind the hulking mass of his Land Rover sat Eliza's little blue car. He couldn't get that lucky, could he? Pulse thudding like he'd run a marathon, Jack somehow managed to navigate his way through paying the taxi driver and getting Noah out of the car without banging his arm.

It could mean anything, she could've popped in to check on his mum, or it might not even be her. It could be Sam come to collect Owen. Hoisting their bag onto his shoulder, Jack took

Noah by the hand and led him into the farmhouse. The distinctive silence of an empty building struck him as he walked into the kitchen. A host of mugs resting upside down on the draining rack was the only sign of recent life. 'Let's go and find Nanna, shall we?'

Jack led Noah back outside. The moment they turned the corner of the farmhouse the strains of a radio and laughter drifted on the air. He followed the sounds to the open door of the processing barn and stopped dead. Sam and Owen stood beside the vats, each one leaning on a pitchfork. Their clothes were coated in dust, faces streaked with sweat and dirt. Laughter rose from the benches where his mum was showing Beth and Libby how to decant and separate the essential oil from the weaker lavender water solution it floated upon.

He took them all in in the blink of an eye, his focus all for the woman clad in baggy denim dungarees, a bright red cloth bound around her head to keep her sandy curls off her face. Bits of lavender clung to the legs of her trousers, and her once-white trainers were a dusty brown from wielding the wide-headed broom in her hands. Red-faced with exertion, she looked hot and bothered, and was the most gorgeous sight he'd ever laid his eyes on. As though sensing his presence, she glanced up and a wide grin drew his attention to the beautiful plumpness of her mouth. 'There you are!'

She said it like it was the most natural thing in the world, like their conversation the previous night hadn't happened. Like she had been waiting for him, like she would always be waiting for him if he would only let her.

Noah slipped his grasp and barrelled into the shed to throw his arms around Eliza. 'You're okay, you're okay!' There was a catch in his voice as Eliza ducked down to cuddle him close.

'Yes, sweetheart, I'm fine. Just a silly scratch, nothing more.' She drew back. 'But what about you? Look at this cast on your arm, does it feel funny?' And with just a couple of words, she distracted Noah from his worries and he was chatting a mile a minute about his adventures at the hospital. Jack's mum hurried over, and Noah was swept away with her to show off his trophy to the others, leaving Jack and Eliza facing each other.

'I'm sorry.' The words weren't nearly enough to express everything he was feeling, but he had to start somewhere.

'It's okay.' She smiled so sweetly, and he ached to drag her into his arms and claim that smile for his own.

Knowing that he could, he allowed himself to relax and close the distance between them. His hands found the perfect hollow of her waist even through the baggy denim. 'I'm an idiot.'

She nestled closer against his chest. 'I'll let you off…this time.'

'Eliza—' All the apologies he owed her, all the promises to do better, to *be* better were cut off by the noisy 'toot toot' of a car horn in the yard.

Keeping her close in his arms—because there was no way in hell he was letting her go again anytime soon—Jack swung around to see a man about his mum's age slide out of the front seat and walk around to open the back doors. He reappeared carrying a large cardboard tray filled with white paper parcels. 'Grub's up!' the man yelled cheerily as he entered the shed.

'Dad! You're a bloody superstar, I'm so hungry my guts are about to gnaw their way out.' Libby skirted around the bench to greet the man with a smacking kiss on the cheek as he placed the tray down on an empty spot.

'Such a charming way with words,' Owen drawled, as he reached for one of the wrappers. Libby slapped his hand away to snatch up the package for herself then poked her tongue out at him. Owen turned to Jack. 'So, Jack, looks like we might be seeing a bit more of each other. Your mum and I have been chatting about doing up the cottage like you mentioned. She's promised to pay me in lasagne, so I've offered to do the plans for free.'

Jack might have worried about her reaction, but the huge grin on his mum's face put paid to that. 'I know we talked about it before,' she said, 'but I wasn't sure what with Jason and everything how you'd manage on your own.'

'I don't want you to feel like I'm pushing you out...'

'Nonsense!' She shook her head. 'Owen reckons we can have the cottage ship-shape by Christmas. I'll be glad of my own space, and I'm sure you will too.' The look she cast towards Eliza spoke volumes.

'We'll talk about this later,' he cut in desperately, before she said something completely outrageous. He and Eliza were only just finding their way together, and he come so close to throwing it all away. It was too soon to be thinking about moving her in... wasn't it? Although by the time Christmas came around...

'I think it sounds like a great idea.'

He stared down into Eliza's smiling eyes. It was hard to tell which smudges on her cheeks were dirt and which were the freckles he'd come to love so much. He could check later, perhaps if he could persuade her to share a shower with him. Once she moved in with him, he'd be able to shower with her every morning. *Christmas can't come soon enough.*

A warm blush suffused her pale skin. 'Hold that thought, whatever it is. Come on, I'm starving.'

Head whirling with plans for their future, Jack let Eliza tow him away. The scent of vinegar and crisp, hot batter filled his nostrils, and his stomach grumbled, reminding him he hadn't eaten anything but half a stale sandwich and a nasty cup of coffee the night before. The man who'd pulled up in the van offered him a paper-wrapped parcel then stuck out his hand. 'Mick Stone, pleasure to meet you. When my Libby told me what had happened, I was happy to do my bit to help out.' He gestured at the food, looking a bit embarrassed at his own enthusiasm. 'It's not much...'

Jack grasped his hand and shook it. 'It is, though. It's so much more than I could've asked for.' Mick retreated with a pleased smile on his face to dish out the rest of the food.

Eliza's arms slipped around Jack's waist, and he turned in her hold to stare down into her moss green gaze. 'The thing about family is that you don't need to ask for help, we're just going to do it anyway.'

The impact of that simple truth rocked him. Putting his still-wrapped food on the bench beside them, Jack drew Eliza away from the noisy impromptu meal. He led her to the other side of the shed to a spot where they'd be hidden from the others by the heavy curtains of drying lavender. Taking Eliza into his arms, he backed her against the wall and followed until his body rested hard against her.

Seeking the soft skin on the side of her neck, he pressed a kiss to her pulse. The breathy catch in her throat turned everything inside him hot and tight and he nibbled higher. 'Eliza…?' He whispered her name against the shell of her ear, followed it with a quick trace of his tongue.

'Yes.'

He grinned against her cheek. There was no hesitation in her response. 'You don't even know what I was going to ask you yet.'

She nestled closer. 'It doesn't matter what you ask me, Jack, the answer will always be yes.'

Overwhelmed, he whispered a silent prayer to whatever entity might be listening. He didn't know what he'd done to deserve this—to deserve her—but he would give thanks every day for the rest of his life. Turning his mouth, he captured her lips and sank into the sweet warmth of his future. The scent of lavender wreathed around him, blending with Eliza's own unique perfume into a marker he would, from that moment on, always associate with coming home.

Acknowledgements

Welcome back to Lavender Bay!

I am so delighted with all the wonderful feedback I received for *Spring at Lavender Bay* and for the love you've shown to Beth, Eliza and Libby. The more I get to know them, the more delighted I am to share their stories with you. I hope you love Eliza and Jack because they both really deserve their happy ending.

To my husband. I never knew how big I could dream until I met you. Thanks, bun xx

To my number one fan, my mum. Thank you for everything you do for me, it means the world.

To my fabulous editor, Charlotte Mursell. Thank you for your endless patience and support. We got there in the end! Prosecco is on me next time x

Team HQ – Superstars one and all. I see you x

To Rachel, Cathy, Darcie, Virginia, Nat, Jean and the other A** Kicking Word Wranglers. Without you, this book simply wouldn't have happened. Have I mentioned the deadline for Book Three???

And, as ever, to you the reader – that the words I write find a place in your hearts is a gift beyond measure. Thank you x

Turn the page for an exclusive extract from *Spring at Lavender Bay*, the first book in the enchanting Lavender Bay series from Sarah Bennett…

Chapter One

'Sort this for me, Beth.' A green project folder thumped down on the side of Beth Reynold's desk, sending her mouse arrow skittering across the screen and scattering the calculation in her head. Startled, she glanced up to see a wide expanse of pink-shirted back already retreating from her corner desk pod. Darren Green was her team leader, and the laziest person to grace the twelfth floor of Buckland Sheridan in the three years she'd been working there. She eyed the folder with a growing sense of trepidation. Whatever he'd dumped on her—she glanced at the clock—at quarter to four on a Friday afternoon was unlikely to be good news. Well, it would just have to wait. Sick and tired of Darren expecting her to drop everything, she ground her teeth and forced herself to ignore the file and focus on the spreadsheet in front of her.

Fifteen minutes later, with the workbook updated, saved and an extract emailed to the client, Beth straightened up from her screen. Her right ankle ached from where she'd hooked her foot behind one of the chair legs and there was a distinct grumble from the base of her spine. Shuffling her bottom back from where she'd perched on the edge of the cushioned seat, she gave herself a mental telling off. There was no point in the company spending money on a half-decent orthopaedic chair when she managed to contort herself into the worst possible sitting positions.

Her eyes strayed to the left where the file lurked like a malevolent toad. If she turned just so, she could accidentally catch it with her elbow and knock it into the wastepaper basket sitting beside her desk. Brushing off the tempting idea, she grabbed her mug and stood up. Her eyes met Ravi's over the ugly blue partition dividing their desks and she waggled her cup at him. 'Fancy a brew?'

He glanced at his watch, then laughed, showing a set of gorgeous white teeth. 'Why am I even checking the time; it's not like I'm going to refuse a coffee, is it?'

Everything about Ravi was gorgeous, she mused on the way to the kitchenette which served their half of the huge open-plan office. From his thick black hair and matching dark eyes, to the hint of muscle beneath his close-fitting white shirt—the only thing more gorgeous than Ravi was his boyfriend, Callum.

Though she'd never admit it to anyone other than Eliza and Libby, she had a huge crush on her co-worker. Not that she would, or could, ever do anything about it, but that wasn't the point. Ravi being unobtainable and entirely uninterested in her as anything other than a friend and co-worker made him perfectly safe. And it gave her a good excuse for not being interested in anyone else. An excuse to avoid dipping her badly-scorched toes back into the dating pool. Once had been more than enough.

Until she recovered from the unrequited attraction, there wasn't room in her heart for anyone else. She could marvel at the length of the black lashes framing his eyes and go home alone, entirely content to do so. He was the best non-boyfriend she'd had since Mr Lassiter, her Year Ten history teacher. He also provided a foil on those rare occasions she spoke to her mother these days. Lying to her didn't sit well with Beth, but it was better than the alternative—being nagged to 'get back on the horse', to 'put herself out there', to 'settle down'.

Eliza and Libby knew all about both the hopeless crush and her using a fake relationship with Ravi as a shield against her mother's interference. And if they didn't entirely support the white lie, they at least understood the reasons behind it. Just like they'd known everything about her since the first day they'd started at primary school together. They knew what her mum was like, and they understood why Beth preferred the harmless pretence of an unrequited crush. She'd never been one for boyfriends growing up, and the more her mum had pushed her, the more she'd dug her heels in.

Beth had been eight years old when her dad had walked out with not so much as a backward glance. Her mum had spent the rest of Beth's formative years obsessed with finding a replacement for him—only one who could provide the financial security she craved. Before he'd left, there'd been too many times her mum had gone to pay a bill only to find the meagre contents of their account missing. If Allan Reynolds hadn't frittered it away in the bookies, he'd blown it on his next get-rich-quick scheme. Given the uncertainty of those early years, she had some sympathy for her mum's position. If only she'd been less mercenary about it. A flush of embarrassed heat caught Beth off guard as she remembered the not-so whispered comments about Linda Reynolds' shameless campaign to catch the eye—and the wallet—of newly-widowed Reg Walters, her now husband.

Determined not to emulate Linda, Beth had clung fiercely to the idea of true love. She had even thought she'd found it for a while, only to have her heart broken in the most clinical fashion the previous summer. Trying to talk to her mother about it had been an exercise in futility. Linda had no time for broken hearts. Move on, there's plenty more fish in the sea. She'd even gone so far as to encourage Beth to flirt with her useless lump of a boss for God's sake. Beth shuddered at the very idea. In the end, she'd resorted to making up a romance with Ravi just to keep Linda off her back.

Beth clattered the teaspoon hard against Ravi's coffee cup, scattering her wandering thoughts. Balancing the tea and coffee mugs in hand, she returned to her coveted corner of the office. People had offered her bribes for her spot, but she'd always refused, even if sitting under the air-conditioning tract meant she spent half the summer in a thick cardigan. Her cubicle with a view over the grimy rooftops of London was worth its weight in gold. When her work threatened to overwhelm her, she needed only to swivel on her chair and glance out at the world beyond to remind herself how much she'd achieved. The ant-sized people on the pavement scurried around, travelling through the arteries and veins of the city, pumping lifeblood into the heart of the capital.

Moving to London had been another sop to Linda. Based on her mother's opinion, a stranger would believe Lavender Bay, the place where Beth had been born and raised, was akin to hell on earth. A shabby little seaside town where nothing happened. She'd moved there after marrying Beth's father and being stuck on the edge of the country had chafed her raw, leaving her feeling like the world was passing her by. When her new husband, Reg, had whisked her off to an apartment in Florida, weeks before Beth's fourteenth birthday, all of Linda's dreams had come true. She'd never stopped to consider her daughter's dreams in the process.

Though she'd never been foolish enough to offer a contradictory opinion, Beth had always loved Lavender Bay. The fresh scent of the sea blowing in through her bedroom window; the sweeter, stickier smells of candy floss and popcorn during high season. Running free on the beach, or exploring the woods and rolling fields which provided a backdrop to their little town. And, of course, there was Eleanor.

The older woman had taken Beth under her wing and given her a Saturday morning job at the quirky seaside emporium she owned. The emporium had always been a place of wonder to Beth, with new secrets to be discovered on the crowded shelves.

Hiding out in there had also given her a haven from Linda's never-ending parade of boyfriends. Beth suspected she'd been offered the few hours work more to provide Eleanor with some companionship than any real requirement for help.

When it had looked like Beth would have to quit school because of Linda and Reg's relocation plans, Eleanor had intervened and offered to take her in. Linda had bitten her hand off, not wanting the third-wheel of an awkward teenage daughter to interrupt her plans. It hadn't mattered a jot that a single woman nearing seventy might not be the ideal person to raise a shy fourteen-year-old. Thankfully, Eleanor had been young at heart and delighted to have Beth live with her. She'd treated her as the daughter she'd never had, and Beth had soaked up the love she offered like a sponge.

Under Eleanor's steady, gentle discipline Beth had finally started to come into her own, Desperate not to disappoint her mum in the way everyone else had seemed to do, Beth worked hard to get first the GCSEs and then A levels she'd needed in order to go to university. With no real career prospects in Lavender Bay, she'd headed for the capital, much to Linda's delight. Her mother's influence had been too pervasive and those early lessons in needing a man to complete her had stuck fast. When Charlie had approached her one night in a club, Beth had been primed and ready to fall in love.

For the first couple of years working at the prestigious project management company of Buckland Sheridan, she'd convinced herself that these were her own dreams she was following, and that her hard work and diligence would pay off. Lately she'd come to the realisation she was being used whilst others reaped the rewards. Demotivated and demoralised, she was well and truly stuck in a cubicle-shaped rut.

Raising the mug of tea to her lips, Beth watched as the street lights flickered on below, highlighting the lucky workers spilling out of the surrounding office blocks. Some rushing towards the tube station at the end of the road, others moving with equal enthusiasm in the opposite direction towards the pubs and restaurants, rubbing their hands together at the thought of twofers and happy hour. Good luck to them. Those heady nights in crowded bars with Charlie and his friends had never really suited her.

Checking the calendar, Beth bit back a sigh. She was overdue a weekend visit to the bay, not that Eleanor would ever scold or complain about how much time it had been since she'd last seen her. She'd tuck Beth onto the sofa with a cup of tea and listen avidly to all the goings on in her life. Not that there'd been much of anything to report other than work lately. Unless she counted the disastrous Christmas visit to see her mum and Reg in Florida, and Beth had spent the entire month of January trying to forget it.

Even surrounded by Charlie's upper-class pals she'd never felt more like a fish out of water than she had during that week of perma-tanned brunches and barbecues. She would much rather have gone back to Lavender Bay and Eleanor's loving warmth, but Linda had organised a huge party to celebrate her 10th wedding anniversary to Reg, and insisted she needed Beth by her side. Having people believe she had the perfect family had always mattered more to Linda than making it a reality.

With a silent promise to call Eleanor for a long chat on Sunday, Beth drained her tea and turned back to her work. The dreaded contents of the file Darren had dumped on her had to be better than thinking about than the surprise date her mum had set her up with on New Year's Eve. She glanced across the partition between their desks. Ravi might be gay, but at least he had all his own teeth and didn't dye his hair an alarming shade Beth had only been able to describe to a hysterical Eliza and Libby as 'marmalade'.

Ravi caught her eye and smiled. 'Hey, Beth?' He pointed to the phone tucked against his ear. 'Callum wants to know if you're busy on Sunday. We're having a few friends around for a bite to eat. Nothing fancy.' They exchanged a grin. Nothing fancy in

Callum's terms would be four courses followed by a selection of desserts.

'Sounds great. Can I let you guys know tomorrow?' It wasn't like she had anything else planned, but going on Darren's past record whatever was hiding in the file he'd dumped on her would likely mean she'd be working most of the weekend.

Ravi nodded and conveyed her reply into the handset. He rolled his eyes at something Callum said in reply and Beth propped her hands on her hips. 'If he's telling you about this great guy he knows who'd be just perfect for me then I'm not coming. Not even for a double helping of dessert.' The only person more disastrous at matchmaking than her mother was Callum.

Her friend laughed. 'You're busted!' he said into the phone then tilted it away from his mouth to say to Beth in a teasing, sing-song voice, 'He's a very fine man with good prospects. All his own teeth!' She closed her eyes, regretting confessing all about the New Year's date to Ravi on their first day back after the Christmas break. He'd never let her live it down.

She shook her head. 'Aren't they all? I'll message you tomorrow.' Which was as good as accepting the invitation. There was always a good mix at their parties and the atmosphere relaxed. Leaving Ravi to finish off his conversation, she turned her attention to the dreaded file.

Three hours and several coins added to the swear jar on her desk later, she decided she had enough information together to be able to complete the required draft report and presentation at home. Darren had left the office on the dot of five, laughing with his usual pack of cronies as they made their way towards the lifts. He'd not even bothered to check in with her on his way out, assuming she would do whatever was necessary to ensure their department was ready for the client meeting on Tuesday. The project had been passed to him by one of the directors a fortnight previously, but either through incompetence or arrogance he'd chosen to do absolutely nothing with it.

Stuffing the file, a stack of printouts, and her phone into the backpack she used in lieu of a handbag, Beth swapped her heels for the comfy trainers under her desk and disconnected her laptop from the desk terminal. Coat on and scarf tucked around the lower half of her face, she waved goodnight to Sandie, the cleaner, and trudged out of the office.

The worst of the commuting crowd had thinned so at least she had a seat on the train as it hurtled through the dank Victorian tunnels of the Underground. The heating had been turned up full blast against the February chill but, like most of the hardened travellers around her, Beth ignored the sweat pooling at the base of her spine and kept her eyes glued on the screen of her phone. Music filled her ears from the buds she'd tucked in the moment she'd stepped on board, drowning out the scritch-scritch of a dozen other people doing exactly the same thing.

She never felt further from home than when crammed in with a load of strangers who made ignoring each other into an artform. In Lavender Bay everyone waved, nodded or smiled at each other, and passing someone you knew without stopping for a ten-minute chat was unthinkable. After three years in London, there were people she recognised on her regular commute, but they'd never acknowledged each other. Nothing would point a person out as not belonging faster than being so gauche as to strike up a conversation on public transport.

The anonymity had appealed at first, a sign of the sophistication of London where people were too busy doing important stuff to waste their precious time with inane conversations. Not knowing the daily minutiae of her friends and neighbours, the who'd said what to whom, was something she'd never expected to miss quite so much. Having everyone in her business had seemed unbearable throughout her teenage years, especially with a mother like Linda. But on nights like this, knowing even the people who shared the sprawling semi in the leafy suburbs where she rented a room for an eyewatering amount wouldn't be interested in anything other than whether she'd helped herself to their milk, loneliness rode her hard.

Cancelling the impending pity party, Beth swayed with the motion of the train as she made her way towards the doors when they approached her station. A quick text to Eliza and Libby would chase the blues away. The odds of either of them having Friday night plans were as slim as her own so a Skype chat could probably be arranged. Smiling at the thought, she stepped out of the shelter of the station and into the freezing January evening air.

Clad in a pair of her cosiest pyjamas, Beth settled cross-legged in the centre of her bed as she waited for her laptop to connect to the app. The piles of papers she'd been working from for the past hour had been replaced by the reheated takeaway she'd picked up on her way home, and a large bottle of ice-cold Sauvignon Blanc. With perfect timing, Eliza's sweetly-beaming face popped up in one corner of her screen just as Beth shovelled a forkful of chow mien into her mouth. 'Mmmpf.' Not the most elegant of greetings, but it served to spread that smile into an outright laugh.

'Hello, Beth, darling!' Eliza glanced back over her shoulder as though checking no one was behind her then leant in towards the camera to whisper. 'I'm so glad you texted. Martin's obsessed with this latest bloody game of his, so you've saved me from an evening of pretending to be interested in battle spells and troll hammers.' She rolled her eyes then took a swig from an impressively large glass of rosé to emphasise her point.

Fighting her natural instinct to say something derogatory about her best friend's husband, Beth contented herself with a mouthful of her own wine. It wasn't that she disliked Martin, per se. It was almost impossible to dislike someone so utterly inoffensive, she just wished her friend didn't seem so unhappy. The two of them had made a sweet couple at school, but Beth had always assumed the attraction would wear off once Eliza gained a bit more confidence and expanded her horizons beyond the delicate wash of purple fields encircling their home town.

When Martin had chosen the same university as them both though, her friend had declared herself delighted so Beth had swallowed her misgivings and watched as they progressed to an engagement and then marriage. They'd moved north for Martin's job, and fallen into a kind of domestic routine more suited to a middle-aged couple. Eliza never said a word against him, other than the odd jokey comment about his obsession with computer games, but there was no hiding the flatness in her eyes. Beth suspected she was unhappy, but after her own spectacular crash-and-burn romance, she was in no position to pass judgment on anyone else's relationship.

Opting yet again for discretion over valour, Beth raised her glass to toast her friend. 'Bad luck for you, but great for me. I miss you guys so much and after the day I've had I need my girls for a moan.'

A sympathetic frown shadowed Eliza's green eyes. 'What's that horrible boss of yours done this time?' She held up a hand almost immediately. 'No, wait, don't tell me yet, let's wait for Libs. She'll be along any minute, I'm sure.'

Beth checked her watch before forking up another mouthful of noodles. It was just after half past nine. The fish and chip shop Libby helped her father to run on the seafront at Lavender Bay closed at 9 p.m. out of season. With any luck she'd be finished with the clean up right about now…

The app chirped to signal an incoming connection and a pale and harassed-looking Libby peered out from a box on the screen. 'Hello, hello! Sorry I'm late. Mac Murdoch decided to try and charm his wife with a saveloy and extra chips to make up for staying two pints over in The Siren.'

Beth's snort of laughter was echoed by Eliza as she pictured the expression on Betty Murdoch's face when her husband rolled in waving the greasy peace offering. Considering she looked like a bulldog chewing a wasp on the best of days, she didn't fancy Mac's chances.

Eliza waggled her eyebrows. 'She won't be sharing his sausage anytime soon.'

'Oh, God! Eliza!' Libby clapped her hands over her eyes, shaking her head at the same time. 'That's an image I never wanted in my poor innocent brain!' The three of them burst into howls of laughter.

Gasping for breath, Beth waved a hand at her screen. 'Stop, stop! You'll make me spill my bloody wine.' Which was a horrifying enough thought to quell them all into silence as they paused to take a reverent drink from their glasses.

Libby lifted a hank of her hair, dyed some shade of blue that Beth had no name for, and gave it a rueful sniff. 'So, I get why I'm all alone apart from the smell of fried fish, but what's up with you two that we're hanging out on this fine Friday night?'

'Work,' Beth muttered, digging into her takeaway.

'Age of Myths and bloody Legends.' Eliza said.

'Ah.' Libby nodded in quiet sympathy. She knew enough about them both that nothing else was needed. People who didn't know them well found their continuing friendship odd. Those bonds formed in the classroom through proximity and necessity often stretched to breaking point once they moved beyond the daily routine. Beth and Eliza had left their home town of Lavender Bay, whilst Libby stayed at home to help her father after the untimely death of her mum to cancer when Libby had been just fourteen.

They made a good trio—studious Beth, keeping her head down and out of trouble; warm, steady Eliza who preferred a book or working on a craft project to almost anything else; and snarky Libby with her black-painted nails and penchant for depressing music. She'd taken immense pride in being Lavender Bay's only goth, but both Beth and Eliza had seen beyond the shield of baggy jumpers and too-much eyeliner to the generous heart beneath it. Though it might be difficult to tell from the hard face she turned to the world, Libby was the most sensitive of them all.

A sound off-screen made Libby turn around. She glanced back quickly at the screen. 'Hold on, Dad wants something.' Beth took the opportunity to finish off her takeaway while they waited for her.

Pushing the heavy purple-shaded fringe out of her red-rimmed eyes, Libby stared into the camera in a way that it made it feel like she was looking directly at Beth. 'Oh, Beth love. I've got some bad news, I'm afraid.'

A sense of dread sent a shiver up her spine and Beth took another quick mouthful of wine. 'What's up, not your dad?'

Her friend shook her head. 'No. He's fine. Miserable as ever, grumpy old git.' There was no hiding the affection in her voice. Mick Stone was a gruff, some would say sullen, bear of a man, but he loved his girl with a fierce, protective heart. 'It's about Eleanor. She had a funny turn this evening as she was closing up the emporium, and by the time the ambulance arrived she'd gone. Massive heart attack according to what Dad's just been told. I'm so sorry, Beth.' Streaks of black eyeliner tracked down Libby's cheeks as the tears started to flow.

The glass slipped from Beth's limp fingers, spilling the last third of her wine across her knees and onto the quilt. 'But…I only spoke to her last week and she sounded fine. Said she was a bit tired, but had been onto the school about getting a new Saturday girl in to help her. It can't be…'

'Oh, Beth.' If Eliza said any more, Beth didn't hear it as she closed her eyes against the physical pain of realisation. Eleanor Bishop had been a fixture in her life for so long, Beth had believed her invincible. From the first wonder-filled visits she'd made as a little girl to the sprawling shop Eleanor ran on the promenade, to the firm and abiding friendship when she'd taken Beth on as her Saturday girl. The bright-eyed spinster had come to mean the world to her. All those years of acting as a sounding board when Beth was having problems at home, dispensing advice without judgement, encouraging her to spread her wings and fly, letting Beth know she always had a place to return to it. A home.

If she'd only known, if she'd only had some kind of warning, she would have made sure Eleanor understood how much she meant to her, how grateful she was for her love and friendship. Now though, it was too late. She'd never hear Eleanor's raucous, inelegant laugh ringing around the emporium as she made a joke to one of her customers, or passed comment on the latest shenanigans of the band of busybodies who made up the Lavender Bay Improvement Society.

The unpleasant dampness of her pyjama trouser leg finally registered, and she righted the glass with trembling fingers. Through the haze of tears obscuring her vision, she saw the worried, tear-stained faces of her friends staring back at her from the computer screen. 'I'm all right,' she whispered, knowing they would hear the lie in her voice if she spoke any louder. 'Poor Eleanor.'

Libby scrubbed the cuff of her shirt beneath one of her eyes. 'I don't think she suffered, at least. Dad reckoned she was gone before she would have known anything about it. At least there's that.' Her voice trailed off and then she shook her head angrily. 'What a load of bollocks. Why do we say such stupid things at times like this?' Noisy sobs followed her outburst and Beth ached at the distance between them.

Eliza pressed her fingers to the screen, as though she could somehow reach through and offer comfort. 'Don't cry, darling, I can't bear it.' She addressed her next words to Beth. 'What are you going to do about the arrangements? I'm sure Mum and Dad will be happy to host the wake. Eleanor doesn't have any other family, does she?'

Eliza was right. Eleanor had been an only child, never married and apart from some distant cousins she'd mentioned whose parents had emigrated to Australia somewhere under the old Ten Pound Poms scheme, there was no one. Which meant one thing—it would be up to Beth to make sure her beloved friend had a decent send off. She sucked in a breath as she shoved her sorrow down as deep as she could manage. There would be time to deal with that later. 'I'll sort it out. I don't think it can be Monday as I'll have to straighten up a few things at work, but I'll be down on the first train on Tuesday morning. Can you let your dad know, Libs? See if he'll have a word with Mr Bradshaw for me.' There was only one funeral director in town so they were bound to be dealing with the arrangements.

Libby sniffled then nodded as she too straightened her shoulders. 'I'll give Doc Williams a call as well and then we'll track down whoever's got the keys for the emporium. Make sure it's properly locked up until you get here. You won't be doing this alone, Beth. We'll sort it out together.'

'Yes, we will,' Eliza added. 'I've got some leave accrued at work and Martin can look after himself for a few days. I'll call Mum and ask her to get my room ready. If there's not a spare available at the pub, you can bunk in with me for a couple of days.' The Siren had guest rooms as well as accommodation for the family, and although the bay would be quiet this time of year, they were one of the few places to offer rooms year-round so they got some passing trade from visiting businessmen and families of local people who didn't have room to accommodate their own guests. Eliza paused, then added softly. 'If you'd rather stay at the emporium, I'll sleep over with you.'

The thought of being in the flat above the shop without Eleanor's bright presence was something Beth couldn't bear to contemplate. She shook her head. 'No, I think with you would be best.'

'Of course, darling. Whatever you need.' Eliza's face crumpled. 'Oh, Beth, I'm so sorry.'

Beth nodded, but couldn't speak to acknowledge the love and

sympathy in those words. If she gave in, she'd never get through the next couple of days. She stared down at the papers she'd set aside until the lump in her throat subsided. Darren would never give her the time off unless she got that bloody report finished. 'Look, I'd better go. I've got an urgent project to sort out for Monday.'

'Message me if you need anything, promise me?' Eliza raised her fingers to her lips and blew a kiss.

Beth nodded. 'Promise.'

'Me too. Love you both, and I'm sorry to be the bearer of such awful news.' Libby gave them both a little wave. 'I know it's terrible, but I'm so looking forward to seeing you both even under such awful circumstances. It's been too long.'

They signed off with a quick round of goodbyes, and the screen went dark in front of Beth. The greasy smell from her plate churned her stomach and she gathered it up, together with her glass and the bottle of wine. Trudging down to the kitchen, she thought about what Libby had said. She was right, it had been too long since the three of them had been together. They'd been drifting apart, not consciously, but life had pulled them in different directions. No more though, not if Beth could help it.

Now that Eleanor was gone, they were all she had left in the world. Crawling beneath the covers, Beth curled around the spare pillow and let her tears flow once more. The one person in the world she needed to talk to more than Eliza and Libby would never pick up the phone again. What was she going to do?

Don't miss *Snowflakes at Lavender Bay* the delightful new book in the Lavender Bay series from Sarah Bennett, coming in October 2018!

If you enjoyed *Summer at Lavender Bay*, then why not try another delightfully uplifting romance from HQ Digital?

Dear Reader,

Thank you so much for taking the time to read this book – we hope you enjoyed it! If you did, we'd be so appreciative if you left a review.

Here at HQ Digital we are dedicated to publishing fiction that will keep you turning the pages into the early hours. We publish a variety of genres, from heartwarming romance, to thrilling crime and sweeping historical fiction.

To find out more about our books, enter competitions and discover exclusive content, please join our community of readers by following us at:

@HQDigitalUK

facebook.com/HQDigitalUK

Are you a budding writer? We're also looking for authors to join the HQ Digital family! Please submit your manuscript to:

HQDigital@harpercollins.co.uk.

Hope to hear from you soon!